The Other AJ Hartford

Addison Michael

PAGES & PIE PUBLISHING
Author Services

2023 Pages & Pie Publishing

ISBN: 979-8-9862920-4-5

Library of Congress Cataloguing-in-Publication Data

Michael, Addison.

The other aj hartford / Addison Michael

Cover Design by Art by Karri

Editing by Tiffany Avery

While set in real places, this novel is a work of fiction. All characters, events, and police agencies portrayed are products of the author's imagination. Any resemblance to established practices or similarity that may depict actual people, either alive or deceased, are entirely fictional and purely coincidental.

www.addisonmichael.com

To families of victims who can't travel back in time to save
your loved ones... my heart goes out to you.

Prologue

AJ Hartford, 1995

It was one of those iconic days that would change their lives forever. They would all remember where they were, as if time froze forever in the moment before she went missing. There was no reason to suspect anything out of the ordinary would happen. Some say that's why she was taken. Because no one suspected a thing.

The sun shot yellow rays of unexpected warmth down on the small town where nothing bad had ever happened. A group of eleven people were gathered in the backyard. The smell of seasoned hamburgers and hot charcoal hung in the air.

"Another Night" by Real McCoy was playing from a stereo. The girls danced to the song that had stayed at the top of the charts most of the year as they sipped drinks out of red plastic cups and giggled about boys. The guys raised their voices to talk over the tune, pretending not to like the song that had been popular this year, like they were immune to the pop singers' sex appeal.

It was unseasonably warm for April, which drew all the

important people in her life to the same place at the same time for an impromptu barbecue. The last barbecue AJ would ever have with her friends.

Sitting on a swing in the backyard of her best friend's house, AJ Hartford stretched her legs out to catch the bright rays, letting them warm her with an unspoken promise to change her coloring from pasty-white to an inevitable shade of pink.

"The eighties were the best era ever!" One voice rose argumentatively over the dull roar of voices. AJ immediately knew that voice.

Her best friend, Lacey Miller, flipped her strawberry-blond ponytail while arguing with AJ's boyfriend, Chance. The two of them picked at each other like they were brother and sister which wasn't too far from the truth. They were cousins and had been best friends since before kindergarten. Lacey had introduced Chance to AJ. AJ had instantly fallen for his boyish good looks, light brown hair, and mischievous blue eyes.

"Oh yeah? You like big hair and tight-rolled jeans?" Chance shot back. He might as well stick out his tongue. In this moment, he looked closer to eleven years old than twenty-one.

Bell bottoms, which were also called hip huggers, were the current "in" jeans of the day. Most of the girls here wore a pair with a little cropped shirt, showing off their flat stomachs.

"Well, no. Thank gawd that's out!" Lacey rolled her eyes emphatically.

AJ watched Lacey tilt her head toward her dad. Jerry, Lacey's dad, was grilling hamburgers for everyone. Lacey and Chance walked over, seemingly to get Jerry to weigh in on their debate. Jerry was off work today, so it was no big thing for him to throw a few burgers on the grill for Lacey, who'd made a rare appearance back in town from college. They were all taking a break from their college routines to sit and bask in the sun during what they assumed to be a perfect day.

AJ watched with a smile on her face as Jerry declined to participate in their argument but instead pulled Chance into a conversation he was having with Skip, Jerry's best friend. The two dads grilled burgers while drinking beers. They were all talking and laughing loudly. It sounded like they were discussing Michael Jordan's return to the NBA.

"Hey!" Jerry said suddenly. "You worked on DOS yet?"

"No," Skip responded. "What the hell is that? I'm in construction, remember?"

"It's this computer operating system. It'll make those machines do a lot more. Been out for five years but there are new programs coming out everyday..."

Chance waved at them but walked away, leaving Lacey standing awkwardly behind, pretending to be interested in their computer talk. Chance sauntered over to AJ and plopped down next to her. He rubbed her growing abdomen.

"How are my girls?" he asked.

"We're fine," AJ responded with a smile. She thought the baby was a boy, but she would let Chance have his fun.

"You havin' fun?" Chance asked.

"I love everything about today," AJ responded with a wide smile.

"You can't plan fun, you just gotta let it happen, ya

know?" Chance smiled happily. His blue eyes turned a shade brighter in the sunlight. He leaned over to kiss her. "Speaking of *not* planning, when are we gonna do this thing?" he asked as he twisted the modest diamond AJ wore on her finger.

AJ sighed. She had dreamed about a fairytale wedding her whole life. She'd already put a deposit down on Shaylee Barn north of town but hadn't given them a date yet. She'd picked out her colors. She'd picked out the dress.

It was the exact dress she'd always wanted. The satin collar snapped at the back of her neck. Lace cut from the neck to a plunging v-line, where a satin bodice fit her snugly, accentuating her curves. It was tight through the waist, then fell into a full, puffy skirt that looked a little like a tutu. The skirt cut off at the knees, revealing her legs and the ballerina slippers she planned to wear. She had taken ballet as a child and loved it.

The dress fit her perfectly—before she found out she was pregnant. Despite the rumors her small town loved to spread, Chance had proposed to her before she'd found out.

AJ sighed and put her hand on top on Chance's hand which rested on her belly. She wanted to wait until after the baby was born to get married. But she hadn't found the right moment to talk to Chance about that. If she left it up to him, they would be married tomorrow. She just didn't want to rush the planning. They had more than enough time for that.

"I don't know yet, Chance," AJ finally answered. "We have plenty of time to decide."

"Burgers are ready!" Jerry called.

AJ's stomach growled in response. She and Chance laughed as they got up to fill their plates. Jerry quickly blessed the food like a good host dad. AJ pretended to close her eyes. Really, she peeked around at all her friends, who she considered family. These were her classmates whom she had gone to school with, danced at dances with, talked about boys with, and was now in college with. They had all found each other here today. The way they always had over the years.

Time was an illusion, and it was passing them by. Weren't they all just in kindergarten together? Now they were turning twenty-one. AJ had always been the first one in the group to try something new. The first to drink. The first to try weed. The first to lose her virginity. Trust AJ to be the first one to get engaged and the first one to get *knocked up* as they had all lovingly teased her.

In truth, they could not be happier for her. The happiest of them all was AJ's mother. She was about to become a grandmother. Her only daughter was about to marry her high-school sweetheart and produce her first grand baby.

You can't be a bank teller forever, her mama liked to say. *Good thing you're going to college. Even better that you'll have someone by your side to share life's ups and downs. Because Amy Jo, there are going to be some ups and downs.*

AJ shook that off. She hadn't experienced any *downs*. She was popular in school, she was beloved by the people she worked with, her college professors thought she was the best student in the class. It was most likely because she was kind to everybody. She didn't care what she did for a job so long as she helped people in life. She knew not everyone had a life as good as hers.

As AJ finished filling her plate with food, Lacey ran up and linked her arm in AJ's, steering her toward the group of girls sitting on a blanket in the corner of the yard.

"We want to talk about the wedding plans. Let's plan this thing!" Lacey gushed.

"Lacey!" AJ protested. "If I sit down on that blanket, I might not get back up!"

"Stop it, you're barely showing," Lacey said. She looked around the yard and grabbed a seat cushion for AJ to sit down.

AJ had no more than sat when Chance came jogging up.

"Uh-uh, Chance, it's girl time." Lacey put up a hand to stop him from joining.

"No worries," Chance panted. "I need to take off."

AJ looked up at him in surprise and disappointment.

"Now?" she asked. "Why?"

"Mom just got called in to work. I need to go watch Bella," Chance explained as he got down on his knees to kiss his future bride.

"Okay, you need me to take you?" AJ asked.

"Nah, mom's coming to get me. Have fun, ladies." Chance wiggled his fingers at the girls who sat watching.

"Okay, I'll come over later after I leave here," AJ promised. Chance's car was propped up on blocks in his garage. The transmission was acting up again.

"You better." Chance smiled at her.

The girls exploded into a pandemonium of teasing and giggling.

Prologue

AJ watched her fiancé and father of her baby walk away. She felt a strange tug in her heart, unaware she would not make it to Chance's house after all. Nor would she any other night after.

It was a full day of fun with friends. As the sun set on a perfect day, AJ said her goodbyes. She was leaving the barbecue well after dark.

As she climbed into her car and began the drive home, she felt the full force of her exhaustion.

"Oh, shoot!" AJ snapped her fingers, remembering her promise to stop by Chance's after she left. She pulled her car into the empty grocery store parking lot where there was a payphone. She needed to call Chance before it got too late. She picked up the receiver, inserted her quarter, and dialed the number she knew by heart. She listened to it ring.

"I'm sorry, Chance. I got sunburnt and I'm exhausted. I pulled over to a payphone to call you when I remembered," she told him when he picked up the phone. She could see the grocery store at the front of the parking lot. The lights were off, signifying the store was closed. Her car was the only one in the parking lot. "Not to mention, those burgers gave me pretty severe acid reflux."

"Come on," Chance whined, trying to talk her into coming over.

AJ watched as a truck pulled up and parked between her and her car.

"You just saw me today," she protested.

"It's been hours! I miss you!"

"Hey," AJ interrupted him in a low voice. "There's a guy standing here. I think he's waiting to use the payphone."

"Wait, where are you?" Chance asked.

"The grocery store on Jackson," AJ answered.

"Ask him if he needs to use the phone," Chance suggested.

AJ turned to the man. The receiver was still pressed against her ear. The man was visibly dirty and his appearance was unkempt. He wore stained overalls, a white 'wife-beater' undershirt, and a flannel shirt. His dirty, brown hair was long and scruffy. There were bags under his eyes and acne marks all over his face.

"Do you need to use the phone?" AJ asked him politely, resisting the urge to wrinkle her nose as his smell assailed her senses.

The man slowly shook his head back and forth. AJ turned her back on him and lowered her voice to a whisper. "He stinks and he's just standing there. He's creeping me out. And his truck is still running. I can smell the exhaust."

"What's he driving?" Chance asked.

AJ looked over her shoulder and suppressed a shiver. Had he stepped closer?

"A puke green pickup truck with some green faded fish decal in the back win—"

Those were the last words AJ would utter to Chance. It would be the last time she would speak to anyone again. Her screams were so high-pitched, so shrill, it was impossible *not* to hear them through the telephone receiver that now dangled and swayed in the wind at the telephone booth.

Chapter 1
AJ Hartford, 2015

The large, almost empty train station sent drafts of cold air straight into her bones. AJ Hartford was now acutely aware why Chicago was dubbed *The Windy City*. AJ was not a fan of all that wind and was thankful she was heading home. As if the wind wasn't enough, the Chicago train station *looked* cold. The colors were not warm. It was not a place to loiter. The station reminded AJ of a public library. Only AJ liked libraries.

She had also liked the teacher's conference she had just attended in Chicago. Continuing education was a vital part of the role she played at the school where she taught. AJ was a teacher and a peer leader. Teacher was a dreaded position these days. In fact, there had been a mass exodus of teachers from the work force this year. *Rightfully so*, AJ thought. It's not like she didn't suffer the same fear and anxiety as her former co-workers. Many of them, having been miffed at the mistreatment from children and parents coupled with the low pay, had used the most recent school shooting as an excuse to permanently leave the profession.

AJ had volunteered to step up and take professional development classes during her summer breaks in order to bring the concepts back to the team and teach her co-workers important techniques, such as how to defend oneself without a weapon.

This particular conference had sessions that ranged from how to defuse a violent situation with a non-violent confrontation to disarming a child with a loaded gun. AJ was still shaking her head at that. One conference presenter had told them that when it came to guns, inexperienced people typically rested their finger on the trigger of a gun, which was an accident waiting to happen. The technique they showed at the conference to disarm someone would take a lot of courage, but AJ was willing to try if it might save her students.

She walked quickly through the depot, listening to the sound of her heels clip on the hard, unforgiving floor. She boarded the train, her eyes scanning the people sitting sprinkled throughout the train car. She looked for a seat where she could be alone. The seats were blue and gray. Two seats sat side by side, some faced forward, and some were against the wall, lining the edge. In each section, the seats were arranged like a small box as if to make conversation conducive, should one be traveling with friends. AJ knew when she sat down the seats would be cold and uncomfortable. By the end of the trip, her back would likely be sore.

The smell of day-old greasy hamburgers permeated the air. Her stomach lurched. She wasn't sure if it was the smell or the anticipation of what motion would do to her that made her stomach roll.

The train brought you here with no problems and the train will take you home, AJ Hartford reminded herself as she sat two seats down from the window. She perched stiffly on the edge of her seat. Sitting did nothing to calm her anxiety. She made a mental note of where the guardrail was so she was prepared when the train went into motion.

Her phone notified her of a breaking news story from back home. Her hometown was ten miles west of St. Louis. AJ checked her watch. The train would take off in less than five minutes. She clicked on the story, hoping to take her mind off the dreaded travel. She touched the earbud she was wearing and listened as the story came to life on her phone.

In 1995, AJ Hartford disappeared from this very phone booth without a trace... A pretty reporter with brown hair that whipped in her face from the gusts of wind paused and pointed to a phone booth in an abandoned parking lot.

AJ jumped a little at the mention of her name. She checked the date. She remembered this story when it originally happened because a girl with her name had gone missing an hour from her house. Her parents assured her it was merely a coincidence. So, AJ didn't concern herself with it. Except on anniversary years when they ran a story about the day AJ Hartford was taken.

Hard to believe it's another anniversary, she thought. She must have been staring into space because the sound of the train engines caught her off guard. The lights flickered just once inside the train car. AJ's breath caught. She held it absently. Then, she released it slowly. She quickly tapped her earbud, pausing the story, and she shut down her phone screen. She stowed her phone in her pocket.

As the train lurched and then stopped, AJ quickly gripped her fingers around the cold metal bar that ran along the side of her seat. The metal bar served as a guardrail, but she gripped it tightly for balance. She suffered from vertigo and had since she was a child. It had something to do with an inner ear problem that never quite got fixed. She told herself this was the primary reason she disliked the train. In truth, the anxiety she felt was unrelated to the physical symptoms.

AJ tried to focus on the fact that this train would take her back home. This train was good. Home was a small country town where she lived on her own piece of land in a little farmhouse. It was there where her life felt the most comfortable and made the most sense. It was a place where her daughter liked to remind her *nothing ever happened*. Which is exactly how AJ liked it.

AJ squeezed her cold fingers around the metal bar. She took a deep breath in through her nose and slowly exhaled out through her mouth. She had a love/hate relationship with these conferences. She knew they were necessary and some of the sessions were actually fun. But with the rise in violence among students, which was so unbearable to think about, AJ knew it was necessary to train in the art of non-violent confrontation and learn how to defuse an emotionally charged situation.

AJ stayed at her job because she viewed it as a place to serve. She was there to change the lives of middle school children. She knew when she taught about prepositional phrases, she was really teaching a child the ability to open his or her mind to learn new things. When she taught about comma splices, the kids weren't learning how to become best-selling novelists, they were learning they were worth the time it took AJ to explain these new concepts to them. Sometimes, when a child approached her with questions about last night's homework, they really needed a caring glance and reassurance because they didn't get any sleep last night on account of parental drama going on around them.

AJ looked out the window to see the train platform was empty. The place where she had stood minutes before was dimly lit. An empty bench sat just outside her window. She yearned to be sitting on it. Not in a train that would take off any minute.

Instant anxiety shot into her veins. She almost felt light-headed just thinking about the motion. The train moved forward. She could feel her long, blond hair whip behind her as if a sudden wind had blown through the train. It hadn't. It took minutes for the train to accelerate to its top speed.

That's when AJ saw her. At first, AJ only saw a hand that now smeared the window as it slowly brushed its fingertips along the glass surface. The hand hit the window loudly and AJ jumped back, gasping and startled.

Just past that hand, a woman peered at her from outside her window. Except there was no platform and no way for her to stand, let alone keep pace with the accelerating train. Yet there she was, hovering, looking like she was standing still. Right outside AJ's train window. AJ could barely see past that hand. She moved her face closer to the window, attempting to focus her eyes to block the movement of the train around the woman.

The woman's features filled in and AJ could now see the woman outside the train as clearly as she could see the man sitting across the aisle. The man paid no attention to AJ or the apparition she was seeing.

AJ felt her eyes widen in shock and she forgot to hold the rail as she covered her mouth with both hands. The woman looked exactly like AJ! Long, straight, blond hair flew opposite the direction they were moving. Hair whipped across the woman's face, which was the only evidence of the speed of the train as the woman floated seemingly in stillness.

The ice-blue eyes that stared urgently into AJ's seemed to be sending her a message. It was a message AJ could not understand. She blinked and moved to the seat closest to the window in an effort to see the woman more clearly. Time ceased to exist as AJ came to a realization. She didn't just look like AJ. She *was* AJ. An older version of herself stared back into AJ's eyes. The woman's face was gaunt. Her skin was thinner than AJ's. It looked translucent. There were no wrinkles on her face because it appeared any extra skin had sunk to form a thin, tight line around skeletal cheek bones and eye sockets.

AJ leaned forward to see the woman better.

"Help!" pink plump lips formed the word. AJ's brain heard the word as audibly as if she'd spoken it herself. The woman's hand was still pressed firmly against the window outside the train car.

AJ put her hand up to match the hand on the window. For a minute, they were suspended in time like that. Time was an illusion. They knew each other. They had lived each other's lives. Only this woman had lived more of hers than AJ had lived.

AJ could feel her hand on the glass, opposite the woman's hand, getting warmer. The glass beneath her palm was no longer cold. She stared into the woman's eyes and leaned in until her nose touched the window. Her hand appeared to be melding through the glass is if conforming to the woman's hand.

That's when AJ realized the glass was gone! Her brain registered with surprise that the woman hovering outside the train was now holding her hand. Only the woman wasn't just holding AJ's hand, she was gripping it tightly. Panic rose as AJ tried to reclaim her hand but couldn't. She put up her other hand to push away and gain the advantage. Instead, AJ found her other hand firmly in the grasp of the woman's other hand.

AJ's whole body locked up as she felt herself move through the window. The window glass was gone. AJ's body began spiraling at breakneck speed through a black abyss. She no longer felt the grip of the woman's hands on hers. Fear swelled inside her chest as she squeezed her eyes shut against a seemingly endless blackness. The only sound she heard was the whirling of her hair as it whipped against her face. Over and over, she spun. Her brain could not process what was happening.

Suddenly, her body slammed against the hard ground and bright lights flooded into her face.

"Ma'am? Are you okay?" asked a male voice.

AJ squinted at the light and put her hand up to ward off the sudden brightness. She did a quick mental check and found she was back in control of her body. She could move her arms and her hands were free.

From her place lying on the floor, she was looking up at the ceiling. She could see a nice green-and-orange striped pattern asymmetrically offsetting the white dome overhead. The half-circle dome windows had a consistent stained-glass pattern. Seven images of Jesus crucified hung in a semi-circle around one big half-circle window. Her eyes slowly traveled down the walls to take in a tiled floor that had similar green and orange patterns.

"Am I at Union Station St. Louis?" AJ asked as she struggled to push herself up to a seated position. She clearly wasn't on the train anymore. She just couldn't understand how that was possible. She could hear the sound of traffic outside. Loud horns were honking and an ambulance drove by, blaring its sirens. She could smell something like burnt rubber and her stomach flipped.

"Yes," the man answered slowly. "Ma'am, are you okay?"

"What happened?" AJ focused on the concerned man leaning over her.

"You fell," he said.

"Did you see me fall?" she asked.

"No. You were just on the floor when I came around the corner." He looked at her with an odd expression on his face.

"I'll be fine," AJ said, still attempting to sit up.

She was not fine. One minute she was tightly gripping the guardrail inside the train, the next minute she was spiraling through a window with no glass. Her mind was racing. The train had just left the Chicago train station when she saw the woman. In a matter of minutes, or maybe seconds, she was in St. Louis. She shook her head.

She rubbed her shoulder, feeling the kind of pain her body might feel if she'd been hurtling through the air and landed on a hard cement floor. Sharp pain radiated from what she'd equate to a bruise. Pain shot deep into her shoulder, as if her bone could bruise, then a pulsing pain ached down her arm, to the left side of her body, and into her hip. AJ could not understand how she was here when two minutes ago, the train from Chicago was just leaving the station.

Nor would she openly talk about what her body confirmed had been a very real experience. An admission like that would get her thrown back into a psychiatric hospital. AJ shuddered at the thought. That was one place she never wanted to end up again.

Chapter 2
AJ Hartford, 2015

AJ heard the front door open and close.

"Kiera?" she called from the kitchen where she'd been making a sandwich. "That you?"

"Of course it's me," Kiera responded as AJ heard her sixteen-year-old daughter slam a heavy bag down on the floor and walk into the kitchen. She'd gotten a ride home with a friend. "If it wasn't, you'd already be dead."

"Thank God it's you, then!" AJ stilled the butter knife she'd been using and gave her daughter a one-handed hug.

Kiera grinned at AJ, her bright blue eyes mirroring her mother's. While Kiera's face also resembled her mother's, that was where all similarities stopped. Kiera's long brown hair was pulled up into a messy ponytail and waved halfway down her back. AJ's hair was blond, straight, and flat. Kiera was tall, thin, and graceful where AJ stood several inches shorter and had two left feet.

"I missed you, kiddo. How was practice?" AJ asked.

"Hot," Kiera said as she made a face. Her normally pale

face was already turning pink. She rolled her eyes and grabbed a handful of Lay's potato chips. She munched on them while AJ turned back to making her sandwich. AJ was not one of those moms who lectured her daughter about what she ate. Kiera was active and life was short.

"They're making you practice soccer in the middle of the summer. What did you expect?" AJ asked. She grabbed a plate, dropped the sandwich on it, and handed it to Kiera.

"I expected an air-conditioned super dome," Kiera quipped. "How was the conference?" she asked with her mouth full, having taken a huge bite. She walked to the table and set the plate down. Many a late-night conversation had happened at that table. AJ was glad to be home with her daughter.

"It was good. A lot of information. I'm still processing it." AJ refrained from telling Kiera about the ghostly image of herself she had seen on the train. After all, a story like that would get her locked up for good this time. "They say guns are the leading cause of death among American children and teens."

"Truly? Well, don't practice any of that non-violent confrontation stuff on me. It won't work. I'll karate chop you in half." Kiera had put the plate down but still held half the sandwich in her hand. With her free hand, Kiera chopped the air.

AJ gave her the *mom* look. "I'd like to see you try it."

Kiera grinned as AJ brought her own sandwich to the table. Kiera popped another bite into her mouth. "How was the train?"

"Oh," AJ swished her hand in front of her like she was shewing a fly and lied. "Uneventful."

"Really?" Kiera looked surprised. "You're making progress. You hate trains!"

"I know," AJ shuddered. "I wish I could just drive but they don't reimburse gas. Anyway, tell me all about practice."

"Oh! Amelia broke her toe!" Kiera said with horror and morbid excitement as she delivered the latest gossip.

"Oh no! A toe? That's terrible!" AJ said.

"Yeah, we had an ambulance come and everything. She thought it was her foot, but they said it was just her toe."

"Well, thank you for not breaking *your* toe today."

"I try," Kiera answered.

"Anything new on Mars?" AJ asked, skillfully redirecting the conversation.

Kiera's eyes lit up. She bounced out of her chair and disappeared into the living room. She returned seconds later with a journal in her hand. She sat back down and opened it. "Ohmigosh, I can't believe I didn't tell you. There's a strawberry moon coming up in a week."

AJ snorted. Kiera had begged AJ for a telescope for her birthday when she learned in January that each full moon this year would bring a different type of moon. Kiera carried her red journal with her to document scientific observations. She was religious about her research. Now she flipped pages excitedly.

"There's a wolf moon, a snow moon, a worm moon, a pink moon..." Kiera rattled off all the types of moons. AJ zoned out at some point. AJ was not a science teacher and wondered often where Kiera had inherited her passion for the subject. Certainly not from her father either. His only passion appeared to be the new craft beer that came out on special occasions, though AJ knew he wasn't that sophisticated about what he drank. Truth be told, they didn't know anything about him anymore and that was the way she preferred it.

AJ had made Kiera promise to use the telescope and true to her word, Kiera had been out on the flat part of the roof with her telescope for every full moon. She'd even coaxed AJ out with her a few times.

Kiera ate the last of her sandwich, put her plate in the dishwasher, and grabbed her journal. Kiera moved to the living room where she'd dropped her bag when she'd first walked in. AJ could hear her grunt as she picked up her duffle bag to go to her room.

"You all packed for soccer camp?" AJ called.

"Of course. I just need to wash a few things from practice today," Kiera answered back. She came out with a small load of clothes in her arms and disappeared down the hallway.

AJ smiled when she thought about Kiera's decision to go to camp this year. Kiera had dragged her feet for weeks before AJ came right out and asked her. *Well, what's it gonna be, kiddo. Camp or no camp?*

Kiera had blushed and shrugged.

What's the problem? AJ had asked her.

I can't bear the thought of leaving you alone all summer! Kiera had wailed.

What? I'm the problem? AJ had gasped. *Don't worry about me. I can't wait to have this place all to myself. No offense but I have half a dozen books I plan to read this summer and you won't be around to distract me from them.* AJ pointed to a stack of books piled on the bottom shelf of the bookcase.

Kiera believed AJ and had signed up for camp that day.

AJ grabbed her plate and brushed up Kiera's crumbs. She walked out to the living room, thinking she might want to dust and deep clean while Kiera was gone too. She glanced critically around their modest little home. It was small but clean and it was hers. She loved this place.

The home had popped up for sale on the market at the exact time when AJ had no home of her own and needed a place for her and Kiera. This home had been the home where she'd grown up. She remembered some of her fondest childhood memories here. It had felt like fate. Having just moved back to the area, which was an idyllic country town called Wimmswick located west of St. Louis, AJ had bought the home. The town felt like a throwback to a simpler time with its historic buildings, dark green trees, and river that bordered the town.

While it's true AJ had grown distant from her parents as she grew up and realized how imperfect they were—her dad with his constant traveling and her mom with her increasing coldness and distance from AJ—still, AJ never wanted to forget this place. It represented a time when she had been truly happy as a kid. A time long before Kiera's dad had come into AJ's life bringing abuse and financial ruin in his wake. Thank God for that restraining order that mandated they never see him again.

AJ had bought the home cheap. It had been in foreclosure when she inquired about it. AJ had restored the hardwood floors, lovingly sanding and polishing them to their original finish. She had repainted every square inch of the walls with white and gray tones. She had crafted old doors and window frames into rustic pieces that now hung on the walls, creating the modern farmhouse look she loved. The furniture was the only thing she'd bought new. It provided a pop of color with its deep burgundy but gave comfort with its overstuffed, fluffy pillows. AJ had felt the pride of owning her own home as a single parent. It had been a consolation prize for the battle scars Johnny, her ex-husband, had left them.

"Uh, mom? You need to see this," Kiera called. "Betz just emailed me this link." It wasn't what Kiera said exactly, it was the way she said it that made AJ move. She sounded spooked. Kiera didn't get spooked.

AJ curiously followed the sound of Kiera's voice to find her in the hallway. She was looking at the news app on her phone. She turned up the volume so AJ could hear the reporter and turned her phone to show her.

"In 1995, AJ Hartford was abducted while using this very payphone."

"That's my name," AJ laughed, remembering the broadcast she'd started to watch on the train. She'd forgotten about that. It was the anniversary date of her disappearance. The other AJ Hartford.

Kiera nodded with a finger to her lips.

The camera panned out to show an empty parking lot of an abandoned, boarded-up grocery store. A lone payphone sat on the edge of the lot.

"She was calling her boyfriend to let him know she wouldn't be coming over that night. Nor would she ever come over again..."

AJ rolled her eyes at the news anchor's obvious efforts

to be clever. Sometimes you just needed to say the thing. Kiera looked at AJ expectantly. She was watching for her reaction with an odd look on her face.

"...new evidence is being released that this was a case of mistaken identity. Here's Officer Sheridan to tell us more."

A tall slender man with a muscular build, scruffy mustache, and tired but kind green eyes filled the screen.

"He's good looking!" AJ exclaimed.

Kiera gave her a look and rolled her eyes.

"Officer Parker Sheridan," AJ read aloud as his name flashed on the bottom of the screen when he spoke.

"We received this note that came to the father of the *intended* victim. The father of AJ Hartford—the *other* AJ Hartford, who was *not* taken—was a drug narc and the kidnappers had found out he was taking them down from the inside by reporting their actions to the authorities without them knowing," Officer Sheridan said from Kiera's phone.

"Wait. That's new!" AJ said, her attention now glued to the tiny screen.

Officer Sheridan held up the note and for a minute, the note filled the screen. Words and letters of all different shapes and sizes had been cut and pasted onto the paper to form sentences.

"That's pretty," Kiera said sarcastically.

AJ clasped her hands together tightly as if in prayer. She leaned in closer to the tiny screen.

What does it all mean? AJ wondered. Her brain was moving fast. She'd known about the abduction since it happened. She had not known about the note.

One day someone could snatch you out of your bed, AJ. Be thankful and live your life like it matters. Her mother's words came back to her with startling clarity. It was something she used to say to AJ almost daily. AJ had internalized those words. As time went on, it became the source of self-pressure and stress that made AJ excel at any job she worked—sometimes overworked—in her life.

As she watched the news and processed the story, the world had stopped spinning. She quickly scanned the note and scanned it a second time. Déjà vu hit AJ like a ton of bricks over her head. This note was somehow familiar, but she was certain she'd never seen it before in her life.

We know who you are ~~#6786854~~. We found your hot daughter. Now say good-bye. Too bad for your wife, you'll never see your daughter again.

Chills ran up and down AJ's spine. It was a hot summer day, and the sun was shining outside. Despite that, AJ felt cold. Her body began to shake as she reacted to the information with a truth she felt she'd always known somewhere inside. Perhaps it was a truth AJ worked hard to block out.

"The other AJ Hartford was abducted that very day from this very payphone. Thanks to this new evidence, two county police stations have collaborated to determine AJ Hartford from Chritten, Missouri, was not the intended target. We believe she was mistaken for the daughter of this police informant..." Officer Parker Sheridan pointed to the letter. What was he doing? Trying to drum up new leads on an old cold case?

Then a terrible thought occurred to AJ. What if this caught attention from the wrong people? Surely, the same person or people who took AJ Hartford weren't still out there. And if they were, would they still care after all these years? AJ's gut told her they were. AJ had learned to trust her gut.

Now her mind was processing what Officer Parker Sheridan had just done. Had the Chritten Missouri Police Force just painted a target on AJ's back, and any other *AJ* in the area who shared her name? *AJ Hartford* had to be a common enough name but if those drug lords were still out there, they had just been alerted they hadn't succeeded in killing their intended victim. It would only be a matter of time before they found her.

"We need to go," AJ reacted. Her thoughts were illogical, but her gut was telling her to move. She went to her room and threw a couple things in a tote bag.

"Go where?" Kiera followed her mother. In her hand, she still held her red journal full of her science notes. She looked stunned and confused.

"To my mother's," AJ said. "Why did I go back to my maiden name after the divorce? Why did I come back to this tiny little town?"

Kiera was watching AJ.

"You need to grab your soccer things. We won't be back for a few days."

"Are you serious right now?" Kiera asked. "We haven't seen Grandma in seven years. What about soccer camp?"

"Kiera, unless you want to wear the same clothes every day, grab your bag. Now!" AJ snapped loudly.

"Okay, don't yell." Kiera hustled down the hallway to her room.

It took Kiera less than one minute to grab her bag. Kiera still wore shoes on her feet. AJ quickly stuffed her feet in a pair.

The sound of breaking glass interrupted their movement. It came from the living room. AJ met Kiera in the hallway, eyes round and wide. AJ felt the same surprise.

The front door flew open with a loud bang. AJ pointed to her bedroom wordlessly. Kiera followed AJ. Soundlessly, they shut the door and locked it. It wouldn't hold long but it might buy some time. AJ scooped car keys off the dresser. She grabbed her purse. She opened the bedroom window.

"Jump," AJ hissed in a whisper.

AJ could see fear in Kiera's eyes. Still, she swung her body out the window. The jump was less than a story. AJ knew Kiera didn't want to twist an ankle on account of soccer camp. Kiera jumped down first and landed on her bottom. She jumped up quickly, brushing off the dirt. AJ climbed through the window. Somehow, she managed to land on her feet, which was surprising considering she was constantly tripping.

"Run," AJ whispered.

Kiera took off in the wrong direction.

"Not to my car..." AJ whispered loudly. "To that one."

AJ pointed to a detached garage. There, they stored odds and ends—the extras that didn't fit in the house. *Extras* like a 2001 Jeep Cherokee. It was Kiera's car. Only, Kiera had no desire to drive yet. AJ kept the car gassed up and ready to go should her car not start one day. Or should a drug lord decided to break into the house to kill them.

They ran to the garage. AJ quickly released the garage lever. It easily lifted on account of the old spring. Kiera got in and buckled herself in the passenger seat, looking bewildered. AJ got into the driver's seat and started the car.

AJ floored it and drove through the grass. Parked in the driveway was an old, rusted, camo-green truck with a faded fish decal peeling in the back window.

Once on the dusty gravel road, AJ pushed the gas pedal. She drove like she expected someone to come flying out of the house any minute.

They didn't.

AJ checked her rearview mirror. The green truck was still parked in their driveway.

"Mom," Kiera finally spoke. "What's going on here? Is this for real?"

They had edged out onto the highway. AJ hit the gas pedal harder than normal.

"I'm gonna check the alarm cameras." Kiera picked up AJ's phone, opened the app, and gasped. The cameras in the house were set to begin recording when movement was detected. Kiera scrolled through the video frames.

"Mom," Kiera whispered, sounding spooked. "A man is in our house! Look!"

AJ saw the man and let out a little shriek. How long before he figured out they'd jumped out the window?

"What's he doing?" AJ asked, feeling horrified.

"He sat down on the couch. He has his feet up," Kiera's voice sounded bewildered. "He was looking through the house, but I guess he gave up and decided to make himself at home."

At a stoplight, Kiera angled the phone so AJ could see the feed from the security cameras. The man was watching TV. He must have missed them escaping and decided to wait for them to return.

AJ punched the gas faster. He'd found them fast. Too fast. Faster than any human should be able to track another. With a slight shiver that had nothing to do with the air conditioning, AJ wondered if he'd already been tracking them. Perhaps he knew the truth about who AJ really was far before the media had broadcasted that story.

Feeling the violation of her privacy and the sudden exposure of who her dad might really have been made AJ feel like she was walking naked in a high school hallway. The sooner they exited this highway to the long backroad to her mom's house, the better.

Chapter 3
AJ Hartford, 2015

"I am the *intended* missing AJ," AJ said, processing aloud while keeping her eyes on the road in front of her as she drove. "At least, I think I am. I must be. It's coming back to me now. It's like this weird memory I had locked away and forgotten—"

"Or blocked." Kiera gave her mom a knowing look.

"There was another girl named AJ Hartford who went missing back in 1995. She was four years older than me. She disappeared and was never found."

AJ felt a chill run down her spine. Had the disappearance of the other AJ Hartford granted her life? AJ was quiet for a minute, suddenly transported to a different dimension in her mind. Memories were things they didn't talk about in her family growing up. There were secrets that were supposed to be buried with her dad. When he was buried, they should have had the freedom to speak freely. But they didn't. AJ's mom had never spoke about anything of significance. Still, AJ wasn't afraid of repercussions anymore. There had been so much more than grief to process.

For instance, as an adult, AJ had decided her dad had shown all the signs of being a drug abuser. He wasn't a *junkie*. He held a job, he interacted with people, and he provided for his family. But he'd always loved reminiscing about the glory days. Those days in high school when he outran the cops when he was driving under the influence and if they caught him, he'd be booked. Or the time he'd hidden a pouch of drugs under his tongue when a teacher walked by at exactly the wrong time.

It all fit. Her dad's prior childhood involvement with drugs and the wrong crowd would have given him a connection to the wrong people. Which could have cost him his life. Instead, those people had targeted the other AJ Hartford, who had suffered needlessly for them all. Until now when they were back to targeting and had found her, the intended AJ Hartford.

"Okay, mom," Kiera said, breaking her mother's brooding silence. "Let's say you're right. Why is this happening now? It was so long ago! Your dad is gone. What good does it do to kill you now that he's gone? What happened to you that day?"

"It wasn't *that* long ago," AJ said, bristling the way she always did when talking about her age. "But I do remember things I haven't thought about for years." She shook her head but could not ward off the memories as they came flooding back to her.

"Such as...?" Kiera prompted.

"I had just gone on a lunch break from work. I worked at this local grocery store on the corner of two very busy intersecting streets. That day, I'd left work on a lunch break to go pick up drive thru. On a whim, I pulled into an abandoned parking lot to call my dad. We didn't have cell phones back then, you know—"

"What? You didn't have cell phones?" Kiera asked in mock surprise and sarcasm. "I know, mom. You tell me that all the time." Kiera rolled her eyes and turned to the road ahead. She liked to keep an eye out to warn AJ about changing yellow and red lights or cops she saw hiding on the side roads.

"I just felt like I needed to check in. I did that from time to time. But I didn't usually do it in the middle of a work shift." AJ shook her head. Even now, AJ wondered at her behavior and the break from her norm. "I never left my car when I went to a payphone. I always just drove up and rolled down the window to put in my quarter. Which is exactly what I did that day. Then, I listened to the phone ring.

"*AJ?* my dad's gruff voice demanded when he knew it was me. *Where the hell are you? You need to get home right now!*

"*What?* I almost laughed. I said, *It's the middle of the day and I'm on lunch. I need to get back to work.*

"*No,* he said. *You get home and stay put with your mother. You hear me? You don't stop anywhere on the way home. Just get home.*

"So, I did. I made some lame excuse at work about a family emergency and drove home. My dad was used to getting his way when he used that tone of voice, and that day was no exception.

"*Thank God!* he said the minute he saw me. He

grabbed my arm and sat me down. Not that I had a choice, his grip was too firm to pull away. He gestured toward the TV, then he told me, *A girl named AJ Hartford just went missing in Chritten, Missouri. It's all over the news. I didn't know where you were.* His look was fiercely protective.

"I told him, *Okay, I'm sorry that scared you. I was at work. I told mom before I left.* I'd looked from him to mom, who had just come back in the room. Then I told him, *Clearly, I'm fine. Can you just back off?*

"*No, don't you get that tone with me,* dad had said. *You're not too old to bend you over my knee, you know. For now, you're grounded. From here on out, you need to ask permission when you want to leave and tell us when you want to come back.*

"*Okay, but this isn't my fault,* I remembered insisting. Really, I'd felt so ashamed. I hadn't even done anything wrong, but I felt dirty and sinful at the hint of accusation. I went straight to my room."

"Mom, I didn't know that!" Kiera exclaimed. "What do you think is happening now?"

"I feel like the news story we just heard put the puzzle pieces in place. What if my dad was the narc who'd received the letter? Do you understand what that would mean?" AJ took the exit off the highway, thankful she only had to go through town for a short distance. Businesses lined what was usually a busy street, but it was afternoon and traffic was light and flowing easily. AJ hated the commercial hustle and bustle of this area. It was all business and no charm. The buildings were cold, with reflective glass that seemed to judge her as she drove by. But this was the only busy road they had to travel before she took the backroad that would take her to her mother's home. She glanced in her rearview, feeling thankful no one had followed them.

"You *were* the intended AJ Hartford. You must have been." Kiera sat upright, her head snapped to the front of the car, and she squinted at something ahead.

AJ nodded absently, agreeing with Kiera's comment but wondering what she was peering at. AJ didn't see her until it was too late.

"Mom, look out!"

Chapter 4
AJ Hartford, 2015

"Look out!" Kiera cried again, this time louder and with more urgency.

A translucent, gauzy material floated through the air and landed on the windshield, temporarily blurring AJ's vision. Then it floated high into the air, floating slowly until it disappeared into the clouds.

AJ slammed on the brakes at the moment her brain registered a woman standing in front of her car. But it was too late. AJ's eyes locked with the figure of a woman who'd appeared suddenly in the road. The woman was standing in front of AJ's car. The car didn't have time to slow before it slammed into the woman.

In that moment, everything appeared to be moving slowly. Before impact, AJ's brain connected with a recent, vivid memory. AJ knew this woman. She was the woman from the train stop. The woman who had AJ's face! Her older doppelgänger crumpled to the ground as AJ's car crashed into her.

They heard the loud, sickening crunch of the hard

plastic bumper. Without thinking, AJ threw the car in park before it was fully stopped. It was hard to tell if the sound the car made was purely due to the collision or also from the sound of the gears grinding as she forced the car into park. Regardless, AJ's mind had registered the woman too late.

"Mom!" Kiera screamed. "You hit her!"

AJ's heart raced and panic flooded her veins. She immediately turned on her flashers. Then AJ threw open her car door.

"What are you doing!" Kiera screeched. No doubt, Kiera was assessing the danger of stopping in the middle of a two-lane split road. The speed limit was fifty-five through here, so Kiera had a right to worry.

"I have to see if she's alive! Wave the cars around, would you?" AJ ordered as she jumped out of the car.

"We're going to die!" Kiera protested fearfully as she climbed out of the vehicle.

AJ ran to the front of her car. Only, there was no body. Had she dreamed the whole thing? She looked at her bumper. The big dent that crumpled in her bumper answered her question.

"That wasn't there before." AJ quickly dropped to her knees. She had to consider maybe the body had rolled underneath the car. But there was no one under the car.

"Mom?" Kiera called. "What's going on?"

"We did hit someone, didn't we, Kiera?" AJ called uncertainly.

"Most definitely. I saw her a second before you did. It happened really fast." Kiera sounded as if she was rehearsing what she would say to the police.

AJ checked the bumper one last time. She was looking for blood or some evidence of what she'd hit.

"I'm missing a body," AJ called. The hilarity of what she'd just said coupled with the severe circumstance struck her wrong. She giggled until she realized how insane it made her sound. AJ's reactions were often wrong in intense situations.

"What?" Kiera forgot to wave cars for a moment as she hurried to where her mom stood. Her eyes grew large as she, too, dropped to look under the car. She popped up quickly and immediately spun around. There was no sign of an injured woman anywhere.

A horn interrupted the search. An angry driver jerked his car over at the last minute, swerving and swearing at them through an opened window. AJ cursed under her breath. She hated this city. It was one reason she'd stayed in her small rural community. She'd only left that community once when she'd married Kiera's dad, Johnny. She thought she could be happy there in the city but really, she was miserable. Though she realized now, the blame did not belong to the city.

They ran back to the car. Kiera jumped in and buckled her seatbelt. AJ did the same and turned off the flashers. She hit the gas. The car took off.

"What's the plan, mom?" Kiera asked.

"The plan would have been *don't hit a woman who appears in front of the car. Don't dent the bumper of the car. And don't lose the woman you hit.* But that all went out the window. So, it's safe to say, there's no plan."

After a few minutes of silence, Kiera tried again. "Are we still going to grandma's?"

"Right, grandma's. That's where we were headed." AJ tilted her head in thought for a minute. "We need to go the last place anyone would look for us. Don't forget someone is after us."

"Grandma is crazy, though," Kiera lowered her voice when she said the word *crazy*.

"Well, you'd be crazy, too, if you were married to a man like my dad. Let's just say it's a wonder any of us made it out alive."

"Dramatic much?"

A sudden groan from the back seat interrupted further conversation. AJ jerked the steering wheel in surprise. The sound of a horn responded beside them. They weren't alone in the car! AJ could feel a presence behind her. Traffic had picked back up, so she had no time to glance in the rearview mirror.

Kiera, however, whipped her head around and screamed. She covered her mouth, her eyes widened in shock.

AJ veered the car off the road, steering into an empty parking lot a little faster than she should have and slammed on the breaks. Her hands shook violently as she put the car in park. Then, AJ slowly raised her shaking hands. "I'll give you anything you want, just don't kill us."

"I come in peace," the woman's words were soft and wispy. They seemed to float away like the scarf she had been wearing when AJ had first hit her.

AJ knew without turning around what she would see. She would be looking into her own aging face and that was jarring. She glanced at Kiera. Silent tears streamed down Kiera's white face. She was still covering her mouth and appeared frozen in terror. For once, their roles were reversed as Kiera sat unmovable in her fear.

"You're following me," AJ said, acknowledging the train incident. "What do you want with me?"

Kiera's voice was barely more than a whisper. "Why do you look like my mom?"

"Because I am your mom," came the soft reply. "I am your mom from a future universe where I was older than your mom is here now. But now, I am no more."

"What does that mean?" AJ turned now and locked eyes with her. She felt a powerful connection and could not look away.

"I died. At first, I could not tell where I was. I seemed to be stuck floating in the darkness. It could have been minutes or hours or days. Until I started falling, faster than the speed of light. I do not know how long I fell. Then I saw you. You were sitting on that train. At that moment, I knew everything. I knew I was stuck between universes. I am here in yours, but I am nothing more than a glimpse. I have not been able to control when you see me and when you don't. But since I saw you on the train, I have been with you." As if to demonstrate, the woman flickered as if she was a bad connection on a TV screen. "Until our hands touched during the train incident, I had no idea I could transport you. I just took you with me to where I wanted to go."

"Mom," Kiera said, her white face betraying how scared she was. She didn't move her head and barely blinked. "What train incident?"

AJ didn't want to talk about that right now. It was too hard to explain why a strange woman with her face sat in the back seat of their car. It took all of AJ's energy to focus on the woman's words. She was surprised to find she believed the words of this ghostly glimpse.

"We don't have much time," the woman said. "When I arrived here, I understood why I got stuck here. You. You are my purpose before I can leave. There's something we have to do before I can be released from this world."

"We?" Kiera asked. "You and mom?"

"Maybe you can explain on the way?" AJ asked.

"Umm, mom? We can't take this lady with us. Do you believe...? We don't even know her—"

"We have to go, Kiera. Remember, we have an angry man looking for us and I don't want to give him a chance to find us." AJ shuddered and put the car in drive.

"So, it has begun," the woman interrupted with a sigh. "The man has already found you?"

"What has begun?" AJ asked.

"This is the beginning of your end."

Chapter 5
AJ Hartford, 2015

Goosebumps rose on AJ's arms as she drove out of the parking lot and back onto the main road. Before she had time to process the meaning of the woman's cryptic words predicting her death, a loud clap of thunder interrupted the conversation and a bright flash of lightning lit up the sky. AJ put her foot on the break and stared at the sky.

"That's weird," AJ mumbled. "It's afternoon, but did you see how dark it just got? It's dark enough to light up—"

"It has begun," the woman repeated.

"Look, future AJ," Kiera began, clearly forgetting her prior fear as her annoyance won out.

"You can call me Amanda," the ghostly glimpse corrected Kiera.

Of course, that's her first name, thought AJ. It was AJ's first name too. AJ was short for Amanda Jane, a traditional name AJ had always hated.

Now as AJ quickly looked Amanda up and down, she could see her doppelganger had embraced a traditional life not only in her name, but in her clothing. Though the ghost's scarf had fluttered away in the wind, the rest of her clothing matched her missing accessory perfectly. Amanda wore a black turtleneck sweater with a black leather belt cinched at her waist. Her brown slacks flowed loosely down to her sensible black loafers that looked odd in this summer weather in contrast to AJ and Kiera's shorts-clad legs. Amanda's blond hair hung in a tangled mess as if she'd let it air-dry without combing through it after getting out of the shower.

"You need to drive. You are running out of time," Amanda commanded.

"Are you some cosmic being?" Kiera demanded. "Do you know everything because you're dead? How did you die, anyway?"

Lightning cracked so close to the car, AJ touched her breaks again. She could smell the singed earth. AJ drove a little faster as she eased onto the backroad that would lead to her mother's home.

"The same way your mom is going to die," Amanda stated.

"Stop saying that!" AJ gasped. It sounded so final. "Is there no way around this?" It wasn't lost on AJ that she was actually listening to this person who wasn't a person at all but a ghost who appeared to be AJ's "Christmas future."

"The only way to ensure we all survive is to travel to a different universe that is years behind ours and save the other AJ Hartford. The girl who died in your place—"

"Can we call her AJ2 or something?" Kiera asked. "This is gonna get confusing."

"If you don't save AJ2," Amanda continued, "her killers will kill every version of you in every universe which will also destroy Kiera. Kiera must live. She is vital to the future."

"Why am I—" Kiera began.

"I can't tell you that," Amanda cut her off as she turned back to her explanation. "Each universe has us on a course, a path, that is similar, if not exactly, like the one in the next universe. The same men who kidnapped the wrong girl in your universe in 1995—AJ2, also kidnapped her in my universe. The broadcasts in each dimension intentionally put the anniversary story out two days early. It won't be the actual anniversary for two more days."

"I don't understand," Kiera interrupted. "Why would they run the story on the wrong day?"

"The media needed ratings today more than in a couple days, so they broadcast it early. In the future universe, where I'm from, the media dictates the direction, action, and reaction of people in the world," Amanda explained.

"Same here," Kiera snorted. Then she sat up straighter. "Oh yeah, in two days, the trial of that financial tycoon will start and they agreed to allow some media footage in the courtroom."

"Remember, my universe is in the future. When the news story in my universe aired that the wrong AJ Hartford was taken, it took less than an hour for a man to arrive at my home, catch me unaware, and kill me. See," Amanda pulled down her turtleneck to reveal an angry red cut across her neck. AJ watched in the rearview but felt her car run over the rumble strips on the side of the road.

"Gruesome!" AJ gasped.

"Eyes on the road, mom," Kiera warned, though her voice sounded less sure than her words. "So how does this going back in time thing work anyway? In *Back to the Future,* Marty McFly isn't supposed to run into himself. But here you are talking to us. Aren't you supposed to hide from your younger self, my mom, for fear of stunning her or changing some course of history?"

"That's not how this works," Amanda said. AJ could hear the smile in her voice. "You can't base real life on a movie from the eighties. In each universe, there can be only one version of a person in existence."

Kiera crossed her arms defensively. "I'm not basing *all* my knowledge on a movie. I do know science." Kiera reached down in the backpack she had thrown in the car. She pulled out a red journal and waved it at Amanda. "I have scientific notes and research in this. But you're here in this universe and so is mom. So, there are two of you in this universe. If there can only be one person in existence, how are you both here now?"

"I'm not alive, remember? I'm just a glimpse. A ghost from another dimension. This is the longest I've been visible since my death. I don't know how to control how visible I am. I knew nothing when I showed up here. I'm learning as I go. I don't know the science. But I know AJ exists here and I do not. When I take AJ where we need to go, I believe she will exist inside the AJ of that universe."

"What do you mean when you say, *take her with you where you need to go?* Are you taking her on the train?" Kiera was clearly grappling to understand this.

"I think the train is the key to help us travel, yes."

"What happened on that train?" Kiera grumbled in frustration.

"When I was sitting on the train, I saw Amanda," AJ began, her eyes glued to the road. "At first, I only saw her hand, then I saw her face. Only, it was *my* face. I was stunned. I leaned forward and put my hand on the window, right where her hand was. Suddenly, the window was gone. She grabbed me and pulled me through the train. The next thing I knew, I was in the St. Louis train depot instead of on the train just leaving Chicago."

"What?" Kiera practically shouted at AJ. "When I asked how the train ride was, you said it was *uneventful*. You might have mentioned getting thrown out of the train by a ghostly glimpse! You lied to me?" Kiera's voice wobbled and AJ could hear the hurt in her voice.

Kiera and AJ had a made a pact. They agreed never to lie to each other. No matter what happened. Given the situation they had escaped when leaving behind her dad, Kiera knew statistically she was more likely to have an abusive partner as a result of AJ's abusive relationship. AJ and Kiera promised they would look out for each other and keep each other safe. And they had. So far.

"I was afraid to tell you, Kiera," AJ admitted with a lowered voice. "I sort of believed it had been a crazy dream." She didn't have to look at Kiera to know her daughter was glaring at her.

"You promised. We promised. I can't believe you broke that. *No matter what,* we said. Now I know *no matter what* means *only when it's convenient for you.*"

"Amanda, you said you knew your purpose now. What is

it you have to do?" AJ asked, ignoring Kiera's words that were ringing so true at the moment.

There was no answer. Kiera whipped around and AJ adjusted the rearview mirror.

The back seat of the car was empty.

Chapter 6
AJ Harford, 2015

Now that they were alone again, AJ had no choice but to face Kiera's fury. AJ knew well that Kiera had quite the temper when she was crossed, and AJ would have to earn back her trust in time. Kiera was the product of an abusive father and knew how to put her guard up to protect herself.

"I'm sorry I lied to you, Kiera." AJ kept her eyes on the road in front of her. "Surely you can understand why I—"

"No. We're a team. You expect me to tell you the truth. You don't get to pick and choose when you do and don't." Hurt laced Kiera's words.

AJ wanted to defend herself and tell Kiera that technically she hadn't lied. But they'd established the ground rules long ago. Omission was a betrayal. With that thought, AJ's mind returned back to that night. Most of the time, she was content to block it out. Right now, however, it was all returning to her as clearly as if they were reliving it. Kiera was only nine years old back then.

The tears streaming down AJ's face after AJ had left Kiera's abusive father was a hard memory to replay. As AJ had driven away, little Kiera had attempted to comfort her mom.

It's okay, mom. It's gonna be okay. Kiera had patted AJ's hand all the while, her own little hand visibly shaking.

The glass in the back window of the car was shattered and missing large chunks. The back seat was lined with glass shards. Wind blew in from the back, chilling them both, but they didn't care about either of those things at that moment. They felt nothing but fear.

AJ had gotten home late from parent-teacher conferences that night. She paused on the steps of her small home, which was a few streets over from a busy city intersection. She could hear the cars splash through the water on the roads still wet from the afternoon rain. She never knew what she would walk into when she got home. When she walked through the door that night, she saw the living room was in messy disarray. She'd sighed, thinking it was going to be a late night playing pick up.

Her husband, Johnny, had already mentally checked out. He sat on the couch, zoned into the TV while drinking a beer. AJ didn't have to check the trashcan to know he'd drank too much. If Johnny had one, he had too many. Johnny couldn't stop once he'd started. He kept drinking until he'd drank every beer in the house.

Kiera? AJ had called, choosing to ignore Johnny, knowing no good would come of engaging him at this point in the evening. AJ had looked in Kiera's room first. She hadn't seen her, so she'd gone from room to room, feeling more frantic by the minute.

Where's Kiera? AJ hurled the question at Johnny like an accusation.

Johnny had squinted at her, his eyes narrowing dangerously. *Who?*

Kiera! Your daughter! she'd raised her voice.

How the hell should I know? he slurred.

You're supposed to be watching her! AJ didn't wait for an answer. She ran back to Kiera's room. She stood still. She was about to leave when she heard it. A soft whimpering was coming from the closet. *Kiera?*

The closet door opened a crack. AJ lunged forward, opened the door wider, and sank to her knees. She gasped as she saw her daughter crying softly. An angry red mark lined nine-year-old Kiera's cheek.

It was my fault, mommy, Kiera sniffled.

Anger radiated through AJ's whole body. *No! Whatever you did, you did not deserve this!* AJ helped Kiera to her feet and threw a few articles of clothing into a small overnight bag. Holding Kiera's hand, AJ went to her room and did the same thing for herself.

When Johnny had caught AJ and Kiera sneaking out of the house, he hadn't said a word. At first, AJ was relieved. She'd always believed him when he said he'd kill her if she ever left him. But he'd seemed so passive as he watched them pick up speed and run to the Range Rover AJ had parked at the front of the house. AJ should have known he was a little *too* quiet. As she focused on Kiera buckling the passenger seat, AJ had missed Johnny's quick movement. He'd gone into the house and come back out with a shotgun.

As AJ had started the car, she'd heard the loud gunshot and the glass shatter all at the same time. The noise was deafening, and AJ had ducked and turned the car key.

Johnny had pointed a shotgun at the car, pulled the trigger, and tried to kill them. Just like he'd promised.

AJ had found the gas pedal and pushed it to the ground. The truck took off with a jump. Wheels spun in the gravel for less than a second before the truck gained traction and took off.

AJ called the police to report him once they'd hit the highway. After years of planning and stashing money away, AJ still didn't feel prepared enough to leave. But what happened to Kiera was enough to push her into action. Now AJ knew they couldn't go back if they wanted to.

When AJ hung up the phone, she'd noticed Kiera was sobbing.

Oh, baby girl! AJ wanted to stop the car and scoop Kiera up with promises that it would all be okay. But she knew better than to stop the car right now.

It's all my fault! Kiera had wailed.

No way! AJ glanced at Kiera with anger. She'd clenched her jaw.

I never should have told you! she'd cried harder.

Listen to me, it is not your fault that your daddy put a bruise on you when I was working. It's my fault for leaving you alone with him. He did it to me too. For years... I didn't think he'd do it to you, baby girl, I just didn't know... AJ's voice trailed off as a sob caught in her throat and the floodgate of tears broke. She was crying so hard she almost couldn't see the road.

No more secrets, mom. Kiera had held up her pinky finger.

AJ had laughed unexpectedly and wiped her tears. She

wondered if she was losing her mind. She wrapped her pinky around Kiera's in agreement.

No more secrets, AJ agreed. *Not telling something important is also a lie. From here on out, we tell each other everything.*

Yes, Kiera had agreed. And they had. Until today.

"I don't want to end up back in the psych ward," AJ blurted now as she watched the road in front of her. There were tears in AJ's eyes, but she didn't know if they were because of the memory of that horrible night or the fear of what she'd just admitted.

Kiera softened slightly and turned toward her mother. But AJ could tell she wasn't quite ready to let her mom off the hook yet. "Grandma said it was a behavioral health hospital and it was where you would get better."

"Grandma tells herself a lot of things so she can sleep at night," AJ said with anger. After she'd left Johnny that night, AJ had driven to her parent's house. She hadn't known where else to go. Her mother assessed her and decided AJ was having a mental breakdown and she needed help.

AJ still blamed her mother for pushing her to go to the hospital that night. At first, AJ had refused to go, but her mother was stronger than AJ. Especially in AJ's fragile and broken state. Her mother had marched AJ out to the car and put her in the passenger seat. She'd buckled her in the same way AJ had buckled Kiera. Kiera had stayed with her grandfather.

AJ would never forgive her mother for separating her from Kiera at a time when Kiera needed her the most. AJ had checked herself in, which meant she could check herself out. Which is exactly what she did, a week later. The staff had advised against it. In the beginning, she had listened to them. She had been too weak to protest. After AJ's return from the behavioral health facility, she took Kiera and left without a word to her mom. That was seven years ago.

AJ had seen her mother briefly at her dad's funeral two years ago, but AJ refused to talk to her mother, and she hadn't brought Kiera along.

"Kiera, we're only going to my mother's to get answers about what happened the day AJ2 was taken. I want to know what mother knows. I need to look her in the eyes. I'll know the truth." Not to mention, no one would look for them at her mother's house. Not even her own mother.

Which is precisely why Maria Hartford looked so surprised to see them when they knocked on her door a short time later. It was the house Maria had built after AJ's dad had died. AJ had no memories here.

As they stood on her mother's front porch, the home that resembled a small version of a southern plantation home, AJ scanned the sky.

The clouds now fully covered the sun and the afternoon had turned dark. Thunder rumbled constantly in the sky and lightning was striking the ground with more frequency than AJ had ever witnessed.

Shocked was an understatement to describe the look on Maria's face when she answered their knocks. AJ had to reintroduce Kiera, whom Maria had not seen since that week seven years ago. AJ looked around her mother, then pushed her way through the door.

"I don't understand," Maria tucked a strand of gray hair

behind her ear and smoothed the wayward waves. Clearly, Maria did not feel dressed for company, and immediately protested when AJ announced they would be staying.

AJ tried to squash the irritation. Her mother had never been a particularly warm or caring mom. Seeing her now and smelling her familiar clean scent of soap and lavender took AJ back to her childhood. AJ could hear her mother's words she'd carried with her through life like a mantra. Only now, she realized with startling clarity they held a different meaning. They made AJ think her mother must have known about that day when AJ2 was taken.

One day someone could snatch you out of your bed, AJ. Be thankful and live your life like it matters, Maria had always told AJ. Had her mother known her daughter was the intended target that day?

A sudden terrifying thought occurred to AJ. What if AJ's presence right now made Kiera and her mother potential targets? Should AJ go somewhere else and hide out until this settled?

"Why are you here?" Maria asked again more directly.

"Something happened," AJ said. "I need to talk to you."

"So, you and the child are here to talk?" Maria asked uncertainly.

"The *child* has a name. It's Kiera. And you would know that if you ever came around." AJ shifted from foot to foot, well aware of her hypocrisy. AJ was the one who'd forbidden her mother from coming.

Maria remained silent.

AJ looked around at her mother's home. It wasn't huge but it was immaculate. The hardwood floors were polished and clean. There was not a rug or carpet in sight. There was nothing here to give a sense of warmth. The couches that lined the front room looked stiff and uncomfortable. There was a wide staircase that curved up to the second floor. AJ wondered if they were slippery or if Maria had even used them. Knowing the degree of perfectionism her mother possessed in her, none of this décor, or lack of décor, surprised AJ.

Maria had paid cash for this house after her dad's life insurance had kicked in. Who knew? Of all the shitty things her mother had to put up with from her husband, Terrance, the one thing he'd done right was leave her with life insurance money.

"Mother, I need to ask you something." AJ crossed her arms across her chest.

Ever the ice queen, Maria said nothing and lifted one eyebrow in response.

"Do you remember when another girl named AJ Hartford went missing when I was younger?"

"I'd rather not talk about that nightmare," Maria answered abruptly, attempting to shut down the conversation.

"Please, I need to talk about this," AJ said in a quiet but firm voice.

"Oh, that day was an awful day," Maria touched her temples with her forefingers.

"Please, mom. It's important to me," AJ pleaded softly.

"Your dad had called. He was frantic. Your dad was many things. But he certainly loved you. He told me when you got home not let you out of my sight. He told me about *her*. That another girl named AJ Hartford had been kidnapped. I thought it an odd coincidence until..." she stopped talking abruptly, her eyes looked in the distance, seeming to relive the past.

"Please, go on. Whatever it is. I can handle it."

"I found a note when I was going through your father's things. After he passed away. It was this awful threatening letter. It had cut-out letters and it looked like a ransom note you'd see on TV. Only there was no request. The letter said something like, *We know who you are. We've found your daughter. Say goodbye.* Only they didn't take you." Maria lowered her voice to a whisper. "They took *her*."

"Did you know?" AJ asked. Her heart was thumping wildly in her chest. Her mother was confirming everything AJ had begun to remember as she watched the news story.

"Not at the time. God, I was in such denial about your father. I never would've thought he'd put us in that situation."

"What did you do with the letter?" AJ asked.

"What else? I turned it over to the police, of course."

"Okay, did you see the news today?" AJ asked.

"No, why?" Maria asked.

"The police released that note. Less than ten minutes after we saw the news story, someone broke into our house. It's not over. It's just begun." AJ repeated Amanda's ominous words, wondering vaguely why she believed her. AJ went to the window and peered out.

"What has begun? Is someone following you?" Maria asked, suddenly worried. She went to stand beside AJ, peering out the window with her.

"No, we weren't followed." AJ glanced at Kiera who was following the conversation with visible anxiety. She was clasping and unclasping her hands.

"That we know of..." Kiera muttered behind them.

"Maybe you should park your car in the garage, just in case," Maria suggested.

AJ nodded but spoke out loud as thoughts came to her mind. She paced around. "Dad died two years ago. The police knew for two years and sat on the note without releasing it to the public. I suppose I should feel thankful. But with dad gone, what prompted the grudge? Who did you give the letter to?" AJ wondered.

"It was a detective. Detective Sheridan, I think. They told me he was communicating with Chritten police. AJ, are you okay?"

"Yes, why?" AJ sank onto a nearby couch which was too stiff, just as she'd assumed. She was feeling jittery.

"The color just left your face."

"Why didn't you tell me?" AJ whispered.

"I didn't want you to have survivor's guilt. It's a real thing, you know." She sat down opposite AJ. Kiera followed quietly.

Too late, AJ thought. "I always knew about her, but I had somehow forgotten," AJ puzzled aloud. "Even back then, I got the feeling it wasn't a coincidence. I had a lot of guilt at the time. I felt like *why her* and *not me*. I remember talking to dad on the phone—a payphone. Just like AJ2 had done when she was snatched."

"You were younger than that at the time. You weren't driving yet."

"But I remember—" AJ shook her head, feeling confused.

"And who is AJ2?" Maria asked, struggling to keep up. AJ ignored her, deep in thought.

You get home and stay put with your mother. You hear me? You don't stop anywhere on the way home. Just get home, her dad had said. The memory was strong. AJ furrowed her brow. "It's like something I'd forgotten is coming to me so clearly now."

"Don't do that," Maria reached out and smoothed the crease in AJ's forehead. "It'll age you."

"Memories are imperfect," Amanda's soft voice floated to AJ through the dark room. "We need to go."

Chapter 7

AJ Harford, 2015

At Amanda's urgent words, AJ snapped her head up and looked at Kiera.

"Did you hear that?"

"Hear what?" Kiera asked.

"What's happening?" Maria's voice was sharp and confused.

"Kiera, can I talk to you in private?" AJ asked.

Kiera nodded. They found an empty bedroom. The bed was perfectly made with a heavy comforter that was gray with a maroon flower pattern on it. There was a single white dresser and a matching chair in the corner. AJ was about to recount the words she had heard when Amanda flickered into view. Amanda put out a hand to touch Kiera's shoulder.

"You touched me," Kiera squeaked in surprise but quickly covered her mouth to muffle the noise. "I didn't know you could touch people."

"Neither did I," Amanda responded.

"What did you mean when you said *memories are imperfect*?" AJ asked Amanda.

"I figured something out. When I died in my universe, the memories of AJ2's kidnapping implanted back into your brain, AJ. Your brain had blocked out much of the incident. I mentioned the time differences in each universe. As I said, my universe is ahead. I also know there's a universe directly below this universe that's behind—"

"Below?" Kiera asked excitedly. "Like actually underneath this one?" She began looking around. "I'm going to grab my journal."

"I don't understand what you're saying." AJ crossed her arms and looked from Amanda to Kiera.

"Hang on, mom. I'll be right back." Kiera ran. True to her word, she returned with her red journal a moment later. She flipped through it.

"There are other universes?" AJ asked.

"Mom, I've heard of this. There are scientific theories about parallel universes. When there's more than one, they call it a multiverse and scientists have kicked around an idea that there's a universe directly below us. Maybe even upside down! Then there's this theory about inflation. They hypothesize that even before the Big Bang, there was inflation. That's a rapid expansion where more universes are thought to have formed. But they've never proven it, of course." Kiera's eyes were wild with excitement.

"Right, this is starting to hurt my head." AJ was picking and choosing her limits on what she would believe.

"We don't have much time," Amanda cut in. "Though time moves differently in every universe, people are similar in every universe. They are likely to make the same choices. Though each universe has subtle differences, it's very difficult to make a different life choice than one a future version of you has already made somewhere else."

"Yeah! There's this theory..." Kiera paused and thumbed through her journal. "I can't remember the guy's name but I'll find it... They put this cat in a box and when they opened the box—however many days later—the cat was dead. Only, they said the dead cat was just our perception. They thought the cat could have been alive in a parallel universe. Aha!" Kiera interrupted herself. "Schrodinger. It was Schrodinger's cat."

"Poor cat," AJ mumbled as she tried to wrap her mind around it. She thought about the Mandela effect. The Mandela effect was a phenomenon named after Nelson Mandela. Some people remember Nelson Mandela, who lived until 2013, as the president of South Africa, and some people claim to remember that he died in jail in the 80s. This felt like that. People don't remember things the same. Could that be because everyone exists in their own reality, realities that are distinctly different from one another?

What had happened the day of the other AJ Hartford's disappearance had been a vague memory in AJ's distant past. Now, the memory was as clear and strong as if this all just happened yesterday. And it was affecting AJ's future.

"I think my memories dumped into your head when I died," Amanda said, reading AJ's mind. "That's the side effect of me being here in this universe, I think. I have to take you from here in order to save you in every other universe. Lucky for us, and thanks to the media, we have a two-day jump start. It will all start over again in the universe below with AJ2's kidnapping. If you save AJ2 there, it will save you here, and it will save me in my universe," Amanda answered. "So, we have to go."

"If life is a foregone conclusion, why live it at all?" AJ cut in.

"Life is a series of sliding-glass moments. Each choice we make determines the direction our life takes. Even the tiniest decisions can change the course of our life path. It's hard to veer from the choices that have been made ahead of you in a different universe. When you feel like you're reliving a moment here, you probably are. It's the universe telling you you're exactly where you were meant to be—"

"Like déjà vu?" Kiera broke in.

"Yes, exactly." Amanda seemed to stand taller.

At first, AJ thought Amanda was on her tiptoes but then AJ noticed Amanda's feet weren't exactly touching the floor. She was hovering.

"What now?" AJ wondered.

"Let's go back and prevent the kidnapping. If you prevent that, it prevents my future death and your imminent death."

"You really think mom's gonna die?" Kiera asked with big eyes.

"You both are. In less than a week, unless we do something fast." Amanda went to the window, moved the curtains that matched the bedspread, and peeked out the blinds. "It's only a matter of time before the man who killed AJ2 finds you. He is determined and will not give up until you are dead."

"So one guy is determined to kill me, the intended AJ,

after all these years?" AJ felt the air leave the room with a rush as she processed the foreign concepts quickly, trying to make sense of them.

"He's not working alone," Amanda informed her quietly. "He works with a team but he's the one who does the *dirty* work."

"You're telling me I have to go to another universe to save AJ2, in order to prevent our deaths which will occur in less than one week?" AJ felt faint. She couldn't even travel on a train without anxiety. How would she travel through universes?

"How does it work?" Kiera asked the question on AJ's mind.

Amanda turned from the window and looked at them. "The same way we traveled through the train depot."

"You never told me how that happened," Kiera responded.

"My theory is because we are the same person, and because I am dead, my touch along with the speed of the train, caused AJ to move through the window and through time that day, to where she landed in the St. Louis train depot. I think I can do the same thing here and help AJ travel to this other dimension to save AJ2."

"Wait, so you were able to move my mom into a different state?" Kiera's voice sounded awed.

"Yes."

"Can't *you* go save AJ2?" AJ asked.

Amanda shook her head. "As you know, I cannot control when I show myself. Nor can I communicate with anyone else. But I've been tied to you since my death."

A chill ran down AJ's spine.

"Does that mean, once mom gets there, to the new universe, she might not be able to see you or know how to get back?" Kiera asked, horror in her eyes.

Amanda nodded. "I'm afraid so."

"That settles it. I'm not going. We'll have to take our chances here, Kiera. We could live on the run." AJ stuck out her chin with determination.

"But I have soccer camp," Kiera's voice was small, her eyes worried.

"Don't worry, I'll take you tomorrow. We're aware and that's half the battle. We can dodge these guys. We'll go to the police. They can help us." AJ felt optimistic.

"You try that. They don't believe you. It only wastes your time," Amanda said with a shake of her head.

AJ looked at Kiera. If she left, there was a chance AJ would never see her again. If she stayed, Kiera could die.

"Why don't we all three go?" AJ suggested suddenly.

"Kiera is not born yet in the other universe. She does not exist there."

"You can't expect me to make such a hard decision right here, right now," AJ protested.

There was a sudden knock at the door and Amanda glitched out.

Chapter 8
AJ Harford, 2015

"Kiera, there you are." Maria walked right into the room and moved to Kiera's side. "Why don't you find a room to stay the night tonight?"

AJ gave her mom a weird look. Had she been listening at the door? She hoped not.

"Go on, Kiera, pick a room," Maria repeated patting Kiera's back awkwardly. "And I'll get started on dinner soon."

Was she trying to act motherly? AJ wondered.

Kiera gave AJ a confused look, but AJ nodded her encouragement. Kiera walked out the door with a look of doubt on her face.

"It sounds like you're suiting up for some big mission, Amanda Jane." Maria folded her arms.

"I go by AJ. And I cannot believe you were listening at the door!" AJ crossed her hand over her chest and resisted the urge to stomp her foot. Why did she always feel like she was seventeen years old again when she was in her mother's presence?

"It's hard not to when my daughter who I haven't seen in two years barges into my home without so much as a phone call and demands I tell her about the past." Maria waved a hand flippantly in the air. "I couldn't make head or tails of it, but it sounds like you're going on an important trip."

AJ wondered if her mother was purposely vague because she didn't want to acknowledge that this plan, and anything she'd heard, made AJ sound off her rocker.

"I'm not leaving my daughter with you again!" AJ protested with more anger than she realized she had in her.

"You didn't leave her before," Maria stated quietly. "I made you go. Pushed you into it. I see that now."

AJ's mouth flew open, but nothing came out. She had no words. She had always blamed her mother for that night. She never would have guessed her mother would admit her mistakes. Now that she had, AJ had no idea what to say.

Maria patted the bed in the room as she sat down. AJ sank down next to her in shock, processing this unexpected shift.

"I was always so worried about losing your father, I catered to him when I should have been prioritizing you. You were the one I needed to protect. It became clear that night you showed up on my doorstep with your daughter. Not at the time, of course. I handled that rather badly. I saw the lengths you went to in order to protect Kiera. I was wracked with guilt realizing you might not have even married Johnny if I hadn't married your father. They were quite alike, you know."

"I guess I never really thought about it," AJ murmured. "Why are you telling me this now?"

"Because I don't think I can wait another seven years for you to come back when you leave here. I've had a long time to process all of this. It's been very lonely."

"You could have called me or come to see me," AJ pointed out.

Maria shook her head. "You made it clear when you left you wanted nothing to do with me. I wanted to give you space. I wanted to wait until you came back to me. This might be my only shot. I apologize."

AJ shook her head, not ready to give up so many years of resentment. "I spent a week in a psych ward because you couldn't handle the fact that I was sad and scared when I left Johnny. They just affirmed that my emotions were normal. They assured me I was going to be okay. And I was."

Maria nodded. "I know that now. Seven lonely years without you made me see that. Whatever you're planning, wherever you're going, do it for the right reasons and you'll have the right outcome."

AJ's heart sped up in her chest with a heavy dose of anxiety and urgency. If AJ believed this futuristic version of herself, and heaven help her she actually did, she had two possible choices. Stay and always be on the run looking over her shoulder, jumping at shadows, and hiding from bad guys. Or she could go and find a way to save AJ2 while saving herself and her daughter in the process. She could live in fear or save three people.

"Make choices today you won't regret tomorrow."

AJ knew the choice she was about to make. She only

hoped she'd live to see tomorrow and make it back to see her daughter.

"I found a room," Kiera came back in sounding breathless. AJ wondered if she'd run so she didn't miss the conversation.

"Lovely, dear," Maria said as she stood, still talking, as she scooted out the door. "I'll be in the kitchen, making lasagna. Kiera, do you like lasagna? It was your mom's favorite..."

Kiera stared at AJ silently for what seemed like an entire minute. "You're going to go, aren't you?"

AJ nodded slowly.

Kiera took off a locket she wore from around her neck. She never took it off. AJ knew without looking that inside the locket there was a picture of her and a much younger version of Kiera. She'd given it to Kiera when she'd stayed the night with a friend for the first time after the divorce.

See, Kiera, I'll be with you the whole weekend. I'll never leave you...

AJ teared up recognizing the symbolism. "Kiera, maybe you should keep it. It's my promise that I'll always be with you."

Kiera shook her head adamantly. "Where you plan to go, you might need a reminder of what you have waiting back home for you."

"Kiera, I would never forget you." AJ felt shocked as Kiera's meaning set in.

"Think about it. If you're going to a universe where you become young again, isn't there a chance that *her* memories will fuse into yours as you're immersed in that world? Please take it. It'll be your anchor to remind you of what you have waiting in the universe where you belong."

"How did you get to be so smart?" AJ hugged her daughter as tears streamed down her cheeks. It was unfathomable that AJ would forget the one person who kept her going every day.

"Mom," Kiera said suddenly as she stepped back. "Amanda is... unreliable. You never know when she'll glitch in or glitch out. What if you can't find her when you need her. What if—"

"Don't say it, Kiera," AJ said softly.

"What if you don't make it back?" Kiera finished.

"I'm going to be fine, Kiera," AJ said, trying to convince herself. "The universe jump might not even work."

"No, you aren't going to be fine. You've never been that far from me before. What if it's not safe? I just need more time to research this stuff," Kiera begged with her eyes.

"You said yourself there's been no proof. Look, most likely, nothing will happen, and I'll be back in an hour." *Then we'll be on the run*, AJ silently added.

"Mom, I love you," Kiera's eyes flooded with tears. "Please, don't leave me here forever with crazy grandma."

AJ smiled. "She's actually not as bad as she used to be. She surprised me earlier."

"How?" Kiera wiped her tears.

"With an apology." AJ smiled. "She has a lot of regret. That's a terrible way to live life, with regret."

Kiera made a face. "Is that what convinced you to leave your daughter and go back to save a perfect stranger?"

"Kiera, you know me better than that." AJ wiped a few

tears from her face. "If I save AJ2, I save all of us and we won't have to live our lives on the run."

"But it's just you and me, forever. I'm afraid of what will happen if you leave." Kiera suddenly looked nine years old again. AJ saw her as if she was just leaving her dad all over again. Only this time, her mom was leaving her.

A bolt of lightning fell from the sky and hit the Earth. Minutes later, a huge crack of thunder boomed loudly and shook the entire house. AJ moved the heavy curtains to the side and could see the singed, burnt spot it left behind.

"It's time," Amanda was suddenly at AJ's side.

Kiera yelped in surprise. "You gotta quit doing that!"

"Sorry," Amanda shrugged apologetically. She quickly went to the window and held back the curtain.

AJ could see car lights in the distance.

"You have been found," Amanda said.

AJ gasped. "The guy who killed AJ2 in 1995?"

Amanda nodded.

AJ panicked, her thoughts surfacing and colliding, then jumbling. She couldn't breathe for a second. "Kiera and my mother?"

"They will be safe. They are looking for you, not them. We need to go now. We will drive to the train station. We just need to get you on the train. Once we're moving, I can transport you."

"Are you sure?" AJ asked.

Amanda nodded. "That's the only thing I am sure of."

Kiera gave her a quick hug. "Go! I'll explain it to grandma. Well, I'll come up with something."

AJ ran. Car keys in her hand, she opened the front door and took a step off the porch. She jumped back with a yelp.

A large bolt of lightning hit less than a foot from where AJ had almost stepped.

The lightning was increasing in frequency. It was coming closer. It was as if the universe was targeting Amanda. As if it was mad that Amanda was still wandering around in the wrong universe.

As AJ saw the car lights in the distance coming closer, she pushed those thoughts aside. She needed to get to her car. She needed to lead that car away. Which meant she needed to make sure they saw her.

AJ took a deep breath and sprinted for the car.

She jumped in the car, started it, backed the car out of the driveway, and hit the gas hard.

Chapter 9
AJ Hartford, 2015

AJ peeled out, her tires spinning in the gravel as she stomped on the gas pedal. She drove straight toward those car lights that were coming toward her on the road. As she closed the distance between her and her pursuer, she hit her breaks. She needed to slow down enough that the man clearly saw her. She reached overhead and flipped on the interior light in her car.

At that moment, she passed the vehicle pursuing her. It was a man driving a puke green pickup truck. His long unkempt beard and shaggy hair reached his ears. His eyes were pure black as they connected with hers. AJ shivered as she locked eyes with him in that brief moment. She felt like she had peered into the soul of the devil himself.

The intended effect worked. AJ looked in her rearview mirror. The truck whipped a U-turn, making the back skid sideways. She stepped on the gas pedal. She drove as fast as her racing heart would allow her without losing control of her car. She had the advantage of knowing the roads better which was good because she needed the head start.

Once she hit the city limits, she would have no choice but to slow down and blend in with traffic.

She only needed enough time to get on the train. Knowing this would be risky, AJ pulled out her phone. She was driving fast and buying train tickets simultaneously. Given her recent trip, she already had the website up on her phone. Because she'd bought tickets recently, the card she'd used was saved in her phone. It took two minutes to click E-ticket for the next train out. The train was going to Michigan. If the plan worked, AJ would not arrive there.

Then she hit a problem. The next train out was in an hour. It would take her twenty minutes to drive to the train depot. She'd have to hide for forty minutes. It gave too much time for him to find her.

The highway loomed ahead. AJ checked her rearview mirror again. She had put distance between them. She couldn't see headlights. She just hoped she had enough distance so she could find a place to hide once she got to the train, but not too much so they couldn't find her trail.

She made the twenty-minute drive in fifteen minutes. She inhaled sharply as she pulled into the parking lot. It was completely full. She drove around slowly, checking for an open spot. At the same time, her eyes scanned for the lights of the vehicle she knew was following her.

She spotted a parking space at the back corner of the lot. Just as she pulled in, she saw a vehicle circling the lot. She turned off her lights and pulled her car the rest of the way into the spot. She ducked down in her seat, watching as the vehicle drove behind her car. It wasn't the truck. Breathing deeply in relief, AJ threw open the car door. On impulse, she grabbed a zip-down hoodie that she had thrown on the floorboard. It was summer but no one would question why she was wearing it. Long train rides could get cold. She threw it on and pulled the hood up.

Phone in hand, she ditched her car and ran to the depot. She arrived at the check-in counter. The line moved quickly. She was out of breath as she approached the sleepy-eyed Amtrak worker. He eyed her with disinterest. He scanned her E-ticket and waved her through.

AJ had no luggage and no purse. Her wallet was in her back pocket. She carried her phone in her hand. *Would they have phones yet in the other dimension?* she wondered. *Of course not, it's the 90s there.*

AJ's heart sank when she saw the long line of people who were standing still. She adjusted her hoodie. She glanced behind her as the door to the train depot flew open. It was him.

"Excuse me," she smiled apologetically at the person in front of her. She moved up through the line as if she knew exactly what she was doing and she belonged in the front of the line. Before people could grumble, AJ found herself in front of an official-looking female.

"We'll board in ten minutes," the woman said, sounding annoyed. AJ didn't dare look behind her again. She knew he would be there.

AJ leaned in close to the woman, hating herself for using the excuse her students often gave her. "I'm sorry, I have a lady's emergency and the line at the other bathroom is extremely long."

AJ could see her eyes soften.

"Well, I suppose it is just ten minutes. But if I let you

on, I have to let everyone on. Might as well, I suppose." She shrugged.

AJ quickly got on the train and locked herself in the women's bathroom. Maybe in the chaos of boarding, he would lose her. If there was anything AJ knew about men, it's that the women's bathroom was the last place they wanted to enter. Which is why AJ would stay in that bathroom as long as she could.

AJ put the toilet seat down and worked to calm her ragged breathing and slow her racing heart. She just needed to wait him out. She checked the time on her phone. She had a half hour until the train left the station. She typed out a message to Kiera.

AJ: *Made it. I'm on the train. I love you and I'm proud of you. You've really overcome a lot at your age. You're going to do great things.*
Kiera: *Stop it, mom. You're coming back. You promised.*
AJ: *You're right. Sleep well tonight. I'll pick you up from soccer practice.*
Kiera: :)

AJ worked to focus her mind on the task ahead. She pulled out her phone and found a website called findajhartford.com. Reading details and committing them to memory would only help. If Amanda was right, and she better be because it was all AJ had to go on, AJ2 would be kidnapped two days after AJ arrived. She began to read the About page on the website that mirrored the news story from earlier.

Amy Jo Hartford, who answered to the nickname AJ, was a young woman living in Chritten, Missouri. She was abducted from a payphone located in a grocery store parking lot at the corner of Jackson and 4th Street. The grocery store was closed for the evening. The parking lot was empty as AJ stopped her car to make a quick call to tell her boyfriend she would not be coming over that night. Her boyfriend, Chance Miller, recalled that AJ had mentioned a guy standing there while she was on the phone.

"Ask him if he needs to use the phone," Chance had told her. He recalled that he was half-joking at the time. Then he heard AJ ask, and the man, who had a deep, gruff voice, had said "No." AJ then mentioned to Chance that the man was standing a little too close. That's when Chance heard her scream.

Chance dropped his phone and immediately got in his car, which he recalled was not in the best mechanical shape. Regardless, Chance got in the car, hit the gas, and sped to the grocery store. He passed a puke green truck on his way.

AJ paused and thought about this. Why would Chance try to save his girlfriend himself? He should have called the cops. Thinking of Kiera, AJ realized when a loved one is in danger, people just react, and they don't always know what that reaction will be. AJ started reading again.

"Chance, help!" he recalled seeing AJ scream and

lean out of the truck. Chance immediately threw his car in reverse and followed the truck, driving backwards until the transmission on his truck failed and his car broke down. By the time he walked back to the grocery store, his fiancé was long gone.

AJ Hartford was four months pregnant with Chance's child and the two were planning a wedding. AJ was loved by the community. She was working at a local bank while she attended college.

New details were released that point to AJ Hartford's abduction as a case of mistaken identity. Officer Parker Sheridan released a note to the public earlier today in honor of the anniversary:

We know who you are ~~#6786854~~. We found your hot daughter. Now say good-bye. Too bad for your wife, you'll never see your daughter again.

AJ Hartford was abducted that very day from this very payphone. Thanks to this new evidence, police have determined that AJ Hartford from Chritten, Missouri, was not the intended target. We believe she was mistaken for the daughter of this police informant...

A sudden pounding on the bathroom door made AJ gasp. She couldn't leave this bathroom. Not yet. No matter what. What if the man who had killed AJ2 was the same man who was knocking on her door? AJ remained silent.

"Come on, I gotta go pee," a child's voice whined outside her door.

No way, AJ commanded herself. It could be a trick. The man could be on this train at this very minute. Most likely, he was.

AJ sat still and re-read every detail of the abduction three more times in an effort to memorize what was going to happen when she arrived. If she arrived. If she even trusted that this other universe would be similar. There was a very real possibility that Amanda was completely wrong about everything. In a new universe, everything could be different, and likely was. People made different decisions every day. The day could be different. The location could be different. Maybe the grocery store doesn't even exist in the universe she was traveling back to. Maybe they don't have grocery stores at all.

AJ opened a new search on her phone. She needed to read about time travel and parallel universes. She already found the theory Kiera had mentioned about the upside-down universe. She instantly missed her smart daughter. There were theories about black holes in space that led to alternate universes. There were theories about alternate universes coexisting right alongside Earth.

Then she found another theory about the speed of light. This one was the most plausible to AJ. It stated that the world was spinning at the speed of light, which was different when measured at the surface and when measured in the air on a jet, and the only way to travel to another universe was to go as fast as the speed of light and travel across dimensions. One could jump, walk, run, or roll to the universe that co-exists right next to them if only they could match the speed of light.

AJ stared into space. While this train didn't go that fast, she'd experienced the combination of train speed and propulsion from the train through the atmosphere when Amanda had flung her into the train depot. There was no science involved in what had happened there. Just a lot of guess work on Amanda's part. AJ had never felt so uncomfortable with something she was going to attempt in her life.

She turned her focus back to the news story she had now memorized. She needed a plan. Sometimes the simplest plans worked the best. All she needed to do was grab a car, drive to Chritten, Missouri, find the other AJ Hartford, warn her not to stop at that grocery store and maybe even leave town for a while.

Easy, she thought.

Her next thought stopped her. There was a good chance AJ2 wouldn't believe her. That was a chance she had to take. She'd travel through several universes to save a hundred women she didn't know just to keep her daughter safe and living in a world free from day-to-day fear. She didn't even care how crazy it would sound when she warned AJ2.

She continued to think about every possible scenario until AJ felt confident. If she stayed focused and on task, she could go straight to Chritten, Missouri, and start working on her goal. When she arrived, she would immediately locate AJ2.

If she arrived, the little voice of fear nagged her brain. *If* she arrived.

Chapter 10

AJ Hartford, 2015

Pound! Pound! Pound!

AJ jumped and screamed a little.

"Ma'am, are you okay in there?" a stern female voice asked.

AJ felt she had no choice but to answer. "Yes, I'm sorry. I'm just feeling a little sick."

"Well, you've been in there for half an hour. There's a little girl out here who has been very patient but needs to use the restroom."

Weren't there other bathrooms on board? "Okay," AJ said, feeling sheepish. The woman said half an hour had passed. AJ carefully opened the door. Her eyes quickly scanned the train. She'd seen what the man looked like on her security video earlier that day, but it had been a quick look. Then she had seen him when she passed the truck on the road. She didn't see anyone who looked like that on this train.

AJ exited the bathroom and found a window seat. Her

eyes darted around the platform outside the train, but she saw no people milling around. This made sense because this train was about to leave, but it would be a good hour or two before the next train left.

That might mean the man was on this train. Chill bumps rose on AJ's arms. Maybe there was more than one man looking for her. She couldn't be sure. Now, she rescanned the train for any shady-looking passengers. No one was even looking her direction.

The train engines whirred, and AJ shut her eyes for a minute. In all the excitement, AJ had forgotten about her motion sickness. But her body had reminded her. Her stomach lurched. As the train started moving, AJ felt lightheaded. She gripped the guardrails, which reminded her of the first night she'd met Amanda. Only this night, AJ was looking for her, expecting her. But Amanda had yet to make an appearance.

"Come on, Amanda, where are you?" AJ whispered, staring hard at the glass as the train amped up to speed. Normally, AJ wouldn't sit so close to the window but now, she found herself leaning in, watching the alternating pattern of light and dark as the train passed the dark depot and started into the city.

AJ heard a heavy figure plop down into the seat next to her. She slowly raised her eyes to the man sitting beside her. She cursed herself for not keeping her eyes up since leaving the bathroom and finding her seat. She had assumed once the train left, she would be safe.

Now as she felt an uncomfortable metal poke just below her ribcage, she knew who was sitting beside her.

She didn't even have to look into those black soulless eyes to know she had seen this man driving the puke green truck. He had found her. This was the man who was coming to end her life.

She hadn't been safe at all.

Chapter 11

AJ Hartford, 2015

The breath in AJ's chest caught. Instant anxiety left her gasping for air. She opened her mouth to scream but no sound came out.

"I wouldn't do that if I were you," the man had a thick southern accent. There was a distinct odor wafting from his general vicinity. It was the mixture of trash and body odor that made AJ gasp again. She tried to scoot away, but the man put an arm around her and grabbed her hip, scooting her closer.

"Why are you doing this?" AJ managed to get the words out. It was difficult to speak with chattering teeth.

"Just finishing a job. I always finish my job. Even if it takes over a decade," his voice was low and menacing. "Here's what's gonna happen. No need to fuss. At the next train stop, you're going to get off the train and come with me."

"Like hell!" AJ spat loudly. She was rewarded with a few curious glances. She estimated there were ten people in the train car with them. Her outburst was followed by the sound of a gun click.

"Don't make me use this on public transportation," he growled.

"How did you even get that on here? Don't they have metal detectors?" AJ asked. Even as she asked the question, she knew the answer. No one had frisked her either. As she walked through the gate, there had been a detector but there were always workarounds. A devious mind could always find a way.

The man's smirk was his only answer. AJ really looked at him for the first time, but his eyes were not on her. He looked afraid. No, he looked horrified. AJ turned to see what he was looking at and immediately jumped back in her seat a bit.

Amanda was peering in the window. Her face was contorted with rage and for the first time, her neck was visible. Blood seeped through the wound at her neck. She bared her teeth at the man. She kept her focus on him like a dog who was protecting her owner. Then, she put her hand to the glass.

AJ looked away from the terrifying site and focused on Amanda's hand. *Stay with the plan*, AJ commanded herself. Her hand shook as she placed her palm against Amanda's and felt the window disappear, replaced by Amanda's hand.

AJ felt her body lock up. She jerked forward. Amanda had captured her other hand. AJ's body lifted up and through the window. Suddenly, AJ felt her body stop abruptly as she jerked back. Something, or rather someone, had her ankle. Amanda gave her a firm tug and AJ, along with her captor, went flying out the window.

At first, AJ felt like something heavy was weighing her down. Then, inexplicably, the weight lightened, and she felt herself floating in the air.

"What happened?" AJ shouted into the darkness. Amanda had told her she was always there, even when AJ couldn't see her.

Sure enough, Amanda replied. "Once you were through the window, the window closed with such force, it threw your captor backwards. Where we are going, he could not follow."

AJ should have felt bad, but an immense relief flooded her.

"What about Kiera?" she asked.

"He's not after her," Amanda replied.

AJ was so relieved she could have cried.

They were floating into nothingness. The blackness was overwhelming. But AJ felt like she was flying. Then she felt like she was floating in a pool. Floating away from the world and into another one with its own complications and new sets of rules that AJ would have to discover quickly and follow in order to remain alive.

Chapter 12
AJ Hartford, 2015

They were floating for what felt like hours. Time had ceased to exist, and AJ's mind felt like it was floating away with the darkness. It felt like she was sleeping, dreaming, but her eyes were wide open. She wasn't about to miss what was coming next.

"I had a dream about her, you know?" AJ said, listening to the way the darkness cushioned her voice.

"Dream about who?" Amanda asked.

"The other AJ Hartford—"

"AJ2," Amanda corrected. There was a smile in Amanda's voice.

"I felt like AJ2 had saved my life. Like I owed it to her to be the best version of myself I could be." AJ felt dreamy as her mind drifted through space. She felt weightless, like she would be floating forever with no real destination. She couldn't see Amanda though she could still feel her hand tightly gripping her forearm.

"Did you?" Amanda asked. "Live your life as the best version of yourself?"

"God, no!" AJ answered without thought.

"Why not?" she asked.

"I grew up. It was a fairytale to think that was possible. I was an idealistic seventeen year old. Adulthood became a nightmare of survival."

"A nightmare?" Amanda's voice scoffed. "It couldn't have been that bad. What went wrong in your universe?"

"My marriage. It all started way too young with a lot of bad decisions. Followed by years of abuse—mental and physical. Then, it ended in a horrible divorce with a restraining order."

"But you got Kiera so that's a pretty good consolation prize," Amanda responded.

"No doubt," AJ agreed immediately. "Was it the same in your world?"

"No," Amanda said quietly. "I didn't marry him. I got pregnant with my daughter, who I named Kara, and I ran away. He never knew about her. Sometimes I felt guilty for that. But I met John in high school, and I knew who he was. I figured it out after I got pregnant. He was a bad guy. I was fortunate to get out."

"Yes," AJ agreed, thinking about her time with Johnny and shuddering. "You were."

AJ was quiet then, wondering how long they would float around before Amanda propelled them into the other universe. Then she thought about her marriage. She thought about her mother's words. She realized she and Johnny were two broken kids from the beginning trying to make it work. *It* being married life complete with the unexpected pregnancy her senior year in high school, not enough money to live on, and his inability to separate from his mother and just be with AJ. Then there was AJ's inability to stop shopping away what little money they did make... The list was too long to catalogue and ultimately ended with severe incompatibility in marriage and in parenting. It was a wonder they'd made it as long as they had. Still, AJ viewed her divorce as her failure.

"Put your other hand on my arm and hold on tight," Amanda said suddenly with excitement in her tone. "You're going to fall for a while. You'll be okay. When you wake up, you will have arrived."

AJ did as instructed. She tightened her gut and felt her anxiety skyrocket. She prepared herself for a free fall. It would make her motion sickness seem like the flu.

"When you've completed your mission, you must meet me at the train station. It's the only way home," Amanda commanded.

"Okay," AJ felt sick with dread, anticipation, and the feeling of sudden motion as her body lurched downward.

"Don't forget about Kiera!" Amanda's voice whispered one last ghostly warning and then she was gone. Truly gone. AJ knew she was alone.

AJ didn't have time to register the amount of fear that shot through her body. She could see flashes of light and a swirling wind ahead. Then she was hurtling toward it. She felt herself sucked into the blackness. At first, she was spinning out of control as her body flailed around. That only lasted a few minutes. Then she was falling, plunging toward a light, falling faster than she'd ever fallen in her life.

AJ had one thought before she blacked out. *I'm going to die.*

Chapter 13
AJ Hartford, 1995

AJ gasped as she woke in a sudden, almost violent manner. Her heart was thumping hard. Her mind was racing. She had been free falling for so long, it felt like she had passed out. Her eyes flew open, and the sudden light burst into her retinas with such shock, she had to close them again. Involuntary tears streamed out of the corners of her eyes.

"Breathe," AJ whispered to herself. She took a deep breath in, held it for a count, and let it out slowly. "Calm down."

She felt her pulse start to slow. She took inventory. She was lying on a bed. The bed was warm and comfortable. But the room was too bright. Even with her eyes closed, it felt like the sun was burning a hole through her eyelids.

She put her hands on her body. Everything was intact. It was just... different. Her breasts were smaller. Her stomach was flatter. Her arms were thinner.

Holy shit! her mind screamed. She understood everything all at once. She was AJ. But she was the seventeen-year-old version of AJ from the other dimension.

AJ peeked through her eyelids and had to force them to stay open. There was a strange rose-colored hue to the room. She would have guessed it was the way the sun came in through curtains, casting that color. But there were no curtains on the windows, only blinds.

AJ sat up gingerly. As she did, her head instantly began to pulse.

"Amanda Jane!"

AJ heard her name before she saw who uttered it. *Mother.* Only it was a much younger, chubbier version of her mother. She didn't remember her ever looking like this. Her mother, Maria, looked healthy and seemed warm.

"Are you still in bed?" Maria's voice went up an octave with disapproval. "You're going to make me late for work!"

"Work?" AJ asked finding her throat very dry. "You work?"

"Ha ha, funny. You asked for a ride to the police station this morning but if you aren't ready in about five minutes, I'm going to leave you. I can't lose my job."

"Police station?" AJ asked. Why was she going to the police station? Didn't she have school today? Not that she would actually go. She had far more important things to do. Adult things. Didn't she? She just needed to remember what they were...

"Remember, the field trip? Your SADD club? Students against drunk driving. Wake up, sleepy head, and get dressed or I'm leaving you here." Maria turned and left the room.

AJ had wanted her mom to leave her home. In fact, she

could really tell her mom she didn't feel well, and it wouldn't be a lie. Instead, AJ flew into motion. She had the faintest notion that what she needed to do today had everything to do with the police station. Maybe she would remember more when she got there.

She opened her closet and groaned at the clothes she saw hanging there. "Let's see, we were wearing bell bottoms." AJ grabbed a pair and stepped a leg into them. "Size six?" she giggled as she put her other leg in and pulled them up. "I haven't fit a size six since I was... oh yeah, seventeen."

Next, she found a cute little shirt that didn't quite come down to her waist. She found a mirror and stared at her reflection. She looked cute enough. She tugged on the shirt and glanced at the selection in her closet for an alternative. They were all this way. Then AJ remembered. Crop tops were in. Big time.

"Chop, chop," her mother called.

"I know, I know, I'm working on it," AJ mumbled, sure her mother couldn't hear her.

She sat at her vanity and grabbed a hairbrush. She pulled her hair into a quick ponytail. Should she poof her bangs? She caught herself just in time. That was the 80s. This was the 90s. She left her bangs alone. She tried to put on makeup, but the room was still so bright she had a hard time getting any to stick. Her eyes kept watering. She finally managed a light layer of mascara. Wasn't she supposed to cake it on? Nope, she was still thinking of the 80s. She looked around until her eyes settled on a pair of pink-tinted sunglasses.

"Perfect!" AJ grabbed them with relief and jammed

them on her face. One more look in the mirror and she decided it was good enough. Cute enough but functional to make it through the day and save AJ2. She snapped her fingers. That was it! She was here to save AJ2 from the man who would snatch her from the payphone. There was just one problem. She had no idea how to save her.

"I'm leaving," Maria announced.

"I'm ready," AJ answered.

"You sure?" her mother eyed her critically, her tone matching the look on her face. AJ could hear that critical edge in her mother's voice. *Ah, there you are. Hello, mother.*

"Yes," AJ looked around and found a backpack and a purse. Surely, she needed them. She scooped them up off the floor.

"I could wait a minute longer if you want to put on a little more makeup," Maria said, peering into her face. "You're looking so pale today."

"I'm fine," AJ said, fighting an immature urge to comment on how *stiff* her mother was looking today. Maria's hair was up in a tight bun. She also wore a tight but long off-white pencil skirt, a matching blazer and a scarf tied in a bow at her neck. She was wearing pantyhose and a pair of off-white pumps. AJ bit back her response and turned her attention to the house.

So far, this house mirrored the home she'd grown up in. Which is why she knew where everything was. As she walked out of her room, she could see the dining room table through the door to the left with a green and burgundy floral-pattern rug under it. The walls were painted dark green and valences that matched the rug hung at the top of the windows. The same dark green was painted onto the living room walls. Two sofas were covered with cream, red, and green floral print that seemed to be the least busy accessory in the room. AJ wondered if the sofas were as comfortable as they looked. She walked in front of her mom and out the front door.

"I'll be happy when your car is back," Maria grumbled as AJ opened the door to a white station wagon with wood paneling running down the sides. She sat down hard in the passenger seat, listening as the cracked vinyl crunched underneath her.

AJ was happy to hear she had a car out there somewhere.

Even through the pink-tinted sunglasses, the sun seemed to burn into her eyes. She'd have to make a note to find sunglasses that had a darker tint. In the meantime, she might be able to get away with these indoors because they looked more like an accessory than functional sunglasses.

They were quiet on the way to the police station, which was fine by AJ. Waking up in the body of a younger version of herself was a lot to process. AJ supposed she should just be thankful she remembered the life she'd just left. So much about traveling this way had been unknown. There was no way to know if AJ would remember anything. She reached up, surprised to find the locket Kiera had given her before she left. It was still latched around neck, another unexpected detail to be happy about. For several minutes, AJ closed her eyes to give them a rest from the pink sun. Finally, her mother stopped the car.

"Remember the deal, AJ. I gave you a ride here, but you

need to find a ride home. I'll be at the bank until after five today."

"Okay," AJ said. But inside, she was panicking. So much for not accepting rides from strangers. Everyone in this world would be a stranger! Not to mention, AJ didn't even know who her friends were.

"Enjoy your field trip. And hustle. You're late," Maria called.

AJ got out of the car and walked slowly into the police station. The world began to spin. AJ walked through the door, looked at the receptionist, and promptly passed out.

The floor was cold and welcoming as AJ lay there. In truth, it felt good, and she wanted to stay right where she was. Which is why she felt annoyed when she felt someone shaking her. AJ could hear voices. One was female and the other was male.

"I dunno what happened. She just walked through the door and passed out..." the female voice sounded echoey and far away.

"Miss, miss, are you okay?" the male voice asked, and it sounded close to her ear. He was close enough she could smell his cologne. It smelled good but didn't help her nausea. AJ felt her shoulder shake again.

She couldn't lay here forever. She opened her eyes and felt that same burst of pain from before. She could see her pink-tinted glasses laying on the floor where they must have fallen off her face as she hit. She reached for them and jabbed them on her face.

"Miss? Hey..." a hand swiped in front of AJ's face.

She focused on the man who was inches from her, his concerned big green eyes looking into AJ's. He appeared to be studying her for signs of life. But when his eyes connected with hers, her breath stopped in her chest. She'd wager his did as well. Why else would thirty seconds go by as if they were frozen like this?

He was by far the cutest man AJ had ever seen. Though he didn't look like a man. He looked like a teenager wearing a cop uniform. He was a bit on the skinny side. She could tell he was tall from the uncomfortable way he had contorted his body to look down at her. His dishwater blond hair was long on the top, and he had to brush it out of his face as he looked down at AJ. From this proximity, she could see the light smattering of freckles across the bridge of his nose.

Still looking at her, he grabbed her wrist and felt for her pulse. AJ knew her pulse was racing but not because of her fall. It was because AJ was convinced she had just fallen head over heels in love at first sight, and her heart was singing every cliché love song phrase ever used to acknowledge how she felt.

"Should we call an ambulance?" he called to someone else, a question in his voice.

"Wait," AJ whispered. "I'm okay."

"You're okay?" the man asked. "Thank God! You really scared me. It's my second day on the job. I didn't want someone to die on me so soon!"

He hopped to his feet but stayed in a crouch as he grabbed her arm and gave it a tug.

She used her hands to push into a sitting position, then she allowed him to help her to her feet. She clutched his arm as the world spun again. She swayed.

"Easy there," he said. His voice was deep but betrayed

his age. He was young, just like she'd suspected. "Can you walk?"

"I think so." But AJ wasn't so sure.

He put an arm around her shoulder and gently led her to a dark room with a sofa. Was she in some kind of breakroom?

"I'm gonna get you some help," he said once AJ was settled on the sofa.

"Wait, stay," AJ said weakly. The curtains in the lounge, or maybe it was a breakroom, were drawn. The darkness was already settling her, and she felt her eyes close again. AJ could feel him lean closer. He smelled good. Like some sort of spice mixed with evergreen trees.

"What did you say?" he asked. His voice sounded concerned. His face was leaning over her, hovering just above her own.

"You're cute," AJ giggled right before she passed out again. Apparently, she'd forgotten she was actually in her thirties, not seventeen. A vague thought flitted through her mind. *I wonder how long it will take before more of my memory merges into the version of AJ I've inhabited?*

Chapter 14
AJ Hartford, 1995

When AJ woke, she immediately noticed two things. Her head was pounding, and there were three uniformed police officers staring at her like they were studying a science experiment. Little did they know...

She stared back at them. One was older with a scruffy gray mustache, one was bald and looked around her mom's age, and the third was the young, cute officer who'd helped her off the floor.

AJ blinked and looked away to find she was still lying on a sofa in the break room. The lights were off, but sunlight filtered in from a window. There was a round table in the middle of the room and a refrigerator in the corner.

"Oh, thank God!" the cute officer exclaimed when AJ's eyes opened.

"Miss, why are you here?" This question came from the bald officer. He seemed grumpy and put out by her disturbance in his day.

"I—" AJ's voice cracked. She was so very thirsty. "Do you have any water?"

"Get her some water!" the cute officer ordered, unwilling to leave her side.

The older man with a gray mustache gave him a surprised look but shrugged and got up. "Okay, Parker."

Within minutes, he had returned and put a cup of water in her hands. AJ sat up carefully and drank it. The cold liquid ran down her throat, soothing it. It was the best thing she'd ever drank.

"I have a message," AJ managed. She looked at the cute cop. She pointed to Parker. At least, that's what the other officer had called him. "But I'll only talk to him."

The other cops looked skeptical. Then they looked at each other, got up, and walked out of the room.

"Let us know if you need anything, Rookie," the bald dark officer called as he left.

"Are you okay?" Parker said. "You don't seem okay. Can I call someone for you?"

"I have a lead for you," AJ pushed up into a sitting position and closed her eyes for a minute. The room was spinning again. Luckily, there was a trashcan within reach. She grabbed it. For a minute, she thought she was going to be sick. Then she changed her mind and sat upright again.

"A lead? Like for a case?" Parker asked.

AJ nodded.

"Okay, what is it?" Parker was an eager, brand-new rookie cop. He leaned forward with excitement.

"There's a girl. She's going to be taken—"

"Taken? When? How?" Parker interrupted.

"Please, let me finish." AJ weakly lifted a hand and laid back down. She was trying to remember the date and time.

Her head was pulsing. She wondered if this was what jetlag felt like.

"Go on," he encouraged.

"I'm sorry. I don't feel well. I'm trying to remember the details."

Parker looked crushed. "Maybe it's best if you go home and rest. I can give you my number and you can call me when it comes back to you?"

AJ nodded.

Parker paused. "Wait, are you safe? Is there someone out there after you?"

"Not yet, but they will be." AJ closed her eyes.

"What do you mean? You're not making any sense. What's your name?" he asked.

"AJ Hartford," she said.

"Okay, that's a good start," he said. "You came to the police station to give us a lead? You don't feel well but it was important enough that you came anyway?"

AJ nodded again.

"AJ Hartford, there you are!" an older female voice interrupted their conversation. "What in the world are you doing?"

AJ opened her eyes and squinted. This person seemed vaguely familiar, but she couldn't place her. She must be a teacher.

"I'm sorry, after my mom dropped me off, I passed out. I guess I'm not feeling well today." AJ tried to sit up again. Sweat was now trickling down her face.

The teacher seemed to soften. "You don't look so well. Maybe I can call your mom to come pick you back up?"

"No," AJ said quickly. "Please don't. She has a busy day at work today. I promised her I'd find a ride home."

"I could take her," Parker volunteered.

The teacher eyed him skeptically for a minute but seemed to decide it was safe on account of the police uniform.

She shrugged. "Okay, but I need to at least check in with your mom to let her know what's happening."

Ugh, AJ barely stopped herself from groaning aloud. *At what age do teachers stop playing babysitter?*

When the double check was completed, AJ found herself in a squad car alone with Officer Parker. AJ wondered vaguely what his first name was.

He seemed irritated as he threw his car in drive and hit the gas. She rattled off her home address.

"You're a student?" he asked sharply. "You were at the station for a field trip?"

"Yes and no," AJ mumbled.

"So, all that stuff about a girl getting taken, what was that? Were you messing with me?" He sounded mad and disappointed at the same time.

"No!" she exclaimed. "That's the most important thing. Nothing else matters."

"Okay," he relaxed a little. "But you can't remember the details?"

"I'm sorry. I feel like it's going to happen in the next couple days."

"How do you know?" he asked.

AJ shook her head slowly. "That's where you wouldn't believe me if I told you. It doesn't matter how I know, just that I know, and we need to stop it."

"We?" he asked.

"Yes, my whole life I felt this sense of guilt, call it survivor's guilt, that I survived a tragedy when someone else didn't. Come to find out, that's exactly what happened. My mother used to say, *One day someone could snatch you out of your bed, AJ. Be thankful and live your life like it matters.*"

"Heavy. I'd hate to hear her bedtime stories!" Parker snickered then sobered up. "Seriously, though, saving someone else's life isn't your responsibility, it's mine."

"That's where you're wrong, officer. My whole purpose right now is to save her. This one small change, saving her life, will alter the course of the future for the good of many."

"Call me Parker. Save who?" he asked, sounding confused. He parked his car in her driveway.

"AJ Hartford," AJ said as she watched the postman slide mail through the slot in her front door, then move on to the next house. Her house was exactly as she'd remembered it as a kid, long before she'd moved back in as an adult and made changes. It was a small, two-story, white house with green shutters. Shutters she had repainted blue later in life.

"Wait, I thought that was *your* name!" Parker got out of the car and followed her. She felt dizzy again and hesitated. Parker grabbed her arm to steady her and helped her walk up the porch stairs. AJ felt electricity shoot up her arm at his touch.

They walked toward the door together. AJ found the key under the doormat and opened the door. She left the door open as she scooped up the mail. She had a hunch, a gut feeling, and followed it. She looked quickly through the mail until she found what she thought might be there. There it was: a nondescript envelope labeled with letters cut-out from a magazine and addressed to her dad.

"Your dad is Terrance Hartford?" Parker was standing so close to her she could feel his breath on her cheek as he peered over her shoulder.

Her heart beat a little quicker at his proximity. "Yes." AJ dropped the other letters and tore open the envelope.

Holy shit! It was the note threatening her kidnapping. Like on the envelope, the note was composed of individual letters cut out from a magazine and pasted onto paper.

We know who you are ~~#6786854~~. We found your hot daughter. Now say goodbye. Too bad for your wife, you'll never see your daughter again.

"I remember now," AJ said. It was all coming back to her.

"What is this letter—"

"It's intended for my dad," AJ lowered her voice to a whisper. "I believe he's a drug informant and I'm the intended target, only they get it wrong, and they don't take me."

"Who do they take?" he asked. Parker leaned forward and peered more closely at the letter.

AJ looked up from the letter and found herself looking into his concerned eyes. He was so close. Her heart beat so fast.

"The other AJ Hartford. She has my same name. They

mistake her for me and take her instead. She lives about an hour from here."

"It's like you knew this letter would be here. How did you know? How do you know any of this?" he asked.

Before AJ could answer, the world started spinning again and she crumbled to the ground, vaguely aware of the strong arms that caught her and cradled her close.

Chapter 15
AJ Hartford, 1995

AJ did not wake up in Officer Parker's arms later that afternoon. She'd woken up in a sterile room. A sterile room with a pink tint to it. Despite drawn curtains, the sun filtering in cast a pink hue. AJ closed her eyes again.

She had formed a theory. The pink-tint and bright sun were causing her nausea, dizziness, headache, and dehydration. At the thought of dehydration, she opened her eyes again. She wasn't thirsty anymore. Clear bags of fluid were half full and hanging to the side of her bed. There were tubes pumping the fluid into her arms.

"AJ? You're awake." Her mom sat with her legs crossed. She had been reading a book. AJ glanced at the cover of the book. It was *The Discipline* by Dr. M. Sange.

"You're reading a business book? Weird!" AJ mumbled in response.

Maria sighed. "I don't know what's going on with you today, AJ. But you know I started this job a year ago and in order to advance in the company, I have to read books to help me get there."

"What's wrong with me?" AJ changed the subject as she squinted at the IVs in her arms.

"Dehydration," her mom said as she shut the book. She leaned closer to peer at AJ. "They told me this is the third time you passed out today. Why didn't you tell me you weren't feeling well this morning? I would have left you at home."

"They?" AJ asked.

"The nurses filled me in when I got here. Also, there was a cop here who'd taken you home, then to the hospital. He had a lot to say about your day." Maria clicked her tongue, her voice telling AJ she did not approve.

"What did he tell you?" AJ's mind went in overdrive, wondering if he told her about the letter.

"When you got to the station, you immediately passed out on the floor. When you came to, they got you to a couch in the lounge where you were in and out of consciousness, talking nonsense. Finally, the cop took you home. You passed out on the doorstep, and he took you to the hospital."

Talking nonsense? So, he didn't believe her. That was fine. She'd fix all of this the minute she got out of this bed.

"When are they releasing me?" AJ asked.

"That depends on your symptoms," her mom replied smartly. "How do you feel now?"

AJ paused to assess. "Better, actually." Maybe the fluids were what she'd needed to acclimate. Though the room was still too bright. "Did you see a pair of pink sunglasses in my stuff?"

Her mom turned around and found a bag with her

clothes in it. She grabbed the sunglasses but held them as she turned to study AJ.

"May I please have them? I'm better but my head still hurts a little. It's so bright in here."

She gave AJ a strange look but handed her the sunglasses and watched her put them on. "AJ, the curtains are drawn, and the lights are off. It's really not bright at all."

"Well, maybe that headache is more of a migraine," AJ tried to laugh it off. "Mom, where's dad?" she asked, remembering she hadn't seen him since she'd arrived. *Was he alive in this dimension?*

Her mom made a surprised face and leaned forward to feel AJ's forehead. "You must really be sick," she said. "You know your dad left a year ago. We haven't heard from him since."

"Oh!" AJ's eyes widened over this information. Given the letter, the kidnappers must not know he'd left either. What did that mean exactly?

"The doctor will be back this afternoon," she said. "I'm sure he'll release you."

AJ nodded, feeling happy about that. A knock sounded at the door. AJ and Maria looked up, surprised to see Officer Parker. He stuck his head in.

"You up for visitors?" he asked, looking at AJ.

AJ nodded.

"I'm going to step out and get some air," Maria announced.

As Parker passed Maria, AJ could see he was carrying daisies wrapped in a plastic bundle.

"Here." He smiled awkwardly, handing AJ the daisies. "How are you feeling?"

"Better," she admitted. For the first time since meeting him, she wished she had taken her mom's suggestion and made more of an effort on her appearance.

Parker doubled back and shut the door to the hospital room. He quickly came back and sat down by her bed. He leaned in.

"After I dropped you off, I had a conversation with my captain. I showed him the note. Clearly, the note is actionable, and you are being targeted as a result of your dad's actions. We've decided we need to protect you." Parker's eyes were lit up with excitement. "Do you know where your dad is?"

AJ shook her head, resisting the urge to tell him she just got here and found out her dad was gone mere minutes ago. It was a lot to process.

"Umm, he left a year ago and we haven't seen him since," AJ told him, repeating what she'd just learned.

Parker looked crestfallen. It was clear he wanted to find her dad.

"Why are you looking for him?" she asked.

He lowered his voice. "It turns out he got involved with the wrong people. He made a deal with us and had been keeping his end of the bargain. But now, he's nowhere to be found. They must know he's a narc but haven't been able to find him either. So, they think targeting you will get him out of hiding. You haven't seen him at all?"

AJ shook her head, but she was only going off what her mom had told her. "Why do you think they know he's a narc?"

"Do you remember the number on the letter?" Parker asked.

"Yes," she said.

"It's an informant number. *His* informant number."

"I see. Did you tell my mom any of this?" AJ asked.

"No, should I?" Parker's eyes looked into hers. He really *was* a rookie cop. *Someday, he'll be the one calling the shots,* she thought. Legally, he needed to tell her guardian she was in danger. But it was 1995, and in her world at that time, she remembered those rules weren't firmly cemented in place. A fact that she used to her advantage now.

"No, please don't tell her anything," AJ requested. "My mom's got a lot on her plate with my dad being gone and having to provide for us... single moms, you know."

"Yeah, okay."

"They're releasing me soon," AJ announced, suddenly feeling antsy to get out of this bed. "Then we can go find her."

"Find who?" Parker looked confused.

"The girl who has my name—the other AJ Hartford. I've been calling her AJ2. The one they're going to target because they think she's me."

Parker's face was blank.

"Remember, I told you earlier. I have a lead on a kidnapping that will happen soon if we don't prevent it. You thought it was nonsense, but it wasn't. These drug lords are coming after me. Only, they won't find me. They'll find the other AJ Hartford who lives an hour away!"

"Okay," Parker looked skeptical. "Let's say I believe you. How do you know all this?"

"Let's just say it's history repeating itself. I've seen this sort of thing happen in the past—"

"Well, well, well, don't you two look cozy." Maria had

returned with a cup of coffee in her hands and a look of disapproval on her face.

Parker jumped up, looking guilty.

Interesting, AJ thought.

"Sorry, ma'am. I was just checking to see if your daughter was alright. It's my second day on the job and I didn't want to write a report about a girl dying on my watch." Parker laughed awkwardly.

"I think there's more to it than that, isn't there Officer..."

"Sheridan," Parker took out his badge to show her. "Parker Sheridan."

So, Parker was his first name. Why did the name Officer Sheridan seem so familiar?

"How old are you, Officer Sheridan?" her mom's voice sounded shrewd.

"Eighteen, ma'am." Parker stood up taller.

"Well, she's seventeen. Surely, you're aware that makes her a minor."

Oh brother, AJ rolled her eyes. She was thirty-something stuck in the body of a seventeen-year-old. Surely, AJ could take care of herself. She couldn't help but smirk over the way Parker's face turned bright red.

"Mom, stop. He's a nice rookie cop who they sent to check on me because no one else has time to deal with a fainting teenager."

Parker opened and shut his mouth like a fish. Clearly, he was debating saying more.

Maria looked at him. Parker looked at AJ. She quickly shook her head to keep him quiet. Before anyone else could say a word, a man in a lab coat walked in and AJ knew he was the doctor.

"Ms. Hartford?"

"Yes," AJ responded.

"Yes," her mom responded at the same time.

The doctor looked between them both with amusement. "Would you like to go home?" he asked, his eyes settling on AJ as he consulted his clipboard.

"I'll wait in the hallway," Parker said respectfully.

"Yes," AJ responded. "I need—would like—to go home."

The doctor flipped back and forth between pages, reading them for a quick second. "Just checking your vitals here so I can send you on your way. How do you feel? Anymore dizziness?"

AJ shook her head to the negative knowing she wouldn't tell him if she did.

AJ knew she should have been thinking about her health as the doctor looked her over. In fact, it could have been important to ask him questions about her condition and file it away. But she wasn't thinking about any of that. She was thinking about AJ2. She was also thinking about the cute cop hanging out in the hallway who had been assigned to keep her safe. Though he was cute, he was brand new. AJ wondered if he would be able to protect her if she really needed him.

Chapter 16

Parker Sheridan, 1995

Parker Sheridan sat in his newly assigned squad car just down the block from AJ Hartford's home. He shook his head when he thought about the conversation he'd had with his supervising officer, Gerome, earlier that day. Gerome was the acting captain until they hired someone permanent for that spot. He was tall, much taller than Parker, he was bald, and had a muscular but trim build. He had to be at least twenty years older than Parker.

I know I'm new here, Parker had slapped the kidnapping note on the table with excitement. *But that girl, the one who kept passing out earlier? This showed up in her mailbox when I took her home.*

Gerome had leaned forward, studied the letter, and whistled lowly.

Mary? he'd shouted through the open door.

An older, pudgy woman with curly brown hair appeared in the doorway. *Yes, Chief?*

Captain, Gerome corrected her absently. There seemed

to be some running joke between them. *Can you bring me the file for Terrance Hartford?*

Sure thing, she'd said respectfully, then she'd disappeared.

Terrance Hartford, AJ's dad? Parker had asked. He'd heard of him in training and recognized the name when the letter showed up on AJ's doorstep, but he couldn't remember why. Now it was coming back to him. They'd used Terrance Hartford as an example to be careful when choosing which informants to trust. Some informants, they had told the class, chose to flee the area and give information on their own terms. The fact that Terrance was still supplying the police with leads might mean he was immersed in the world or hiding from it. Hiding from police or the drug lords, they couldn't say.

Yeah, he's still MIA. We've looked for him of course. Last we knew, he was alive out there, somewhere. We just don't know where. He always calls in on an untraceable payphone.

The payphone is untraceable? Parker had been surprised by that.

Well, no. He hangs up before we can track him. We always figured he stayed in the area. This though... Gerome tapped on the letter, *tells us he's not hanging with his usual crowd because they've found out about him. Especially now that they're targeting his daughter. Where is she now?*

The hospital, sir, Parker said, starting to realize he shouldn't have left her.

Then I suggest you get to the hospital. Gerome turned to

find Mary with the file in her hand. He took it from her with a nod, quickly opened it, and ran a finger through the file, flipping until he found what he was looking for. He tugged out a sheet of paper and compared the informant numbers.

Parker saw the numbers were a match.

Gerome looked up at him. *You're on babysitting duty.*

Babysitting duty? he'd repeated.

Yeah, it's a shit job but you're a rookie who has a connection to the target. Don't let her out of your sight again. Your job is to keep her safe. If you can find her dad, it's bonus points. Gerome seemed agitated, mumbling about Terrance.

Sir, there's something else, Parker had said hesitantly. In truth, Gerome was scary to him, reminding him of an Army drill sergeant.

Gerome looked up at him expectantly.

Parker had cleared his throat. *She doesn't think she's the target. She has this theory that these guys,* Parker had pointed to the threat letter, *are going to take someone else they think is her.*

Why would they do that? They clearly have her address. If they know where she lives, they must know what she looks like. Gerome had frowned at him with intensity.

Shouldn't we alert the other girls in the area with the same name? Just in case? Parker had asked timidly.

Gerome had laughed unexpectedly. It was a short mean laugh that showed his teeth, making him look like a predator. *You want us to spend tax-payer dollars and police resources calling up every Hartford family in the area and ask them if they have a daughter named AJ?*

Parker felt his face go red. *Well, no. I guess that*

wouldn't work. There's no database of families with the names of children listed somewhere?

This time, Gerome had clapped Parker on the back and laughed harder. He doubled over for a minute. When he straightened, his eyes were serious. *See that machine over there, son?*

Parker had followed his gaze and nodded.

That's the closest thing this department has to a computer. It was handed down from a school when it started glitching. It plays an Oregon Trail game and has something called DOS on it. DOS is what you might be referring to as a database, but someone needs to input it all into the computer before it can retain anything. See that filing cabinet over there?

Again, Parker had looked and nodded.

That's all we can track. Those are people with a criminal background. Unless there's another father out there with a daughter named AJ Hartford who has committed crimes, we won't find her. In fact, you got damn lucky with this letter. So, I suggest you do what I asked and go follow her around. Make sure no one grabs her.

How long? Parker had asked uncertainly.

Until we have resolution. Maybe you can find out what she knows about her father. Maybe she can lead us to him.

Okay, Parker had agreed. He'd left then and gone back to the hospital. He'd stayed with her until AJ's mother shewed him away.

Now, as he watched their house in the darkness, Parker wondered when he was supposed to sleep. He'd started his day at eight in the morning, and he was getting pretty sleepy. He thought about when AJ was released from the hospital and leaving. That moment when Parker had fallen in step with her but her mother had put her hand on his chest.

"I appreciate the concern, officer, but don't you have somewhere else to be?" Maria's voice was frigid. She reminded him of Gerome, and he felt intimidated by her, too.

"I do," he said. He turned to AJ who looked at him with pleading eyes. He remembered her request from earlier. *Please don't tell my mom, she's got enough to deal with being a single mom and all...* It was really tying his hands. But as he glanced at her, his heart melted a little more. He was surprised to feel his concern seemed to go farther than normal empathy. That was going to be a big problem.

She had dark blue eyes which were big with fear at that moment. Fear and urgency. Her white-blond hair was pulled back into a messy ponytail. She was average height and thin. But there was something about her that drew him to her. She was only seventeen, but she seemed older than that. She was mature beyond her years. But the powerful attraction he felt for her was the real trouble. She was underage and he was a cop. And as he stood looking at her mom, he could see that she was not going to give him permission to date her any time soon. Nor should he be thinking about such things.

"We'll be fine, Officer Sheridan. We can find our way home from here," Maria had told him.

Parker nodded and fell in step behind her mom, hanging back then and watching them leave the hospital. Without telling her mom, shadowing AJ was going to get tricky. He would have to shadow her from a distance.

Which is exactly where he needed to be. He needed to keep this blond-haired, blue-eyed girl at a distance. With any luck, he might even land his first big case. If he could solve it fast, he would be a rising star. Just the thing he needed for his newly started police career.

Chapter 17
AJ Hartford, 1995

After a good night's sleep, AJ popped out of bed very early. A feeling of panic settled over her. How much time had she lost? How much more time did she have? The sun was barely peeking above the clouds when she looked out the window. That's when she saw him.

A police car was parked on the road down the block and around the corner from her house. She could almost see Parker Sheridan's sleeping form slumped over in the car.

Was he stalking her? She immediately shook her head. *No, of course not.* They'd assigned him to keep an eye on her when she gave him the threatening note. She just didn't expect that he'd sleep outside of her house all night. Since AJ had requested he not tell her mom, she supposed that's why he'd kept an eye on her from a short distance around the corner.

She felt a sense of urgency that they needed to find AJ2. Today. Things were coming back to her with startling clarity. She still couldn't remember the exact day, but she had remembered that AJ2 had gone missing from Chritten, Missouri, and was abducted from a payphone in a grocery store parking lot. That was something, at least.

"AJ, are you awake?" Maria popped her head in and looked surprised to see her daughter up and about. "How do you feel?"

"So much better!" AJ smiled a winning smile. "Ready to get back to school." She gave her a thumbs up and her mom gave her a strange look. AJ guessed she was a little too over the top.

Her mom nodded and turned to leave.

"Hey, mom. I've got a ride to school this morning."

"Oh, thank goodness!" Maria exclaimed. "I need to get to work early to make up for the time I lost yesterday."

"Great," AJ said and proceeded to get ready. This time she opted to spend a little more time with her makeup. Today, she chose a short plaid skirt, a short black top, and a denim jacket. She pulled on a pair of black knee highs and found a pair of clunky black boots. She giggled a little when she looked at her reflection. She remembered wearing this exact outfit in high school. She spritzed her hair with hairspray and ran a hand over the back of her hair to straighten out her flyaways, sighing to herself. She eyed herself critically one more time.

After her mom left, AJ found two cups with lids on them, made two coffees, and walked them to the police car down the road. Parker was sleeping. She giggled a little and tapped on the window. Parker gasped and came awake suddenly. There was a red mark on his cheek from where he'd been leaning against the side of the steering wheel.

"Good morning," she called in a light sing-song voice as

he rolled the window down. "You have drool on you," she teased as she handed him his coffee. Then she got in the passenger side of the car.

Parker quickly wiped his face, shook his head as if to wake up, then stared at AJ as she put on her seatbelt. "What are you doing?" he asked.

"Helping you solve this case," AJ smiled a smile that was a little too bright.

"Well, before we do all that, I need to find a gas station and clean up a bit." Parker had turned on the car and started driving. "Don't you have to go to school or something?"

"No, I won't be here long enough for it to matter."

"What does that mean?" he asked.

"It means we're running out of time. And I remembered where AJ2 is from. She's from Chritten, Missouri," AJ proudly announced.

"About that," Parker said hesitantly. "They aren't putting any credibility into your theory. They aren't connecting why or how you know these things."

AJ crossed her arms. "*They* being your police unit? But you believe me, right?"

"Believe what? You haven't really told me anything."

"I guess you're right." AJ fell silent, knowing her truth would put them farther behind. She had no logical way to explain that. "What if I told you I knew where my dad was?"

"Now that would be a start." Parker perked up.

"He's in Chritten, Missouri."

Parker gave her a suspicious, skeptical look.

"I mean, it's possible, right?"

"Not really. They sent the letter to *your* house. They know who *you* are and where *you* live."

"True." AJ had no answer for that. No answer that would make sense to Parker anyway. "But if I'm with you, they can't get me, can they? What's the harm in a little drive to Chritten, Missouri?"

"Do you really think your dad is out there? In Chritten?" Parker's voice sounded suspicious.

"Truthfully, I have no clue where my dad is," AJ sighed. "You probably have no idea what that's like. I bet your parents have a great marriage and have been together since before you were born."

"Yes, they were together from before I was born until the day they died. Together. In a car accident." Parker delivered the words quietly, staring straight ahead at the road.

"Wow, Parker, I'm sorry. I just assumed..." She gently put her hand on Parker's hand, which was resting on the gearshift. Her eyes were full of apology. Sudden, surprising tears came to her eyes. His words brought to mind the moment in her universe when she'd found out her dad was dead. Her mother had called her. She hadn't been speaking to her mother at the time. She almost hadn't picked up the phone.

AJ, it's your mother, she'd said in her cold, abrupt way.

AJ had sighed inwardly but responded, *I know, mom.*

AJ, her mother had paused. Her words caught in her throat. *It's your father. He's... He's had a heart attack.*

Oh no! What hospital is he in? I'll go right over to see him. AJ had started gathering her things. She'd just finished her school day.

AJ, stop. He's gone. Your father is gone.

Even now, AJ felt the breath catch and hold right in her chest in a way that made it impossible to breathe for half a second.

"You didn't know." Parker's eyes flitted to hers and softened.

Embarrassed, AJ quickly swiped her eyes. She couldn't tell Parker she'd lost a parent too. Because she hadn't yet. Not in this world. AJ thought about her dad and the complicated relationship she'd had with him. She'd found in that moment when he was gone forever that so many of those disagreements hadn't mattered. He was still her dad. He was the one put in her life to fulfill that role.

"That's actually the reason I became a cop," Parker smiled. He seemed at peace, having found his purpose. "They were hit by a drunk driver. I vowed to take a job where I could get those people off the street before they hurt anyone."

AJ nodded. "Very noble of you. We need more people like you out there." She tugged on her short skirt, suddenly feeling ridiculous in this outfit.

"Thank you." Raw emotions showed on Parker's face. Until his eyes followed her movement, then color crept into his cheeks as he quickly glanced away. He slowed the car and pulled into a gas station and the moment was gone.

AJ watched as a new, white Nissan 300 ZX pulled into the gas station. It was blaring "Pump up the Jam." Four girls sat in the car. Each of them looked like a carbon copy of one another. They all had stick-straight, long blond hair and dark makeup. They looked like her.

The ringleader of the girls, who was also the driver, jumped out of the car.

"Amber don't forget to grab donuts," a girl in the back seat hung her head out the window.

"You're gonna get fat!" Amber said as she walked away and into the gas station.

"Hey!" The same girl who was hanging out the window had spotted AJ sitting in the police car. She started waving like a maniac. "AJ! Hey!"

AJ looked around, feeling exposed. This was a busy place. Not knowing what else to do, AJ got out of the car. She caught Parker's eye as he put the nozzle in his gas tank.

"I'll be right back."

"Okay, I'm gonna run inside for a minute," Parker said.

"Hey," AJ greeted as she walked over to the girl. AJ got the feeling she should know her, but she had no idea what to say.

All three girls in the car turned and stared at her. The girl in the passenger seat popped her gum before she addressed AJ.

"What gives, AJ? We went by your house, but you were gone. Rude much?"

"Yeah," another girl lowered her voice. "Why are you riding with a cop? Did you get in trouble?"

All three girls whipped around to see Parker walk by and into the gas station.

"Oh, he's cute, AJ. Totally get it now."

"Becka!" the girl in the passenger seat snorted.

"Hey, slut. Get in. We'll be late to practice." The girl they called Amber shoved AJ's shoulder from behind as she walked by and opened the driver's door. She threw a package of donuts at the girl in the back seat.

AJ hesitated and cast a glance toward the gas station. Parker was still inside. AJ supposed it would take him a minute to get cleaned up after sleeping in his car all night. "No, I've got a ride today."

"Yeah, you do," the mouthy Becka quipped.

The girls laughed.

Amber looked at AJ weird and got in the car. "What'd I miss?"

"AJ's hookin' up with the hot cop in there—" a girl jerked her head in the direction of gas station.

"I beg your pardon?" The voice was familiar and not the one AJ wanted to hear.

"Mom?" AJ half turned, feeling horrified. What was her mom doing here? Was it the only gas station in this little town? She could see her mom's angry face. Maria was glancing from AJ to where Parker had now emerged from the gas station. He walked by, replaced the nozzle at the pump, and looked in her direction. When he saw her mother, he got in his car. He sat waiting for AJ.

"Why is he here, AJ?" Maria seethed. She looked ready to grab AJ's arm and yank her to her car. AJ felt her face flush hot with embarrassment and annoyance.

AJ shrugged casually. "It's a small town. He's getting gas in his car." She opened the door to the car full of girls. "Scoot over."

"Don't think this is over. We'll talk about this later," Maria said as she stormed off to her car.

"I take it your mom doesn't approve of the cop?" Amber said as she started the car. Though the girls had all scooted over, it was a tight fit. AJ felt constricted. No one was wearing a seatbelt. Then she remembered. It was the 90s. No one wore seatbelts back then.

She saw Parker watching her out of the corner of her eye. He casually pulled behind the car she'd gotten in and followed it to the road. He let a car get between them, but AJ knew he'd be there.

"Is it because of Johnny?" Becka asked.

Oh, God, AJ thought. Had she already started dating her no-good ex-husband by this point?

"Are you cheating?" a quieter girl beside her asked.

"Lisa!" Becka sounded shocked. Considering she was the mouthiest, that was saying something.

The car went silent, and all eyes were on her. She even saw Amber's eyes flick to her rearview mirror watching for her answer. She turned down the stereo.

"No, I met the cop, Parker, yesterday at the police station. The field trip—"

"That you didn't show up to." Becka rolled her eyes.

"Oh, I showed up alright. I just didn't stay long. I ended up in the hospital."

Everyone started talking at the same time. Relief flooded over AJ.

"What the hell, AJ?"

"I was severely dehydrated," she explained. "No big deal. But that guy, the cop, was the one who got me to the hospital after I passed out. He just came to check on me this morning, is all."

"That's so romantic," Lisa said. "You should dump Johnny."

"Am I really *with* Johnny?" AJ asked, trying to remember when they'd started dating.

Everyone went silent again.

"Oh, I love this song!" AJ shouted to distract them. "Turn it up!"

Then they all sang the words to "Opposites Attract." She felt panic in the midst of this chaos. She needed to get out of there and back on course as quickly as possible.

Time was running out.

Chapter 18

AJ Hartford, 1995

"Focus, AJ!" Amber snapped for the tenth time that morning. "Geez, it's like you don't remember any of the cheers!"

"Sorry," AJ was panicking. How was she a cheerleader in this universe, anyway? In her universe AJ had zero coordination. She needed to get out of there as quickly as possible. "I was sick yesterday, remember?"

Amber gave her a sideways glance. "That better not be your excuse for the whole week."

By the end of practice, AJ really thought she was starting to get the hang of it. Until she turned the wrong way in a cheer and collided with the girl next to her.

"Hey!" the girl shrieked. The girl bobbled a little but maintained her balance.

AJ, on the other hand, fell clumsily to the floor. Her knee hit the unforgiving wooden gym floor and instant pain shot through her. Well, at least now she had a convenient pass from practice the rest of the week. What wasn't convenient was the way her knee alternated throbbing and shooting pain down her leg.

"Let's call it," Amber said, shaking her head with disgust as she reached down a hand to help AJ up. "Come on, we only have about twenty minutes until the bell rings anyway."

AJ couldn't figure these girls out. They were so snarky but at the same time, really seemed to have each other's back.

Practice over, AJ hobbled slowly and painfully toward the locker room to get dressed. AJ grabbed the small gym bag she had stashed in her locker, which she had somehow known the combination for. She had heard of muscle memory, but she felt surprised by this. She had very little recollection of anything else in this world. She was thrilled she had white tennis shoes and opted to wear them instead of changing back into the clunky shoes she had left the house in. Then, she slowly headed down the hallway. Still hobbling, she walked right out the front doors. The school bell rang just as she exited the building.

"Miss Hartford, where do you think you're going?" a shrill voice sounded behind her.

She could see Parker sitting in his car out in front of the school. He saw her too. She'd never been a good liar and she wasn't clever on the spot. Nothing came to mind.

"I hurt my knee this morning in practice. My mom's picking me up," she tried to lie casually.

"You and your mother know the policy. You can't leave without her calling you out."

"Right," AJ laughed a little. "I thought she did. I can have her call you when she gets back to work."

"Nice try, missy. Come on back inside until she gets here." The principal was tall. She towered over AJ and had such a fierce frown on her face, AJ would have done anything to divert it from her direction.

With a dejected glance in Parker's direction, AJ turned and walked back into the school building with the principal. She would have to make a break for it at lunchtime.

"Have a seat, Miss Hartford." The principal sternly pointed to a chair in her office. Her name badge said *Principal Kelly*. She opened a phone book and picked up the phone sitting on her desk. It was a large, clunky green phone with a curly cord connecting the receiver to the phone. It made noises when the principal pressed the buttons.

"Yes," Principal Kelly said smoothly into the receiver. "May I please speak to Maria Hartford? Yes, I'll wait."

Busted, AJ thought with an inward groan as she slumped further in her seat.

After a few minutes, Principal Kelly spoke. "Good morning, Mrs. Hartford. This is Principal Kelly and I have your daughter here. She told me you were here at the school to pick her up because she hurt her knee—"

The principal listened for a moment, her eyes glaring coldly at AJ.

"Yes, she's sitting right here. Of course, you can speak to her." Principal Kelly handed AJ the phone.

"AJ! What's going on?" Her mom's voice was sharp and disapproving.

AJ sighed, remembering the days when that voice would undo her.

"Well?" Maria asked again. "Were you sneaking out of school?"

"Oh, you want an answer? I thought that was rhetorical. Well, I hurt my knee at practice, and I was leaving school." AJ almost giggled at how needlessly bulky the phone was against her ear. She caught herself just in time.

"Leaving school with whom?" Maria asked.

AJ was silent. She had no answer her mom would find appropriate.

"Does this have anything to do with that cop who's been following you around?"

"Yes, but it's not what you think. I can explain. I just can't get into it right this minute." She could see out the large picture window behind Principal Kelly's desk that Parker's police car was still parked outside the building.

"Without an explanation, you're grounded, young lady," Maria snarled.

"That's fine, mom. I understand." Only AJ wouldn't be here long enough to see that happen. She hung up the phone and looked at the principal.

"I'm grounded," AJ said, hoping to appease the mad woman.

"That's a nice start," Principal Kelly said. "You will also spend the day here in ISS." She peered at AJ, looking for a reaction.

This was great news because she had no idea where her classes were, but AJ knew better than to speak.

"You will have someone watching you all day long. You'll do your homework in isolation. Come with me." She got up and led AJ to the administrative office. She addressed the secretary at the desk who looked surprised to see her. She looked vaguely familiar to AJ, but she could not place her.

"Ms. Quanita, can you please contact AJ's teachers to get her homework for today collected and brought here? AJ is in ISS and will need a pair of eyes on her at all times."

"Yes, ma'am," Ms. Quanita agreed. As she nodded her head, her short, straight black hair swung just below her jawline. Her dark brown eyes regarded the principal seriously. She comfortably filled out the chair she sat in behind a light-wood desk which was pushed against the wall. It was a small single office with windows around each side so Ms. Quanita could see whoever approached the office before they opened the door.

When the principal exited the room, Ms. Quanita smirked at AJ with humor in her eyes. "What'd ya do?"

AJ smiled in spite of herself and the pain in her knee. "I was trying to ditch school."

"AJ Hartford! That's so unlike you. You're normally such a goody-goody! What's come over you?" she asked. Then AJ remembered. Ms. Quanita had been her babysitter growing up. At least she had been in the other universe. She seemed to know AJ here, but she didn't think babysitting was the reason why.

What if the same people in one universe were still in a person's life, just in a different capacity in another? AJ thought. *Like when you see a person you swear you know but can't figure out why.*

"I know. I wouldn't have done it if I didn't think it was absolutely necessary!" AJ wailed and sank onto the couch

Ms. Quanita had in the office. She put a pillow under her knee and propped her leg up.

"What's wrong with your knee?" Ms. Quanita asked.

AJ looked down. Her knee had swollen to the size of a large potato. "It looks bad, huh?"

Ms. Quanita nodded. She picked up her phone which looked a lot like the principal's phone. After a moment, she said, "I've got a student in here who has a swollen knee. Can you bring ice? I'd come get it but she's in ISS. I can't leave her. Thanks, Marissa."

Minutes later, a pretty blond wearing a track suit and a fanny pack around her waist entered the room. She was holding an ice pack. Her green, inquisitive eyes peered at AJ's knee.

"Looks pretty bad, let's keep an eye on that." She gently pushed on a few spots.

AJ screamed and nearly came off the couch.

"Hmm, keep this on it. Ten minutes on, thirty minutes off. If the swelling goes down, you're golden. If not, I say you need to go to the doctor for an x-ray," the nurse advised.

"Thank you!" AJ said with overstated relief. "Do you have any Tylenol?"

"Of course. I'll go grab some, as long as your mom left a note on file." Marissa left the room and returned with a glass of water and two white pills. Job done, Marissa plopped down in one of the two chairs across from Ms. Quanita, crossed her legs in a yoga pose, and began to gossip.

"Did you see the cop car parked outside the school?" Marissa asked.

"No, I've been in here all morning," Ms. Quanita said as she stood and tried to look out the front door. "Do you know why it's here?"

Marissa shook her head. "Though I could speculate about a few delinquent sophomore boys—"

"I assume I can go to the restroom?" AJ broke in. She knew why the cop car was there and had no desire to fill them in. Nor did she need to hear the gossip about kids she didn't even know.

"Of course you can!" Ms. Quanita said dismissively as she turned back to Marissa.

AJ felt relieved as she hobbled out of the office. She'd take her chance while she could get it.

Chapter 19

AJ Hartford, 1995

Her chance wasn't going to come so easily. It was like a force working against her had locked her in this building. She was not getting out any time soon. She could see the front door in her sight. She sped up her hobble when she noticed the principal had her door shut and appeared to be yelling at a student.

AJ was free. That is, until a tall, lanky boy dressed in jeans, white sneakers, and a leather jacket suddenly stood in her path.

"AJ?" he said, his voice deep.

She looked up and recognized Johnny. His brown hair was on the long side and swooped just slightly over his eyes. His vivid blue eyes peered at her with intensity. This boy had swept her off her feet when she was in high school. He symbolized all the things she wasn't. He had come riding into her life on a motorcycle and picked her up for dates. Something she would never allow her own daughter to do. Then AJ had gotten pregnant. They'd had a daughter together. Then he'd abused them. If only her mom had just said *no* to AJ getting on that motorcycle!

Johnny came closer and closer to her. AJ backed up until she bumped up against the wall. He casually leaned an arm over her head and peered down into her face, looking into her eyes.

Oh brother, AJ thought. She remembered she had actually fallen for this act when she'd been younger! She remembered how dangerous he'd seemed and how attracted she was to him. Now, as she gazed into his eyes, her stomach revolted. She wanted to kick him between the legs and run.

"I had fun with you the other night," he said suggestively.

Oh no, what did we do? Was it their first date? "Umm, me too."

"So, when are we going out again?" he asked, his intense eyes boring into hers.

She wanted to scream in his face. *Never! You'll just ruin my life. You'll ruin Kiera's life.* She resisted the urge. "How about I call you?" AJ ducked under his arm and hobbled down the hall away from him. He followed her.

"Johnny, you need to go to class. AJ, is this guy bothering you?" Marissa had just left the administrative office.

AJ wanted to say *yes*, emphatically. Instead, she shrugged. Johnny didn't wait for her answer as he sauntered down the hallway. With Marissa watching her, AJ had no choice but to hobble to the bathroom.

AJ stopped at the sink and turned on the water faucet. She splashed cold water on her face. She felt a sudden hand on her shoulder and gasped in surprise. Water dripped into AJ's eyes when she opened them. She could see Amanda standing behind her in the mirror.

"Hey," Amanda's voice sounded in AJ's ear. "What the hell are you doing?"

AJ covered her heart and tried to slow it down from the fright Amanda had given her. "I'm trying to get out of here. You touched my shoulder. What else can you do?"

"I don't know. I'm figuring out I can do a lot of things," Amanda said. "I meant, what are you doing changing history?"

"Will one day really make that much difference?" AJ asked. "I didn't even mean to go to this building at all today."

"Well, you did. You're changing everything and wasting a lot of time." Amanda sounded put out.

"Tell me about it! I'm trying to get out of here," AJ protested.

"Well, try harder. You have less than twelve hours before your target goes missing. You need to get out of here now."

"A little help would be appreciated," AJ said through clenched teeth.

"Unlike you, I cannot intervene in the sequence of events. But you have a choice. You need to prioritize your daughter. She's the most important thing here. I told you about sliding-glass moments. You get to choose your path in your world. But every change you make here will also affect your life back in your world. For the good or bad. There's no way to go back and undo it. Choose wisely."

"No pressure," AJ muttered. "Hey, I thought you said

when a person dies in one dimension, they're dead in another dimension." AJ was still thinking about her dad.

Amanda shook her head. "I didn't say that. I said when the news story broke about the other AJ, it set off a chain of events that set in motion your death in every dimension. As you're seeing, things are similar here but not exactly the same. Don't assume anything based on your world."

"This is getting complicated," AJ grumbled, but then noticed Amanda had disappeared at the same time she heard a set of feet on the bathroom floor.

"Hello?" a rude, unfamiliar voice sounded when a kid walked in. "Who are you talking to?"

AJ looked at the bratty girl and debated not answering at all. "Myself." She was remembering how much she hated high school and all the nosey kids who thought they had the right to ask these questions.

The girl made a face and went in a stall. AJ left the bathroom, all the while thinking about Amanda's original words about sliding-glass moments.

You get to choose your path in your world. Every change you make here will also affect your world. For the good or bad. There's no way to go back and undo it. Choose wisely.

AJ thought about the way she had blown off Johnny. She also thought about the butterflies in her stomach when she was around Parker. She hadn't really changed anything yet, had she? She hadn't acted on her feelings for Parker and if she knew anything about Johnny, her dismissal had just made him more interested. He loved a challenge.

But she knew Amanda was right. AJ wasn't here to start something with Parker. She was here to save AJ2 and tonight would be her only chance to do that. With determination, AJ quickly hobbled out of the bathroom.

"There you are," Marissa said. She eyed AJ suspiciously.

AJ sighed. That was the thing about getting busted fleeing school. Adults didn't tend to look the other way. AJ knew in the pit of her stomach she would be stuck there the remainder of the day.

Chapter 20

AJ Hartford, 1995

When the final bell rang, no one stopped her as AJ hobbled confidently to Parker's police car. Nor did she stop when she heard her name called. She opened the door and looked into Parker's surprised eyes.

"Man, am I glad to see you," AJ said as she sat down in the passenger seat and buckled her seatbelt. She looked expectantly at Parker who looked back at her but said nothing. "Well, drive," she ordered.

"Where are we going?" Parker asked. "My job is to protect you. Whether you're in that building or in my car, I just need to keep you safe."

She sighed. "Please, Parker. Will you please take me to Chritten?"

"I don't—" Parker's answer was cut short by an abrupt rapping on the window.

AJ spun in her seat and came face-to-face with her angry mother. She took a deep, impatient breath and exhaled it. She held up one finger to her mother and turned back to Parker.

"With or without you, I'm going to Chritten, Missouri, today. I'm going to get there before dark. I don't have a precise time but this event—this kidnapping—happens tonight. I need to get there. I'd like you to take me but if you don't, just know that's where I'll be."

Parker didn't have to respond because his face held quiet resignation. "Wherever you go, I'm on assignment to follow." Then he pointed to the window where AJ's angry mother was still peering in at them. "You would do well to tell her what's happening. I feel like she has grounds to launch a complaint against me and I can't have that so early in my career."

AJ instantly felt contrite. He was right. She knew it. She reluctantly turned back toward the door and paused before opening it. Then she turned back to Parker.

"Tonight at dark, Chritten, Missouri. There's a grocery store on the corner of Jackson and Fourth Street. I'll be there with or without you."

AJ opened the car door and stepped onto the sidewalk. It was a stony silent walk to her mother's car. AJ had no more than buckled her seatbelt when her mom broke the silence.

"What has gotten into you?" she snapped.

AJ shrugged. How could she tell her mother this story? She couldn't think of a way, so she stubbornly remained silent as Maria started the car and drove down the street. AJ assumed they were heading home.

"You just haven't been yourself since yesterday morning," her mom persisted. "Are you still sick?"

"No," AJ stared out the window. "What the..." her words stalled in her throat as she watched the skyline. AJ knew this place. Everything about this home and school in this universe had been familiar. The main difference was the rose-colored hue that AJ had assumed caused her equilibrium imbalance, though the doctor had called it severe dehydration. But now as she spied the skyline, AJ knew it was a lot more than dehydration.

She could see the St. Louis Arch that she'd always taken for granted because she saw it every day when she left her neighborhood and went to school. The presence of the arch here wasn't the shock so much as it was arching in the wrong direction! The St. Louis Arch here looked like the letter U and belled at the bottom. The arch touched the ground and the two ends extended high into the sky, where in AJ's universe, the base of the arch peeked high into the sky.

AJ remembered Kiera and Amanda discussing the "upside down" universe that scientists had theorized was directly under their universe. Suddenly, AJ knew it was true. This universe was underneath her universe and no amount of rose-colored glasses was going to help with that light-headed dizziness AJ had not been able to shake.

"Amanda Jane!" Maria's words broke through AJ's musing.

"Yes?" AJ turned her head back to her mother.

"You've seen The Bell a million times, don't pretend like you've never seen it. I will not be distracted from this. First, you attempt to leave school and you get in-school suspension. Then you jump right into the cop car. Thank God I intercepted you. Is this about that child cop you've been running after?"

"Child cop I've been running after?" AJ sputtered

indignantly. She was still processing that her mom had called the upside-down arch "The Bell."

"Yes, you're practically throwing yourself at him—"

"First of all, he's only a year older than me. Second of all, this isn't romantic. He's concerned I might be in danger. I'm not, but I can't seem to convince him of that. Third, I need his help with something important. Nothing you'd understand."

Her mother groaned. "You're not making any sense, Amanda Jane."

"AJ," she argued. "I go by AJ. Surely, this isn't a new thing here, too. People here have been calling me AJ. Can't you just go with it?"

They had pulled up to the house and AJ took the opportunity to act her age in this world. She opened the car door and slammed it shut a little harder than was necessary. She hobbled awkwardly into the house, her knee still throbbing in pain, eager to change her clothes to something more comfortable.

"What's happening with your knee?" Maria called from behind her. "On the phone earlier, you said you hurt it?"

"It'll be fine," AJ stated without turning around. The last thing she needed was to lose more time in a doctor's office. She caught Parker's cop car pulling down the block as she reached for the front door. She tried to open it but gasped when she found it already ajar. AJ pushed it carefully, so it swung the rest of the way open.

Maria bumped into AJ's back.

"AJ, would you walk? Why did you stop suddenly—" Maria stopped talking mid-sentence.

Both women stood out on the front porch peering into a

semi-lit living room. The living room was barely recognizable from the way AJ had left it earlier that day. Couch cushions were overturned, some were lopsided on the couch, some were laying on the floor. A lamp lay broken and the glass from the light bulb was shattered into big pieces. There were papers strewn all over the room. The TV screen was broken. The phone receiver dangled from its curly cord, still swinging slowly back and forth. As if whoever did this was still there.

AJ took a step back, shielding her mom. "Mom, we need to get out of here right now. I haven't been honest with you, and I think we're in danger."

They turned around and as quick as AJ was able, she limped back to the car.

"There's that cop again," her mom exclaimed with frustration. She bypassed her parked car and walked toward the police car Parker had parked on the street.

"Be thankful he's here, mom!" AJ called as she sat down in the passenger seat. She stared at the front door. Then her eyes flicked to the rearview mirror. She could see from her place in the car that Parker saw Maria and looked surprised. Reluctantly, he rolled down the window.

"Our house has been vandalized," Maria told him loudly. "It looks like a burglary."

"I think someone could still be in there," AJ called out to him after he flung open his car door.

"Officer Sheridan requesting back up," he spoke into a radio on his dash and gave the address. Parker quickly got out of the car. AJ could see his jaw clench as he pulled his gun. "You two need to drive down to the station, now. I'll clear the house and meet you there."

AJ watched him gently approach the door and swing it open further with his toe. She locked the car door as her mom got in and started the car. Maria backed out of the driveway.

"We're just going to leave him here?" AJ asked, shocked Maria would take Parker's instruction like that.

"You heard the officer," Maria responded. "He's been trained for this and I'm obeying his orders."

AJ watched the house, trying to peer into the front door for as long as it took to drive past the house. She wondered if Parker was going to be okay in there by himself. She sighed. Being seventeen was restricting all her freedom. All she wanted to do was follow Parker into that house and confront whoever had ransacked the place.

But AJ had bigger problems. She looked at the clock. It was 2:45 in the afternoon. Time was running out.

Chapter 21
AJ Hartford, 1995

"Amanda Jane, start talking," Maria demanded. AJ could see Maria's knuckles were white as she tightly gripped the steering wheel.

"There was a note. It came in the mail. It was a threat—"

"Against whom?" Maria interrupted impatiently.

"Please, mom, let me finish," AJ watched her nod and continued. "The other day when Parker—"

"Officer Sheridan," Maria interjected.

"When he took me home from the station, the day I kept fainting, I opened the mail before he left the house. There was a letter stating that dad was a police informant, and they knew, so they were going to kidnap me for revenge. I turned the note over to the police."

"Who is *they*?" Maria asked.

"There's a group of drug lords, people who supply drugs, and they learned that dad was a police informant. They mentioned an informant number. Officer Sheridan was able to match the number to dad."

"Your dad is a police narc?" her mother's voice sounded shocked.

"Yes."

"But the drug suppliers found out he was telling on them?"

"Yes."

"So, they threatened to take you for revenge in a letter that came in the mail?"

"Yes."

"The police have this letter?"

"Yes."

They pulled up to the police station. They had parked and Maria threw open the door. AJ followed her lead.

They walked up the steps of the police station and had almost walked through the door when AJ stopped and put a hand in her pocket.

"Oh, no. I left something in the car," AJ said. "Can I have your keys? I'll meet you in there."

Wordlessly, her mom handed over her car keys.

AJ flashed her a smile and watched as her mom walked into the station by herself. Then AJ hobbled as fast as she could to Maria's car. She slid behind the driver's seat and locked the car doors. She turned the car on and drove out of the station. She didn't even look back.

She hit the gas and drove. She shook her head when she saw The Bell and watched it become smaller in her rearview mirror.

When AJ had driven thirty miles without spotting one gas station, she realized she had no idea what direction Chritten was. With no cell phone and no GPS, AJ had no idea how to find the place.

"What did we do back in my childhood without GPS?" AJ mumbled. She remembered a time when she was hopelessly lost, and she'd stopped at a gas station. She would just have to stop at the first gas station she saw.

Only, she didn't see any gas stations. After a few miles of driving aimlessly, AJ checked her gas gauge and saw that it was getting low. She thought through her options. She could drive back the way she came, but she would still be lower on gas and no closer to AJ2. Not to mention, the closer she got to her mom, the more chance she had of being caught and grounded, and unable to leave again.

Her best bet was finding a gas station out here. Panicking, AJ began looking around at houses as she drove by. The houses seemed to be scattered around. Miles of farmland spread out in either direction. On all that land, she could only see one house. Then AJ wouldn't see another house for many more miles.

Considering the lack of safety in her current situation, AJ realized with a start how stupid it would be to knock on the door of a perfect stranger's home. No matter that it was a different era, strangers weren't friends. AJ would do well to remember that.

So, she kept driving and watching as the time on her dashboard ticked away until she'd been driving for over an hour. Time moved so slowly when one was watching. It moved quickly when one had somewhere important to be.

Dread struck deep in AJ's heart. What if this universe was trying to keep the events perfectly in order of how the other universes had played out?

Chapter 22

Parker Sheridan, 1995

By the time his backup showed up, Parker had already cleared the house and was waiting on the porch.

"There's no one inside," Parker informed his coworker, Officer Rogers. "Though the place was definitely vandalized and maybe even robbed. We need to have the victims look around to report if anything was stolen."

"Did you dust for fingerprints?" the officer asked him.

"No, do we need to have someone dust for fingerprints before the family is allowed back in?"

"We always dust for fingerprints, Rookie. The kit is kept behind the driver's seat. Come on, I'll show you where." The officer walked Parker to the car and reached behind his driver's side seat and pulled out a box. Rogers led Parker back inside, put gloves on, and opened the kit.

"Any of this look familiar?" Rogers asked him.

Parker nodded sheepishly. He had learned how to do this in training. Everything was there in the kit. The black powder, the fluffy white brush, the tape, and the index cards. He watched as Rogers opened the black powder and lightly swirled the brush around. Then he eyed the room critically, proceeding to dust.

"It's likely the prints we pull will belong to the family, but we'll hit the main surfaces just in case," Rogers said with his attention on the process.

Parker watched, intently absorbing everything he was seeing. "We don't have a different department do this for us?" he asked innocently.

The officer gave out a short bark of a laugh. "Small town departments like us can't afford a whole department to do fingerprints. We do it all. In fact, if there was a bigger crime happening somewhere in town, we wouldn't even spend time on this one. I hear in the big cities, the ones with a lot of crime, they don't even send people out. They just have the people report what they're missing and try to match 'em up if they recover hot items later."

"Really?" Parker was horrified at the thought and felt grateful he lived in a small town.

"Yeah. Say, you're a little too new to be out on assignment by yourself," Rogers frowned at Parker. "What's the story?"

"I was assigned to watch AJ Hartford, the girl who lives in this house. I was here when they discovered the break-in," Parker explained.

"I see. Where's the family now?" the officer asked as he finished his task and closed up his kit.

"I sent them on to the police station. I thought someone was still here and they might be in danger."

The officer nodded and walked out of the house. He waited for Parker to follow, then he closed the door to the home behind them. He promptly removed his gloves and put them in a disposable bag.

"So, the Captain gave you a busy-work assignment that he thought you could handle on your own. Only, the girl you've been assigned to isn't here," Rogers frowned at him.

Parker felt his face go hot. He didn't know if he should feel flattered or irritated that they'd given him a job before he should have been released to work by himself.

"Look, Rookie, we just don't see a lot of action around these parts. When I joined the force, I was idealistic and wanted to solve crimes and help everyone feel safe. Just like you. But there's not a lot of crime-solving to do. It's a quiet town." With that, he got in his car.

Parker felt his heart sink but followed his actions and got into his car. As he drove back to the station, passing through the small town without really seeing anything, he reflected on his senior officer's words. Parker had to admit to himself he did want to solve big crimes and make sure everyone was safe. But he just wasn't willing to move to a bigger city to get action.

The two police officers arrived at the station at the same time, got out their cars, and walked into the building.

"It's about time you got here," the receptionist whispered to Parker as he approached. "They're looking for you."

"Where's the girl?" asked supervising officer Gerome when he spotted Parker. Gerome was taller and with his chest puffed up in anger, Parker was downright intimidated. His supervising officer had large biceps, a trim build, and a good three inches of height on Parker. He was also old enough to be his dad.

Parker shrugged and shook his head. "I sent her and her mom straight here while I cleared the house and waited for backup."

"You lost the girl?" Gerome thundered at Parker Sheridan so loud all eyes in the office looked in their direction. "And you went in the house before backup arrived? You're a rookie cop. You don't rush ahead in that situation. Next time, you wait."

"Yes, sir," Parker said, looking Gerome in the eyes. Gerome's pupils were dilated in anger. His eyes were usually a medium brown color but now looked black with rage.

There was a moment of utter stillness in the office. Then they heard the clacking of high heels against the tile floor.

Maria Hartford showed up in the open doorway. "Excuse me."

Parker looked up in surprise, his face showing defeat. Both he and Gerome looked expectantly at Maria.

"Officer Parker didn't lose my daughter. I just looked out the window where I parked. She cleverly lied to get my car keys, then stole my car. No telling where she was going." Maria's voice was clipped, and her mouth was drawn into a straight line.

"Mary, put out an APB on AJ Hartford," Gerome said with his booming voice as he snapped his finger several times at his assistant. Gerome had to talk loudly because Mary's desk was in the middle of the room and her back was to him. Still, Parker didn't like the way Gerome addressed Mary, and he wondered if he treated her that way because she was female or because she was his direct command.

"Yes, Chief," she snapped into action, her fluffy brown hair swaying with her sudden movement. She looked frumpy and laid back, but Parker had to admit, she was really moving fast. She didn't seem intimidated by Gerome, just happy to have something to do.

"Captain, acting captain," Gerome snapped as he turned back to Maria. "Please tell Mary there the make and model of your car."

"You don't have to do that," Parker said in a quiet voice as Maria walked over to Mary's desk.

"What?" Gerome asked sharply.

Parker put his hands up. "I'm not telling you how to do your job, sir. I just know where she's going."

"Where?" Gerome demanded.

"Chritten, Missouri, because she's convinced that's where the other girl will be taken," Parker said.

"Other girl?" Gerome looked at him blankly.

"Yes, I'm not sure if you recall what I told you about her suspicions after I turned in the note?" Parker tried to remind him.

"The theory that although the letter showed up in her mailbox, with her dad's informant number, these guys are going to somehow mistake her for another girl with her same name who lives over an hour away? That theory? I thought we decided that was foolish," Gerome snapped impatiently.

"We did, sir. But AJ didn't. She's stubborn and she's determined to find this woman and save her," Parker admitted.

"Well, what are you waiting for?" Gerome asked. "Go get your AJ Hartford and bring her back. We'll put out the APB, that way if someone else finds her first, they'll know to hold her until you get there. Then you can escort her back."

Parker nodded and turned to leave. It was a little under an hour to Chritten, Missouri, and AJ had a nice head start. Chritten was a small town so surely, he would find her once he got there.

"Sheridan?" Gerome boomed from where he stood still in the doorway with his hands on his hips and a frown on his face.

Parker turned around.

"You better hope nothing's happened to her. She's on your watch. If you find her, you need to keep her this time. Do not take your eyes off AJ Hartford."

Parker nodded, his heart thumping in his chest. He'd find her. He had to. Parker knew the fear he felt deep in his heart had little to do with Gerome's ominous command and more to do with the thought that something could happen to AJ before he got there.

Chapter 23
AJ Hartford, 1995

AJ saw a small building up ahead. It looked a little like an abandoned shack. The front of the building was deteriorating wood and the roof looked old. There were two cars in the parking lot.

As she got closer, her heart soared with renewed hope. It was a diner. Her hesitation over her initial judgments were replaced with warm feelings as she pulled into the parking lot. She could see that the windows were clean and had cute flower beds built underneath. An assortment of colorful flowers grew in purple, yellow, and red. The front door was propped open as were the windows. Most likely to create an airflow. Though it was old, the diner was lovingly well-kept.

AJ pulled into a parking space and put her car in park. Before she walked in, she scrounged around for money. She found three dollars. She'd buy a cup of coffee just to get directions if she needed to.

AJ walked in and immediately smelled the aroma of fresh-baked bread and roast beef. The diner was mostly empty, save a woman sitting at a table. The inside of the diner was clean, with a nice wrap-around bar, tables, and booths that had red checked tablecloths on them. When AJ walked in, the woman at the table got up. She was short and curvy with kind eyes and dark red hair pulled back into a ponytail. She looked like a cliché southern mama. As it turned out, she was the waitress.

"Hello!" the bubbly woman greeted her. "Sit wherever you want."

"Actually," AJ smiled sheepishly. "Can you tell me what this town is? I'm afraid I'm a little lost."

"Yes, this here is Eddington. Is that where you need to go?" The waitress quizzically studied AJ.

"No, I'm looking for Chritten, Missouri. Do you know where it is?" AJ asked.

"Hmm," the waitress pursed her lips. "No, but I think we've got a map back there. Would that help?"

"Absolutely!" AJ brightened. There was no substitute for Midwestern hospitality. Within minutes, AJ had found where she was on a map and where she needed to go. Her heart sank again. She had just driven an hour in the wrong direction! Her mom's car was running out of gas. By this map's estimation, it would take an hour and a half to get to Chritten!

She gratefully thanked the waitress and realized she had not eaten today when her stomach growled. The waitress heard it.

"My goodness, somebody's hungry," she giggled. "What can I get you?"

"Nothing, thank you," AJ responded, still looking at the map. "I left my money at home and I'm about to be late to something important." To her horror, tears welled up in her eyes.

"Oh no, none of that," the waitress tsked. "Are you having a rough day?"

AJ nodded and wiped her eyes. "I just drove an hour and a half in the wrong direction!"

"I have just the thing for you," the waitress said and disappeared into the back of the diner. After a few minutes, she came back with a sandwich in a to-go box. "Taste test this and tell me what you think. We're trying a new recipe. You'd be doing us a favor to eat it."

The sandwich looked amazing. AJ's stomach rumbled again. Slices of black forest ham, cheddar cheese, lettuce, and tomato where piled high inside two slices of homemade sandwich bread.

"Thank you." AJ gasped. "It looks wonderful!"

"On the house in exchange for your honest opinion." She winked as she put her hands on her hips.

AJ took a quick bite.

"How about something to drink?" the waitress asked.

"Coffee, please?" AJ was sure her eyes showed the gratefulness she felt.

As she expected, it was the best sandwich she'd ever eaten. AJ tried to leave her three dollars when she finished but to her surprise, the waitress shook her head. Then she quickly leaned down and added a ten-dollar bill to the one-dollar bills.

"I couldn't," AJ tried to protest.

"Of course, you can," the waitress told her. "You can keep that map too. I have a feeling you're gonna need it.

Besides, we have two more back there just like it." She winked again and was gone.

AJ waited a minute, but when the waitress didn't come back, she grabbed a napkin and a pen she saw on another table and wrote the note.

Thank you for your hospitality.

AJ walked out of the restaurant, juggling the map and the coffee, trying to feel hopeful even though time continued to rush by.

Chapter 24
Parker Sheridan, 1995

Parker had arrived in Chritten, Missouri. The first thing he did was check in at the Chritten Police Unit. This town was so small, Parker didn't have to drive far before he spotted the old brick building that looked like it used to be a small schoolhouse back in the day. It had a white weathered sign out front that said Chritten County Police Unit.

"The name of the town and the county are the same?" Parker mused aloud.

When an officer went out of his county following a case, it was important to give a nod to the local authorities. Not only was Parker not in his jurisdiction, but he might also find himself in need of backup later on.

There, he found himself in front of the local town sheriff. *Sheriff Rifkin*, his badge said. After he offered a friendly handshake, Sheriff Rifkin sat down heavily to hear Parker's story. Parker tried not to stare at his large pot belly and chose to give only the facts about his story.

"Well, yeah, I recall the APB we had faxed over today on

this girl. AJ Hartford—her name rung a bell 'cause we got an AJ Hartford here in this county, too."

"You know a girl named AJ Hartford?" Parker's mouth was suddenly dry. Could AJ's story be true after all?

"Well, yeah," the sheriff scratched his head. His graying hair seemed a little long. "She's kinda the town sweetheart around here. Her name is Amy Jo, but her friends and family call her AJ. Was homecoming queen, top of her graduating class... Hell, she's the nicest bank teller you'd ever meet. Before I bring her in, you wanna tell me what this is about?"

Parker paused as he processed the sheriff's words. "She works at a local bank?"

"Sure does. Citizens Memorial Bank of Chritten. Might even be there now... It's right down the block. Can't miss it," he responded.

"Did the fax have a picture of AJ Hartford?" Parker asked.

"Sure did." Sheriff Rifkin leaned back and reached for a piece of paper off a fax machine and slid it toward Parker.

Parker picked it up. It was his AJ Hartford alright. "I'm curious. Does this picture resemble the AJ Hartford who lives here in Chritten?"

Sheriff Rifkin leaned forward for a good look. "Well, yeah. Sure does! But if you're asking me that, I'm guessing we're talking about two different girls?"

Parker nodded, feeling perplexed. "Well, that's curious because this AJ Hartford," he tapped the picture, "the one we're looking for, stole her mother's car and drove here. She's not from Chritten. She's just convinced she's connected somehow to your AJ Hartford. Mind if I look around town a little to see if I can find AJ?"

"Which AJ?" Sheriff Rifkin snorted.

"The AJ from my town. The one who stole the car and ran. I don't believe she's dangerous. She's just stubborn and I need to get her back home," Parker stated.

"You think she's coming here to find Amy Jo, huh?" the sheriff pondered a moment. "Try the bank. Amy Jo works there. There's a good chance she's working today. Sounds like you'll find your AJ there if she's looking for our AJ," Sheriff Rifkin chuckled and shook his head.

Parker suddenly saw the humor in this crazy story. "Our AJ calls your AJ, AJ2. To keep it straight."

"We'll just call her Amy Jo to avoid confusion. Good luck with your search and let me know if I can help you with anything."

Parker got up, thanked him, and left.

The bank was the newest building in town so far and it wasn't hard to find. In fact, nothing in this town was hard to find. It was a tiny little town in the middle of nowhere. Parker pulled his car into the bank parking lot, viewing the new white siding and navy-blue accent corner pieces.

He walked into the lobby. The lobby was more dated than the outside with its linoleum floor and navy-blue shag rug that sat under a vacant desk.

"Hello, can I help you, officer?" a cheerful clerk at the counter greeted him the minute he walked in. She was wearing half of her brown hair down and half of it up in a side ponytail. She had a big bow around her ponytail. She pushed up the puffy sleeves of her otherwise fitted black dress.

"I—" Parker caught sight of the professional-looking cluster of pictures that hung on the wall. There was a picture of Amy Jo Hartford. The name under her picture wasn't necessary. She bore an uncanny resemblance to his AJ Hartford. She looked like an older sister. At the thought of *his* AJ Hartford, his cheeks flushed pink.

The woman cleared her throat.

"I'm sorry. I'm looking for her," Parker pointed to the picture, then scanned the lobby, not seeing the woman anywhere.

"You're outta luck. She's off today. Is there anything I can help you with?" The teller seemed outgoing, but Parker realized it was more than that. Her eyes were scanning him in appreciation. She was flirting with him.

Parker raised an eyebrow. It wasn't the first time he caught attention though he never understood what women saw in him. His nose had a smattering of brown freckles as a result of working outside jobs through high school. He'd heard someone say his hair was dishwater blond. It was true he was tall and muscular but that was only because he worked out to keep himself in shape for the job.

Deciding to use her attraction to his advantage, he gave her his most charming smile. He walked closer, put his elbows on her counter, and leaned in. "I wish you could," he read her name tag, "Melissa."

Melissa smiled brightly. "You're not from around here, are you? Our cops don't fill out their uniforms like that in this town."

"No, I'm not from here. I'm trying to find someone. A distant relative of Amy Jo's, and I was hoping she could help me out," Parker said, shrugging apologetically.

The expression on Melissa's face changed. "AJ, she goes by AJ," she automatically corrected. She looked around, then she leaned forward too. Their faces were inches apart. "Look, if you're looking for that no-good daddy of hers, you tell him to stay the hell away from her. Better yet, lock him up for good. Every time he comes 'round, he breaks her heart. It's not worth it, but she just wants a relationship with that loser."

"I'll keep that in mind," Parker pulled back, his heart racing as he processed her words. He thanked her. Then a thought occurred to him, and he decided to play a hunch. "What makes you think Terrance is so bad?"

Melissa didn't miss a beat and quickly confirmed his suspicion. "Typical dead-beat dad. He makes big promises with zero follow-through. He's left her sittin' at restaurants, no-shows big events, forgets to call on her birthday... you know the type."

Parker nodded, his heart pounding as he worked to remain casual. "Yeah, I know the type. You probably don't have any idea where to find her on an afternoon like this do you?"

Melissa shook her head. "Gawd, isn't it beautiful? One of those unseasonably warm April days... I hope she found a park to sit in and soak up this nice sun. Have you tried her boyfriend, Chance Miller? Bet you a thousand bucks she's with him."

"Thank you," Parker nodded. "You've been a huge help." He gave her a two-fingered wave and left the bank.

He checked his watch. AJ left at least a half hour before he did. Maybe he needed to switch tactics and drive around town to find her. It wasn't such a long shot with a town so small. His thoughts made him feel uneasy. In fact, everything about this situation made him feel uneasy. AJ had to be here somewhere. Unless someone had found her and intercepted her before Parker had even arrived.

What if he was too late?

Chapter 25
AJ Hartford, 1995

The bright sun beat in through the windshield of the car AJ drove. Despite the large, dark sunglasses she had found that must be her mom's, AJ still needed to put the sun visor down to shield her eyes even more. The longer she drove, the more her vertigo returned.

She had been traveling at a nice pace but when she felt nauseated, AJ pulled off the highway and drove a couple miles down the road to a gas station. The town was a small metropolitan city that seemed a little busy for the afternoon. It was like a small city had popped up out of nowhere and everyone seemed to have a place to be and a plan to get there. The buildings that lined the streets were three and four stories. They were old but sturdy. They looked important.

Thankfully, she felt better once she stopped the car and got out. She breathed in the fresh air. She needed to get gas in her car anyway. She grabbed the ten-dollar bill the waitress had generously given her and went inside to pay before she pumped. She did a double take when she saw the price of gas per gallon was ninety-nine cents! She never remembered a time it was this low, but she was glad it was.

She walked in and impulsively grabbed a fountain drink cup and filled it with water. She paid for the cup and prepaid the rest of her ten dollars for gas. After a quick bathroom stop, she turned back toward the door but paused before leaving.

"I'm trying to get to Chritten, Missouri. If I turn right out of the station and follow the highway west, will I really run into it?"

"Hmm," the clerk buzzed as he pulled out a road map. He traced his finger from where they were right now to Chritten. Then he paused.

"Is this what you're looking at?" he asked.

AJ followed his finger as it traced a route to Chritten. She nodded.

"Looks like the most direct route to me. Just take this road right back out to the highway. Head west and watch for the signs to Chritten. You got quite a ways to go, though." He pointed to the road in the direction AJ had just come from. "But just so you know it's about rush hour and just past this gas station, we're down to a one-lane before you get to the highway. It's going to slow you down if you're in a hurry."

"Oh no," AJ sighed. "Thank you. I'll scoot out of here quick."

"Won't make no difference now. It's five."

"Okay," AJ still moved as fast as she could without putting any more strain on her knee.

She put the gas nozzle into the tank and clicked the

nozzle on. She closed her eyes, leaned against the car, and took another deep breath. Her stomach settled and she felt like she might be okay to drive. She took account of her body as she listened to the swishing sound of gas going into her car. Her knee was still in pretty bad shape but otherwise, she was okay.

As the nozzle clicked off, AJ opened her eyes and replaced the nozzle. She got back in her car. Just as the clerk promised, traffic was at a complete standstill. There were already several cars lining up for the gas pump she was leaving. AJ shook her head at how fast that change had happened. As she tried to wedge herself out in the traffic, she got a few honks until one kind soul finally let her out.

AJ adjusted her radio until she found some 80s oldies. She realized with a start that these weren't so old. It was 1995 here after all. She had to marvel how many similarities there were in this world to the world she'd left.

With the exception of the upside-down arch, the rose-colored sunlight, and her consistent vertigo, the miles of open country landscape and the kind people with Midwest manners were all the same.

AJ edged herself out into traffic. No reason to just stay parked at the gas station. As AJ watched the bumper in front of her, she mindlessly reached up and fingered the locket around her neck.

Shocked, she held it a minute remembering what the locket held but realized how easily she had forgotten about its contents and the daughter who had given it to her. The daughter she had waiting at home.

If she ever got back home.

Chapter 26

Amy Jo Hartford, 1995

It was one of those days that changed their lives forever. The type of day that lulled them into a false sense of security. A day that tricked them into believing they were invincible, immortal, and they would all live forever.

When reporters asked them questions in the future, they would recall where they were when it all went wrong. Time forever frozen in the moment before Amy Jo went missing. With no reason to suspect anything was out of the ordinary, they lived in the moment, carefree and happy. Some say that's why Amy Jo was taken. Because no one suspected a thing.

The sun shot rose-colored rays of unexpected warmth down on the small town where nothing bad had ever happened. A group of eleven people were gathered in the backyard. The smell of seasoned hamburgers and hot charcoal hung in the air.

"Another Night" by Real McCoy was playing from a stereo. The girls danced to the song that had stayed at the top of the charts most of the year as they sipped drinks out of red plastic cups and giggled about boys. The guys raised their voices to talk over the tune, pretending not to like the song that had been popular this year, like they were immune to the pop singers' sex appeal.

It was one of those unexpected days where Amy Jo was off work in the middle of the week. Her college classes were paused for a three-day Good Friday holiday, and it was an unseasonably warm April. All the important people in her life were in the same place at the same time for an impromptu barbecue.

Sitting in a swing in the backyard of her best friend's house, Amy Jo Hartford stretched her legs, knowing well the dangers of rose radiation that poured down from the sky. She didn't care. Her skin matched the sun most days. It was an inevitable shade of white tinged with pink.

"Eighties for the win! Best. Era. Ever," one voice rose argumentatively above the voices of the small crowd. Amy Jo immediately knew the voice of her best friend.

Lacey Miller was arguing with Amy Jo's boyfriend, Chance. The two of them picked at each other like they were brother and sister which wasn't too far from the truth. They were cousins and had been best friends since before kindergarten. Lacey had introduced Chance to Amy Jo.

"You would think so. You look better with big hair and tight-rolled jeans, Lacey," Chance shot back. He might as well stick out his tongue. In this moment, he looked closer to eleven-years-old than twenty-one.

Bell bottoms, which were also called hip huggers, were the current "in" jeans of the day. Most of the girls here wore a pair with a little cropped shirt showing off their flat stomachs.

"I do, don't I? But you have a point. Thank gawd we moved on from that!" Lacey rolled her eyes.

Amy Jo watched Lacey who tilted her head toward her dad. Lacey's dad, Jerry, was preoccupied with flipping burgers on the grill. Lacey and Chance walked over to Jerry. Amy Jo couldn't hear him, but she bet they were pulling him into the debate. Jerry had taken off work because it was a rare moment when Lacey made an appearance back in town from college. They were all taking a break from their college routines to sit and bask in the sun during what they assumed to be a perfect day.

Amy Jo watched with a smile on her face as Jerry shook his head, declining to answer their argument. Instead, he pulled Chance into a conversation he was having with Skip, Jerry's best friend, who was helping grill burgers while drinking beers. They were all talking and laughing loudly.

"No, really, it was breaking news. The Hubble telescope showed," Jerry made air quotes with his fingers, "evidence of the existence of supermassive black holes in the center of galaxies."

"You made that up!" Skip laughed while shaking his head. "Black holes..."

"That's my cue to leave," Lacey said. She exited the conversation and ran over to a group of girls.

Chance waved at them but walked away. He sauntered over to Amy Jo instead and plopped down next to her. He rubbed her growing abdomen.

"How are you?" he asked. "And how's my boy?"

"The baby and I are fine," Amy Jo responded with a smile. She thought the baby was a boy, too.

"What are you doing over here by yourself?" Chance asked.

"Soaking it all up. I love everything about today. I wish I could live this moment in a loop and never leave," Amy Jo responded with a wide smile.

"It's the kinda fun that just happens," Chance smiled happily. His blue eyes turned a shade brighter in the sunlight. He leaned over to kiss her. "Speaking of *not* planning, when are we gonna do this thing?" he asked as he twisted the modest diamond Amy Jo wore on her finger.

Amy Jo sighed. "You know how I feel. I want the fairytale dream wedding. The one where my wedding dress is not plus-one sized." She'd already put a deposit down on Shaylee Barn north of town but hadn't given them a date yet. She'd picked out the dress. To be fair, she'd picked it out ten years ago. True, the style had changed, but she could modify the dress easily.

It was the exact dress she'd always wanted. The top was off the shoulders and fitted to the waist. It was simple and elegant. The skirt fell in a simple line to the floor with a long train in the back. No lace, just yards of off-white satin and soft material. She would have a bustle sewn in so she wouldn't trip over the train during the reception. She planned a simple off-white heel to complete the look.

The dress fit her perfectly—before she found out she was pregnant. Chance had also proposed to her before she'd found out she was pregnant. But no one in town believed that. She could tell by the way they whispered when they thought she couldn't hear them. She didn't care. She was happy. She and Chance were happy together.

Amy Jo sighed and patted Chance's hand that rested

on her belly. While she'd hinted that she wanted to wait until after the baby was born to get married, she hadn't found the right moment to talk to him about it. If she left it up to him, they'd already be married. She just didn't want to rush into it. They had plenty of time. Their whole lives were ahead of them.

"I don't know yet, Chance," Amy Jo added. "We have plenty of time to decide."

"Burgers are ready!" Jerry called.

Amy Jo's stomach growled in response. They got up to get food. Jerry quickly blessed the food. Amy Jo closed her eyes but promptly opened them. She peeked around at all her friends, who she considered family. These were her classmates she'd gone to school with, danced at dances with, talked about boys with, and was now in college with. They had all found each other here today. The way they always had over the years.

The illusion of time was passing them by. Just a minute ago, they were all in kindergarten together. Now they were turning twenty-one together. Amy Jo had always been the most impulsive of the group. She was a dive-in-first and think-about-it-later type. She was always the first to try anything new. She was the first to drink. The first to try weed. The first to lose her virginity. Trust Amy Jo to be the first to get engaged. It was certainly no surprise that she was the first to get *knocked up* as they had all lovingly teased her.

In truth, they could not be happier for her. The happiest of all was Amy Jo's mother. She was about to become a grandmother. Her only daughter was about to marry her high-school sweetheart. They'd had their share of trouble growing up with her mom supporting them as a single mom. Amy Jo refused to think about her dead-beat father who never paid a dime in child support and only showed up when it was advantageous for him.

A bank teller job is good enough for now, her mama liked to say, *but you go get that college degree. You make sure you can support yourself. But it'll be nice for you to have someone by your side to share your life. Because Amy, baby, life can get lonely sometimes.*

Amy Jo had disagreed. Life wasn't lonely for her. She was popular in school, she was loved by her coworkers, and her professors thought she was the best student in the class. She was kind to everybody. She didn't care what she did for a living so long as she helped people. Not everyone had as good a life as her. Even without a dad, her life was good. She didn't need a dad because he sure didn't add anything to her life.

As Amy Jo finished filling her plate with food, Lacey ran up and linked her arm.

"Come on, AJ. You're needed over here with the girls." Lacey steered her toward the group of girls sitting on a blanket in the corner of the yard.

Amy Jo groaned playfully.

"We need to start planning the wedding!" Lacey gushed.

"Lacey!" Amy Jo protested. "If I sit down on that blanket, I might not get back up!"

"Hush, you're barely showing!" Lacey said. She looked around the yard and grabbed a seat cushion for Amy Jo to sit on.

Amy Jo sat.

Chance jogged up.

"No boys allowed, Chance. It's girl time." Lacey put up her hand.

"No big deal," Chance panted. "I need to go."

Amy Jo looked up at him, surprised.

"Why?" she asked.

"I need to go watch Bella," Chance explained as he got down on his knees to kiss her. "Mom just got called in to work."

"Okay, need me to drive you home?" Amy Jo asked.

"Nah, mom's coming to get me. Bye, ladies." Chance wiggled his fingers comically at the girls who sat watching the whole thing.

"Okay, I'll be over later," Amy Jo promised.

"You better," Chance smiled at her.

The girls laughed as he ran off.

As the sun set, she tried to say her *goodbyes*. No matter how hard she tried, she got sucked back into conversation. Amy Jo just wasn't ready to end this day.

Chapter 27
Parker Sheridan, 1995

The trip to Chance Miller's house had been a waste of time. The local sheriff had warned Parker there really was no use going over there. Still, Sheriff Rifkin had pointed Parker in the direction of Chance's home.

Don't get your hopes up though... the sheriff had warned him.

Why not? Parker had asked.

Even if he's home, his mama's a real paranoid one. Won't open the door for authorities, let alone anyone she doesn't know.

Is she dangerous? Parker had hesitated, his hand resting on the doorknob ready to leave.

The sheriff had chuckled. *Not at all. She's a good, decent, law-abiding citizen. She just doesn't trust the government and won't let them get a foot in the door. Her exact words.*

Okay, got it, Parker had said.

Optimistically, he'd thought he'd be able to get her to open the door. He thought wrong. He knocked three times before he saw the curtain sway. It was a clear sign she was checking to see who was on her doorstep.

"Ma'am, my name is Parker and I'm with the police department. No one's in trouble. I just want to talk to Chance." Parker paced on the porch. Then he sat down on her porch swing and waited. Fifteen minutes went by before he gave up. He knew she wasn't coming out. And neither was Chance.

Parker drove away and stopped in a parking lot. He scratched his head. He couldn't think of any other lead to take him to either AJ. He might as well loop around town a few times. Surely he'd find his AJ's car. *If* she was in town. If she wasn't in town, Parker had no idea where she was. The thought chilled him.

As he drove, he worked to recall every detail she'd told him about finding the other AJ Hartford, Amy Jo, who she called AJ2. In her strangely confident and prophetic way, AJ had said AJ2 would be taken from a grocery store sometime after dark.

Parker spotted the only grocery store in town as he drove. At least, he assumed this was the one. He didn't see any others. He noticed the grocery store had a payphone at the far corner of the parking lot. This store was also located at the intersection of Jackson and 4th Street. This all sounded familiar. He made a mental note to come back to this corner after dark. He knew this is where he'd find AJ. *If* he found AJ.

Parker drove his car around town one more time to see if he could spot Maria Hartford's car, the one AJ had stolen. He didn't see it anywhere.

How could she possibly hide out in a town this size?

There was nowhere to hide. Parker's mind went to Terrance Hartford who was currently missing and wanted for skipping town and his informant duties.

When informants stop responding, they have to be brought back in. They've broken their agreement and need to be parked in a jail cell, Gerome had explained before Parker had left. *Or worse—*

Worse? Parker had interrupted.

Yeah, they might be dead.

Parker headed back to the station. He went inside and stuck his head in the sheriff's office, tapping on the door.

"What can you tell me about Terrance Hartford?" Parker asked.

The sheriff stared at him for half a minute. He stroked his beard. "Close that door and come in here, would you?"

Parker obeyed.

"Now, mind telling me why you're askin' that? I assume you've connected him in all this to Amy Jo?"

Parker nodded. "He's an informant for our department back in Wimmswick, but he went MIA a while back. I think he's the key to all of this. He's also *our* AJ Hartford's dad. AJ got a kidnapping letter in the mail. It was intended for Terrance. Someone is targeting AJ because they found out Terrance is an informant. They had his informant number and everything. They said they were going to take his daughter."

Sheriff Rifkin stared at Parker, dumbfounded. "Well, son, this is getting weirder by the minute. Amy Jo Hartford is also Terrance's daughter. Which daughter were they targeting?"

Parker shrugged. "AJ thinks they're going after Amy Jo.

Though I'm not sure why she's so convinced. In fact, I'm here to escort AJ back home and make sure she's safe on account of that note. Back home, they don't put much stock in her theory. Truth is, I didn't either until I learned more about Amy Jo."

"Well," Sheriff Rifkin stood and put on his hat. "There's only one person who can help us get to the bottom of this."

Parker stood too. "Who is that, sir?"

"Let's go see Terrance Hartford."

"Terrance is here? In Chritten?" Parker was now dumbfounded.

"Yep, I'll drive you out there. Bit of a drive though," Sheriff Rifkin stated as they walked out to the parking lot.

"How much of a drive? I still haven't found AJ and she's my first priority."

"We've got officers around town looking for her too. It'll take us about twenty minutes to get there," the sheriff said as he led Parker out to the car.

"You understand I'll have to detain him on account of him hiding from us? If an informant refuses to cooperate, we have to take him in," Parker stated.

The sheriff laughed. "No love lost between me and Terrance. He's not a good guy and I'd be happy for you to take him out of my town."

"Great!" Parker's heart beat faster with excitement as he got in the car. Parker might actually bring a wanted criminal informant back into town. That would be a nice jump start to his career!

"Let's do this then!" Sheriff Rifkin whooped as he hit the gas and navigated to the road.

After a long ride on a paved road turned into a short

ride on a dusty dirt road, Sheriff Rifkin slowed his car. He turned in to an isolated piece of land with a single-wide trailer. The only window Parker could see was boarded up with wood. There was a couch sitting outside looking weathered and worn. The most disturbing image of all was the door. The top hinge looked broken, so the door dangled, not quite lining up with the frame. The door lifted and slammed against the side of the trailer when the wind picked up.

Sheriff Rifkin squinted as he pulled the squad car to a stop, jamming it into park. He slowly got out of the car, mumbling as he did.

"Looks like trouble." He drew his gun.

Parker followed his lead.

The two proceeded cautiously, scanning for signs of life outside and inside the trailer.

"Terrance?" the sheriff yelled when he got to the door. "You in there?"

There was no response.

"Hey," he called again, this time knocking on the dangling door. "You decent?"

Again, there was no response. Sheriff Rifkin looked at Parker and signaled for him to follow. They stepped cautiously through the door.

Parker gasped as his eyes adjusted to the dark. A rank odor met his nostrils. He recognized it immediately as a mixture of blood and feces. Was Terrance dead? This would be the first time to see a dead body on the job. He tightened his gut in an effort to prepare himself.

Sheriff Rifkin pulled a small flashlight out of his pocket. Though his eyes had mostly adjusted, the light eased

Parker's sudden fear of unknown attack. Besides, no one was in this trailer. As he looked around, he didn't know how anyone could live like this. Couch cushions and blankets were strewn randomly. Dishes were broken on the floor intermingled with broken beer bottles.

Then there was that stench. Did someone just not flush the toilet? Parker proceeded cautiously. They had searched every square inch of the small trailer and were about to leave when Parker spotted it. A long smear of blood ran down the length of the wall beside the open doorway leading out of the trailer. The floor showed traces of fecal matter.

"What the—" Parker heard a grunt and a loud thump behind him and turned just in time for his face to connect with a hard metal object.

Chapter 28
AJ Hartford, 1995

AJ pulled into Chritten, Missouri, just as the sun was setting and painting a pretty display of reds and purples, in addition to the pink hue, across the sky. Missouri was known for its beautiful sunsets, but these vibrant colors outshone anything she'd seen back home. The beauty in the sky did nothing to dispel the anxiety in her heart.

She had lost so much time in that traffic jam. Then she'd made a wrong turn again. While she was able to get back on track, it still took her another twenty minutes out of her way. All she had to do was find that grocery store.

Jackson and Fourth, Jackson and Fourth, Jackson and Fourth, she repeated to herself like a mantra.

"You know you can't just go rolling up there and let everyone see you, right?" Amanda's sudden voice sounded, and AJ could see the outline of her body fill in on the passenger seat as AJ drove further.

AJ nearly wrecked her car. She jerked the wheel in fright. "Geez! You almost gave me a heart attack! Where have you been?"

"Well, someone needs to tell you that if you park your car anywhere that's visible, you could deter the kidnapping before it even happens."

"That would be great. Wouldn't it?" AJ had no idea how she was going to stop a man who was two times her size.

"No, you need to stop him in the act or after the fact, so he gets put away for a very long time, if not forever. Otherwise, he'll make another attempt," she explained.

"Now you tell me." AJ was starting to feel grouchy. This was not what she'd signed up for. She was regretting leaving town without her police escort. As she drove aimlessly around town searching for Jackson and 4th Street, AJ pondered going to the police. But as the sun set further behind the clouds and the sky turned a shade darker, AJ worried she just didn't have the time.

Before she could contemplate further, in a stroke of destiny, a police car turned on its lights and whooped its siren behind her. AJ gladly pulled her car over. She glanced at the passenger seat. Amanda was gone.

She eagerly rolled down her window as the officer stepped out of the car. He was a tall, thin man with bushy gray eyebrows. He had tired eyes. He looked worn out and disinterested in the world around him.

"Officer, I'm so glad you're—"

"Ma'am, I'm going to ask you to step out of the vehicle with your hands up," he cut her off and commanded in a loud, authoritative voice.

"What did I—"

"Step out and away from the vehicle." He put his hand on his gun.

"Okay," AJ mumbled, feeling shocked. They sure were

excited about out-of-towners here. AJ turned off the ignition, pulled the keys out, slowly opened the door, and got out of the car. She dropped the keys in her back pocket then lifted her hands up. "What's the charge, officer?"

"You're in my town," he snarled as he pulled out a pair of handcuffs. AJ didn't think he looked that strong. She was surprised by the drift of body odor that assaulted her nose. "Did you really think you could steal a car and drive through *my town* without someone catching you?"

AJ felt a giggle bubble up from nowhere. Cops in the real world didn't say things like that, did they?

"Something funny to you?" he asked. "Put your hands behind your back."

AJ slowly lowered her hands. Everything felt surreal. Surely, this was a dream, and she would wake up like Dorothy in Oz. She didn't come all this way only to be arrested and thrown in jail, right?

"There's been a mistake," AJ explained logically, summoning the inner thirty-something voice. "This is my mom's car. It's not stolen. We can call the police station back home and they'll clear me." She felt herself being led to the police car parked behind her.

"Oh yeah, is that the exact police station that faxed an APB to us with your picture and the very license plates on this car to inform us that you stole it?" he laughed humorlessly as he stuffed her head, forcing her to bend down and get into the car.

AJ felt stunned as he closed the door behind her. She'd never been in the back of a squad car in her whole life and it was the worst possible time to be there. The sun was rapidly disappearing. She blinked back tears as she stared out the window, watching the streets mock her as they drove by. She had been so close.

Then she saw it. The grocery store on the corner of Jackson and 4th. She could see the payphone on the corner of the lot. She could see that the parking lot, at this hour, was full of cars.

Hope renewed in her heart as she saw how close the police station was to the grocery store. She just had to make sure she made her break before the officer took her into the station. The only thing she couldn't figure out were these damn handcuffs. How would she get out of those?

As they pulled into the station, she heard the officer radio in.

"Picked up your car thief. Bringing her into the station now."

Like hell you are, AJ thought.

Chapter 29
Parker Sheridan, 1995

Parker groaned as he gained consciousness. He was lying face down on carpet that smelled like mildew. He knew and felt the absolute urgency that he needed to get up. He also felt pain. He tried to rewind his brain to the moment that had led him right here, unconscious on the floor.

He'd been walking around this very trailer looking for Terrance Hartford. He'd noticed how trashed the place had been. While it was possible Terrance lived like this, Parker's mind was making a connection. The place reminded him of how AJ's house had looked after she'd gotten the threat letter. Like someone had ransacked it. What if someone had done the same thing to Terrance's place?

He'd turned around to mention that to Sheriff Rifkin, who had been standing behind him, when something metal had hit him in the face. An uneasy feeling settled over him.

Did Sheriff Rifkin hit me? he wondered. He dismissed that ridiculous notion as quickly as it had come to his mind. Why would the sheriff have taken Parker out here if he was only going to knock him out?

Still, as Parker slowly opened his eyes, he noticed two things. One, he was alone on the floor in this trailer. The second thing was the metal object lying next to him was a tea kettle. He could see a smear of blood on the metal pot. Parker gently reached up and touched his cheek, pulled his hand away, and looked at it. Warm, red-brown liquid marred his fingers.

Slowly, he peeled his face off the ground. He instantly felt dizzy and thought for a moment he might throw up. His dizziness made him identify with AJ. Had he only met her yesterday? At the thought of her, he knew he needed to get moving. He needed to find her. They weren't safe here in this town. In fact, Parker was beginning to think they'd put themselves in more danger than they were in before.

But first, he had to get out of this trailer. He slowly moved his body into prone position. Then, he pushed up to his knees. He crawled forward one knee and one hand at a time. He took a deep breath as he got closer to the door and inhaled fresh air.

He could see outside on account of the broken door that hung off the hinges. *Just one hand and one leg forward, then switch,* he told himself, focusing on the task. He must have gotten hit awful hard. He was having a hard time doing the things that had come naturally to him only minutes before. Or had it been longer than minutes? And where was Sheriff Rifkin?

When he finally made it to the door, Parker used the door frame to pull himself up. He took gulps of fresh air and clung to the frame. When the nausea and dizziness passed, he managed to get down the two steps. He stood for seconds, fighting to keep balance. He sat down on the steps.

Whoever had hit him didn't intend for Parker to walk back out of there tonight. Parker could see it was getting dark. There was something important he needed to do at dark. He just couldn't remember what it was.

He slowly scanned his surroundings. The trailer was sitting on an isolated piece of land. The nearest house was so far off in the distance, it was hard to see it. Parker estimated it to be two miles up the gravel road. He could hear the song of the bullfrogs and the swish of a creek running through the property somewhere.

He needed to call someone. But who? He didn't remember seeing a phone in the trailer.

How had he gotten here? he wondered. He scanned the empty front lot. Then he remembered the police car that had been sitting here. He'd come with the sheriff. Only the sheriff and the police car were now gone. Without those two things, Parker had no idea how to get back to town.

He sat watching the sky get progressively darker, wondering how he could have botched this assignment any worse. If he laid down on this gravel, he felt sure he'd take a long, well-deserved nap. That wouldn't be so bad, would it?

Chapter 30
AJ Hartford, 1995

The officer who'd picked up AJ was now driving the squad car and talking on his walkie. AJ had scooted over to where she could see the car keys dangling from the ignition as the officer drove. She'd bet her life the key to her handcuffs was on that keyring. She just needed to get those keys and run before they made it into the station building.

She watched as the officer pulled the car in to the station, turned off the car, and pulled the keys out of the ignition. As he got out of the car, he slipped the keys into his back pocket, slammed the front door, and opened her back door.

Before she could talk herself out of this plan, AJ kicked her feet out of the car and struck the surprised officer, knocking him to the ground. He fell face first in the gravel. She needed to get down on the ground to grab his keys. She fell hard on her bottom which stung upon impact, her own keys poking into her. Since her hands were cuffed behind her, she used both hands to grope blindly until they found his back pocket.

"Hey!" the officer yelled. He got on his knees. He crawled away from her. Then he jumped to his feet. AJ could see him towering over her. He leaned down and grabbed her arm. He hauled her to her feet.

AJ said nothing as she watched his jerky movements and red face. He grabbed her arm so tight, AJ was sure there would be a bruise there tomorrow. They'd come a long way since the late 90s in her world. Such behavior there would be categorized as abusive. Not in this era. And she was not in her world. She knew better than to try anything again so soon.

He marched her up the steps of the red brick station. When he opened the door, the smell of dust and must assailed her senses and she immediately sneezed. Didn't anyone clean in here?

She'd have to wait for another opportunity to escape later. As he walked her into the station, she passed a large clock on the wall. It was a quarter to eight. Her pulse quickened. She could see as she glanced outside that the sun had set and a dark haze had settled over the town. Dark is when the kidnapping would happen. The longer she was stuck in here, the less chance she had of saving AJ2.

AJ could see a large open room with multiple desks pushed up against the wall. There were a few offices with doors shut and lights turned out. There were two jail cells right in the room with them. AJ bet they didn't get used much.

The officer roughly pushed her into a cell. He shut the cell door with a loud, angry clang.

"Hey, can I get these off me, please?" AJ requested, turning around and indicating her hands were still cuffed.

"No!" he snapped.

AJ watched him stalk around the office as though looking for someone. Finally, he stopped in the middle of the office and glared at a secretary who sat at a desk ignoring him while writing something on a piece of paper.

He waited until she looked up. When she did, his expression held annoyance.

"Can I help you?" Her tone was sarcastic, and AJ assumed she was annoyed that he was staring at her. She was trim with dark, shoulder-length hair, and an older self-assured attitude. She wasn't intimidated by him, she just seemed annoyed. AJ was annoyed too. In fact, everything this man did annoyed AJ. She didn't know how the woman worked with him.

"Where the hell is Sheriff Rifkin?" he demanded.

The woman shrugged. "He and that cop from out of town went out to Terrance Hartford's place. It was over an hour ago. I haven't heard from him yet."

"Why did he go to Terrance Hartford's place?" the officer asked, sounding outraged.

"I truly don't know. I didn't ask. Nor did they tell me." Now she sounded bored. She went back to writing on her paper, clearly dismissing him.

"Well, he's not answering the walkie and I don't know what to do with her," the officer jabbed a finger in AJ's direction.

AJ's mind was spinning as she processed what she heard. Parker was here? Had he come to help her or to take her back home? And was her dad really in this town after all? It had been such a long shot when she proposed that idea to Parker. It was hard to believe he could actually be here.

"Excuse me, don't I get a phone call?" AJ asked, interrupting his adult temper tantrum.

"No," he snapped.

"Yes," the secretary said, giving him a pointed look.

"Fine," he unlocked the jail cell but hesitated. "Don't try anything or I'll slap *assaulting an officer* on you. I should have done it the first time."

AJ shrugged sheepishly. "Can't blame a girl for trying."

The officer held her arm again in the same spot he'd held it before. Her arm was starting to hurt.

"Ow," AJ said a little too loudly and yanked her arm away, making sure the secretary saw the scene. She'd need a witness in case she had to use it later.

The secretary gave him another glance that looked like a warning. The man pulled the phone receiver off the wall and handed it to AJ, but her hands were still behind her back. She gave him a look. He held the phone up to her ear and waited while AJ remembered her mom's phone number and rattled it off to him. It had come right to her. Only, she realized by the second ring, her mom was probably still at the station. AJ had her car after all. And their home was still trashed.

"No one's home," AJ said with a small, embarrassed smile. "Can you call the police precinct? She's probably still there."

"Why would she be there?" he asked.

"Because there's been a mix-up," AJ smiled sweetly. "I

didn't steal a car. That car is my mom's. She can clear this up for me."

The secretary came forward with a number written on a piece of paper. The officer seemed annoyed but took the paper and mumbled his thanks.

This time, he put the phone up to his own ear. "This is Officer Givens down here with the Chritten Police. Listen, I have AJ Hartford here, the missing girl who stole a car. You faxed us about her—"

Clearly someone had interrupted him.

"Yes, she's right here. I'll put her on." The officer put the phone to her ear.

"AJ?" It was Maria.

"Thank God," AJ said. "There's been a mix-up and I'm in jail. They think I stole your car."

"You did steal my car Amanda Jane," Maria said in her most stern voice.

"Did not! I borrowed it to run an errand." AJ knew how lame that sounded.

"An errand that's over an hour away?" Maria's voice was getting louder.

"Mom, I found dad. He's here in this town," AJ interrupted, desperate to bring her mother to her side. Her declaration was met with silence.

"Wait, is your dad—" Officer Givens sputtered.

"Terrance Hartford?" AJ answered mindlessly. "Yes."

"AJ, you're in Chritten?" her mother's voice broke through the line.

"Yes," AJ answered. "Wait, did you know dad was in Chritten?"

Again, there was silence. AJ's mind flew as she processed her mom's response.

"You lied to me," AJ gasped. "You said dad left, and you didn't know where he was."

"I was protecting you. That man... he's not... he's a terrible person, AJ. You would do well to leave him there and come back home."

Rage boiled inside AJ. With an ability she'd worked in her adult years, AJ dropped her voice and kept it steady. "You knew where he was, and you didn't tell me. The least you can do is tell this officer, who has me in handcuffs right now, that I didn't steal your car and that you're not pressing charges. That way I can drive home."

"Put him on the phone," Maria commanded.

AJ looked up at the officer. "She wants to talk to you."

The officer pulled the phone away from AJ's ear and listened. Due to her close proximity, AJ could hear every word. When her mother proclaimed her car wasn't stolen after all, the officer asked to talk to someone in charge.

After some identity verification, followed by a promise to fax the lifted charge, the officer hung up the phone.

"Looks like it's your lucky day," he said. He grabbed the key and reached for her handcuffs.

AJ heard the key click her handcuffs free at the same time she heard the phone ring.

"Hello?" the secretary answered the phone. She listened for a minute. Then she gasped loudly.

"What is it?" The officer asked.

The secretary ignored him for a minute, still listening, her eyes wide in shock. "Ohmigod!"

"What?" the officer looked like he might yank the phone out of her hand.

She put her hand over the mouthpiece. "They found Sheriff Rifkin."

"Great!" the officer said with impatience. "I need to talk to him."

Tears filled her eyes. "You can't. He's dead."

Chapter 31

Parker Sheridan, 1995

Parker was back in the trailer. Getting up had been hard. Slowly, he stood. When he was sure he had his balance, he'd turned around and walked back up the steps. He peered inside. His only goal was to find a phone.

It spooked him to re-enter the trailer. Someone might still be in there. He felt for his sidearm and didn't find one. After a few minutes of searching, Parker was convinced there was no landline inside.

Since then, Parker had been walking down the long gravel and dirt road. After Parker had been walking for what seemed like an hour, he spotted a house. It was officially getting dark. Moonlight lit the road.

He walked up the driveway half hoping someone was home and half hoping they were not. Parker had to remind himself that not everyone was friendly to police officers. If the altercation in the trailer was any indication, Parker would do well to keep his guard up.

It was a small blue house with wood siding. The yard

was clean and picked up. A ten-speed bike leaned against the outer wall.

Parker raised his hand and knocked on the door. A wave of dizziness hit him hard and for a moment, he thought he might throw up right there on the front porch. As the door opened, the moment passed.

A woman with kind eyes and a nice smile greeted him. Then she took in his appearance and her smile became a look of concern. Parker felt relieved. He knew the blood he'd wiped off his cheek earlier must still be visible somewhere on his face by the way she was staring at him. He felt for his badge but didn't find it in the pocket he normally kept it in. Had he left it back at the trailer? Was it with his sidearm?

"Hello, I'm Officer Parker Sheridan. May I please use your phone?" he asked politely.

"Certainly, officer." The woman held the door open and pointed to her phone. A man sat in an overstuffed chair watching TV while a child played with toy cars on the carpet in front of him.

"Thank you," Parker reached for the phone. He picked up the receiver and put it up to his ear. The sound of the TV in the background sounded hollow and far away in his ears.

"Officer? Officer?" a woman's voice echoed.

It felt like the walls were caving in. That's when Parker felt himself falling. His body hit the ground hard. He barely felt it.

Then, he passed out on the floor of their living room.

Chapter 32
AJ Hartford, 1995

AJ rubbed her wrists, unaware of the way the handcuffs had cut into them until she saw the red line. She hesitated for a moment, not sure what to do as the jailhouse drama unfolded. She still stood by the phone where she hadn't moved, all but forgotten by the obnoxious officer who'd brought her in.

The secretary was crying loudly, and the officer tried to formulate a plan. He turned to the secretary.

"I know you're upset. I am too. But I need to know everything. When did Sheriff Rifkin leave for Terrance Hartford's place?"

"Over an hour ago," she sniffled.

"Why was he going out there?" he asked, repeating his question from before.

"I don't know. They didn't tell me."

"They?" he asked. "He and the officer from out of town?"

She nodded.

AJ knew with a sinking heart the other officer was

Parker. She also knew Parker's agenda was to bring Terrance Hartford home in handcuffs.

"That cop that came here looking for her—" the secretary turned to point to AJ just as AJ opened the door. She quickened her pace to hurry outside before the officer could get suspicious and arrest her again for knowing Parker Sheridan or something stupid like that. Once she burst into the dark night air, she ran. She remembered how close the grocery store was to the police station.

With everything in her, she hoped and prayed Parker was still alive. But she could no longer be distracted from the real reason she was here. AJ2 would be kidnapped any minute, if she hadn't been already.

There was no time to find her car. She realized as she ran, she had no plan and no transportation. Panic set in. Once she got there, she had no way to save AJ2. At the thought, she slowed her pace and began to walk.

"Think, AJ, think," she whispered to herself. "Amanda said I have to save AJ after the man takes her." She calmed, knowing she needed to wait until AJ got kidnapped. Maybe she could save her after they got to where they were going.

Once near the grocery store, she found a tree with a very large trunk and leaned against it, catching her breath. She was close enough to the payphone to get there quickly. What if she was too late? What if AJ2 had already been taken?

She scanned the grocery store parking lot. It was still full of cars. She snapped her fingers, remembering something she'd read.

"It was closed," she mumbled. "The grocery store was

closed which is why no one saw her get taken."

She breathed relief. She was in time. In fact, she was early. She sat her bottom on the ground and leaned her back against the tree. She would just wait here all night if that's what it took.

When she heard sirens, AJ scooted around the tree so as not to be seen and tucked her feet up to her chest before she saw the police cars scream out of the station. She peeked out to see the action. Within minutes, she heard and then saw an ambulance go by as well. Her heart seemed to stop in her chest. Then it beat quickly. She knew Sheriff Rifkin was dead but what about Parker?

For minutes, her veins felt like ice. She felt fear, anxiety, and dread flood her all at once. How could she feel such intense emotion for someone she'd met just over twenty-four hours ago? It was like her soul was destined to find his in this universe. She just wished she'd found him in hers.

As the chilly night air washed over her, the sirens settled, and the town grew quiet again. She could hear the crickets sing a nice, peaceful rhythm. She closed her eyes, feeling so sleepy. She just needed a little rest.

AJ was dreaming within five minutes. It wasn't a restful sleep. She felt herself falling. As she fell, AJ saw Kiera's face. First, Kiera was a baby. Then she was walking for the first time. Then she was playing her first soccer game at six years old. Kiera reached out and touched AJ's cheek, wiping away a tear. It must have been after AJ had left Johnny, Kiera's dad. Then Kiera was giving AJ her locket. AJ took it. Before she could say good-bye, AJ was falling again.

Chapter 33
Amy Jo Harford, 1995

Amy Jo finally left the barbecue well after dark.

"AJ!" Lacey's voice came from inside the house. "You forgot this."

Amy Jo stopped to see that Lacey held a necklace belonging to Amy Jo. It had fallen off earlier today when the clasp had broken. It was a favorite gift from Chance. She dared not lose it.

"Thanks! I'd forget my head if it wasn't attached these days," Amy Jo joked.

Lacey's eyes were a little too bright from the day drinking she'd done. "Pregnancy brain," Lacey quipped and giggled.

Amy Jo wiggled her fingers and got back behind the driver's seat. She started the car, put it in drive, and pulled out in the direction of home.

"Oh, shoot!" Amy Jo snapped her fingers as she looked at the necklace. She remembered the promise she'd made to stop by Chance's after she left the barbecue. Pregnancy brain fog was a real thing. She was so foggy these days.

She could see the grocery store sign that lit up the night even though it was closed. She pulled her car into the now empty parking lot when she spotted the payphone. She'd used this payphone many times in her life. Amy Jo wanted to call Chance and explain why she wasn't there before it got too late and Chance went to bed.

"I'm sorry, Chance. I'm exhausted," she told him when he picked up the phone. Her car was the only one in the parking lot. She watched a truck pull up and roll to a stop. "Not to mention, those burgers gave me pretty severe acid reflux."

"Come on," Chance whined. "I miss you!"

"You just saw me today—," she said, suddenly dropping her voice. "Hey, there's a guy standing here. I think he's waiting to use the payphone."

"Ask him," Chance quipped.

Amy Jo turned to the man. The man was visibly dirty and unkempt. He wore stained overalls, a white dirty undershirt, and a flannel shirt over the top. His hair was long and scruffy.

"Do you need to use the phone?" Amy Jo asked him politely.

The man slowly shook his head back and forth.

Amy Jo turned her back on him and lowered her voice to a whisper. "He stinks and he's just standing there staring at me. He's creeping me out."

"What's he driving?" Chance asked.

Amy Jo looked over her shoulder and suppressed a shiver. Had he stepped closer?

"A puke green pickup truck with some green faded fish decal in the back window—"

Amy Jo's sudden screams were so high-pitched and so shrill, it was impossible *not* to hear them through the telephone receiver that now dangled and swayed in the wind. Amy Jo struggled and fought the dirty man, who had just grabbed her and flung her over his shoulder like she weighed nothing.

Chapter 34
AJ Harford, 1995

"Wake up!" Amanda's angry voice sounded in AJ's ear. "You need to go!"

AJ's whole body jerked. She felt an electric shock. She gasped awake. Her eyes were heavy and filled with sand. She rubbed her eyes.

"Did you just shock me? I did not know you could do that!" AJ whined.

"Me either. You need to get up! Now! You're going to miss them!" Amanda's voice was an octave louder, but AJ was sure she was the only one who could hear her.

AJ jumped to her feet. Her hand had been closed over the necklace Kiera had given her. When she woke, she lowered her hand, and the necklace tore off. Unbeknownst to AJ, the necklace fell to the ground. Amanda disappeared from view.

AJ could see a puke green truck which was obstructing her view. She heard a scream. She ran. Then she saw movement of a woman who was struggling to get out of a man's grasp.

AJ was too far away to get there in time. Adrenaline flooded through her veins as AJ ran. She closed the distance quickly but not quickly enough to stop the man from putting the fighting AJ2 in the truck.

The man shoved AJ2 in the truck and locked the car door. Then he went around the front and got in the driver's side. AJ2 was still kicking and fighting.

AJ heard a thump and saw AJ2 go still. The man had punched her face and it had stilled her actions. AJ heard the truck start.

With all the energy she had in her, she closed the gap and lightly hopped into the truck bed.

For a moment, she lay still and prayed the man hadn't heard or felt her get in. Her pulse raced and she willed it to calm down. She didn't know how long the ride was. Nor did she know where they were going. Once she got there, she had no plan on how to get back out, let alone save this woman. All she knew was she had to rescue AJ2. Or die trying.

Chapter 35

Parker Sheridan, 1995

When Parker came to, he was riding on a stretcher in the back of an ambulance. How long had he been out? He tried to lift his body up, but the world spun and this time, there was no stopping the nausea. Parker leaned over the stretcher and emptied his stomach onto the floor.

"Oh!" An EMT worker scooted away quickly to avoid the line of fire.

Parker wiped his mouth. He felt so weak. "I'm sorry," he said. He laid back down and closed his eyes.

"You have a nasty gash on your cheek. It's pretty swollen and bleeding. Any idea how it got there?" The EMT worker had a nice, decidedly feminine voice. Her badge said *Tammy*.

"Someone hit me with a tea kettle," Parker answered.

"Hold this on it for now," Tammy passed Parker an ice pack.

Parker did as he was told but gasped as the cold touched his face. On one hand, the ice felt good. On the other hand, it stung where his face was bleeding. The longer Parker lay there, the more aware he was that something important was about to happen and he was going to miss it.

He moved the ice pack and sat up a little. He immediately felt dizzy. The EMT worker looked surprised.

"I think I feel better," Parker lied. It was coming back to him. Sometime after dark, according to AJ, a woman was going to be abducted from a grocery store parking lot. He'd noted the grocery store earlier. But from here, he had no idea where it might be.

The EMT looked suspicious. He saw her eyes squint at him. "I think you have a concussion and that cut on your cheek looks pretty deep. It might even need a stitch or two."

"Don't you have a butterfly Band-aid or something you could put on it? Can you tell if the bleeding has stopped?" Parker asked.

"Well let's see," Tammy chose to indulge him. She peered at it closely. Then she rooted around in a first aid kit. She put gloves on and pulled out peroxide and a cotton ball. "This will sting a bit."

It did. Parker winced as she carefully cleaned the blood. Then she put two bandages on his face that felt like it was pinching his cut. He took deep breaths and laid back down.

"You okay?" Tammy asked.

"Yes." Parker lay still with his eyes closed for a minute. He just needed this dizziness to go away so he could get out of here when the ambulance stopped. "How far is the hospital from the grocery store?"

"What?" her voice sounded confused.

"I'm supposed to meet someone... official police business," Parker tried to sound professional. He didn't think it was working.

"I don't think you're going anywhere," Tammy said, sounding like his mom. "Hey, you're not falling asleep, are you?"

Parker shook his head, but he thought sleep sounded nice. He opened his eyes.

"You need to stay awake for three hours at least."

"Okay, I can do that. Hey, this is weird but if I give you my insurance card, can you write down my numbers and bill this ambulance trip to that? I really need to get back to the station. I remembered an important meeting I need to get to. Police business..."

Tammy looked skeptical. "I'm not sure we can do that... Let me have a conversation with my co-worker."

"You know, I could pull a badge on you and order you to pull over," Parker smiled a little, knowing his badge was currently missing, trying to be charming enough to pull it off. Suddenly, he felt desperate to get out of this ambulance.

Tammy smirked at him and repositioned her body to talk to the driver. As Parker listened to them talk, he formulated a plan. He sat up and took deep breaths. His temple was pulsing, and he felt a headache forming. The longer he sat up, the more his dizziness seemed to subside. He fumbled around in his back pocket for his wallet. Luckily, it was still there. He pulled out his insurance card as the conversation wrapped up. The two had come to the conclusion that if Parker was stable enough, they didn't see why they couldn't drop him by the station.

He handed his card to Tammy. She took it and jotted down the insurance numbers.

"Listen, we're going to drop you off at the station. We don't usually do that. But we don't usually pick up on-duty cops either. I want you to take this ice pack with you. Ten minutes on, a half hour off. Don't sleep for at least three hours. The longer you stay awake the better."

"Got it," Parker said as he saw the station through the window. He could see his police vehicle too. "Can you point out the direction of the grocery store?"

"It's on Jackson and Fourth," she said.

"I'm not from here, can you point out the direction?" Parker remembered it was such a small town, everything was close by.

"It's over there." She pointed to the grocery store. "See, you can see the lights when it's open, but I think they just closed."

The ambulance stopped and the driver hopped out and opened the back doors. Parker climbed out, careful to make it look like he was perfectly fine.

"Don't make us regret this, officer," Tammy said. She held out her hand.

Parker grasped it. "Thank you," he kept it simple and walked to his car.

He found his key storage box up under his wheel well and opened the car door. Putting his keys there was a habit. He remembered his dad lecturing him for it, but it hadn't backfired on Parker yet.

He turned his attention to the grocery store after he

hopped in his car. He just hoped he wasn't too late. Parker watched the ambulance roll out of the police parking lot. He took a deep breath, realizing everything had brought him to this moment. Ready or not.

As he sat in the driver side of his car, he fumbled with his keys. He started the car. Driving dizzy felt a lot like driving tipsy. Not like he'd never done that before—he had. But it had been on a dirt country road driving in a straight line from his best friend's house to his parents' house. His parents always seemed to know before he walked through the door. They'd make a show of taking his keys for a few days but they always gave them back. Parker was a good kid. He was still a kid, truth be told.

He could do this. Whether he believed a kidnapping was about to go down or not, he did know where he would find AJ. That was his mission. Find AJ and bring her back home. She'd told him exactly where she would be. He just needed to get there.

He pulled into the grocery store parking lot. The grocery store hadn't been far. Nothing in this tiny town was far. Parker drove with a faint light-headedness. He saw the grocery store. He saw the empty phone booth. He watched the way the phone receiver dangled by its cord and swayed in the wind. He was experiencing the eerie sensation that a heinous crime had just occurred. The aftermath of a disappearance. Parker knew in this moment, he was too late.

He saw a car drive by backwards down the road. The car was driving fast. Parker blinked his eyes in confusion. He immediately pulled out of the grocery store to follow and maybe stop the car. That's when Parker's confusion and dizziness hit a peak. The car lights shone right into Parker's eyes. He knew the car was driving backwards down the road. What he didn't know was why. Was his brain playing tricks on him?

Because it looked like the car was coming straight for him.

Chapter 36
Parker Sheridan, 1995

On a deserted dirt country road, Parker could see the pair of headlights looming in the distance. They looked all wrong. He had pulled out of the grocery store parking lot to follow the car that was driving backwards. It hadn't taken long to find himself driving away from town and down a dark dirt road.

The high speed of travel was concern enough. The headlights were pointing right at Parker's car. Once Parker's dizzy brain understood the driver was indeed navigating backwards, Parker pushed the gas pedal and turned on his police sirens.

He saw the driver glance in front of him for half a second. Then the driver veered the car backwards off the road. It came to a sudden halt with the sound of a loud grinding of metal. As Parker slowed down to pull behind him, the man jumped out of the car. He waved his hands.

Parker rolled to a stop. He watched in sheer disbelief as the man ran straight for the passenger door. He flung it open and sat down.

"Thank God, officer! I need your help. My car just broke down. Can you please drive? Like drive fast... My fiancé was just kidnapped. I was in pursuit of the truck, but I think I ruined my transmission."

Parker wordlessly started driving. While the dizziness came and went, the pounding headache persisted. His muddled head felt confused. "Okay, sir, can you slow down and start at the beginning?"

"There!" the man, who didn't look much older than Parker, shouted abruptly.

Parker could see taillights a mile ahead of them. He pushed the gas. Then a thought made him slow down a bit. The last thing he wanted to do was come up on an armed kidnapper and start a high-speed chase.

"My fiancé called me from a payphone. She told me this guy was standing near her. I said, *Ask him if he needs to use the phone.* She did. Then she told me he'd gotten closer. Like she could smell him. *He smelled bad,* she said. The next thing I know, she was screaming. My car's been acting up, but I had to go after her. I knew where the payphone was. On my way to the payphone, I passed her in this ugly green truck. I could see her, but it looked like she was sleeping. Oh God! What if she's already—" the sound of a panic-stricken sob escaped him.

Parker was speechless. It had happened. Just as AJ had predicted. "What's your name?"

"Chance Miller," he answered.

"Of course it is," Parker mumbled.

"What?" Chance asked. He wiped away his tears.

"Nothing. What's your fiancé's name?" Parker asked but already knew the answer.

"Amy Jo, but she goes by AJ," he sniffed.

"Well, it's a bad night to be an AJ," Parker said cryptically, well-aware he was making no sense to Chance. But he had to wonder where his AJ had gone off to. In fact, he wondered if he'd ever see her again. He and Chance were both pondering the same thing.

Parker could see the taillights but didn't close the gap. He had an idea. "Chance, I need you to trust me here. I don't want to alert them we're following, but you might need to help me navigate. I don't know these roads like you probably do."

"Okay," Chance agreed and sat upright.

Parker turned his lights off and focused on the taillights he'd been watching in the distance. He followed them with road instructions from Chance until he saw the brake lights and hit his own brakes. He had to hang back. He couldn't risk the kidnapper knowing he was there.

Chapter 37
AJ Hartford, 1995

The truck rumbled loudly, vibrating underneath AJ's body. She tried to lay as still as possible to not be discovered. Then she almost laughed aloud. There was no way to be heard above the sound of the truck's muffler. Which is why AJ was surprised when she heard Amanda's voice.

"So, what's next?" Amanda asked.

AJ jumped and muffled a scream. "Must you always catch me off guard?"

"If ever there was a time to be on guard, it is now!" Amanda quipped. "What is your plan, AJ?"

"Does it look like I have a plan?" AJ hissed with frustration.

"No, it doesn't," Amanda agreed. "Where's your locket?"

AJ immediately felt for the necklace. The locket! It wasn't there. Tears filled her eyes. "It's gone."

"Don't cry. Just because your locket is gone doesn't mean your daughter is gone."

"Really?" AJ felt hope and relief flood her. She felt a

strong sense of homesickness. She needed to get back home to Kiera. "I need to go home."

"You will. The only way back is to follow through on this plan."

"Really?" AJ felt doubtful. "What plan?"

"You save AJ2. Finish what you set out to do."

"Yes, no matter what. I save her." Then a horrible thought occurred to AJ. "What if I die?"

"You can't," Amanda said simply. "If you die, I stay dead, AJ2 dies along with the daughter she's carrying, and Kiera is never born."

"No pressure," AJ mumbled grumpily.

"There's something else. Something bigger than you even know," Amanda said.

"Great," AJ said sarcastically.

"Kiera will develop a clean water system for economically developing countries that begins a trend of longer lifespans and the development of world resources in countries no one was initially exploring."

AJ was silent for a moment. She wasn't surprised but in that moment, she thought her heart might burst with pride. Then she felt it burst with reality.

"*If* Kiera is born."

"Precisely," Amanda confirmed.

"In every dimension?" AJ asked.

"Yes," Amanda said, her voice resembling what AJ's heart felt.

The realization set in. "You've seen it?"

"Yes, my world is ahead of yours, remember? Kiera was on the path when I was wiped out."

"That's the real reason you came to save me. To save her. To save economically developing countries?"

"Yes."

"My dad is here somewhere. In this town," AJ said. She'd been processing since she learned. Her dad was dead in her dimension. "I might have a chance to save him too—"

"Forget about your dad," Amanda said. "He has made his choices. Now you need to make yours."

"But what if I—" AJ stopped talking abruptly.

Amanda was gone.

The truck rolled to a stop.

Chapter 38
Parker Sheridan, 1995

Parker slowed the car to a crawl and parked it on a side road beside the house. Quietly, they opened the car doors and got out of the cop car. The kidnapper was now parked by a dumpy, dilapidated ranch-style house. They could hear a ferocious dog snarling as the man exited the puke-green truck.

"Shut up!" he said. The dog yiped and then whimpered. Parker assumed he had kicked the dog. The dog went back to the porch with his tail tucked.

As Parker and Chance approached, they could see the man go to the passenger side door and open it. He reached in to grab Amy Jo but jumped back in surprise. Amy Jo kicked him hard between the legs with the heel of her shoe.

As her kidnapper doubled over in pain, Amy Jo jumped out of the truck and ran past him. The kidnapper recovered fast and grabbed her around the waist before she could run too far. He tackled her to the ground. When he had her pinned, he got up and hauled her to her feet, firm hands on both of her arms as he pushed her forward.

Chance was running now. Parker had no choice but to follow his lead. Parker quickly ran to Chance's side. He grabbed Chance's hand in time to stop him from rushing in.

"Wait," Parker hissed as he caught up. "There could be a whole house full of pissed off hillbillies. We would be outnumbered and outgunned. We can't just go running in there. We need a plan."

Chance stopped abruptly and doubled over in an attempt to catch his breath. "What do you propose? We have to hurry," Chance panted.

"Agree. Catch your breath. We'll go wide around the fence line and approach through the back. We'll peek in the window. Assess the situation before we go barging in."

Chance nodded and they walked to the fence line of the property. "Shouldn't you call for backup or something?"

Parker put a finger to his mouth. The truth was, he didn't know this police unit. His CB frequency in the squad car wasn't tuned to theirs. And right now, the sheriff was missing. For all Parker knew, Sheriff Rifkin could be the one who'd hit him over the head.

They quietly stalked to the window. There were no blinds or coverings on the windows and with the lights on, it made it easy to see straight into the small, dilapidated house. In the short time it took to walk the fence line, the man had tied Amy Jo to a chair. She was unconscious again. Parker heard Chance suck in a breath.

They crept quietly to the back of the house. They

rounded the corner and came face to face with a tall, red-headed man with shaggy hair and mean eyes.

Parker immediately kicked the gun out of the man's hand. Parker could hear his gun hit the ground and knew it had disappeared in the tall, uncut grass. Parker, senses on high alert now, prepared for a fight that would no doubt take away their element of surprise.

Parker made fists and put up his hands. But not before the man's fist connected with Parker's nose. Parker lost his balance and fell back in the grass. He immediately swept his foot and connected it to his assailant's foot. When the man went down, Parker jumped on him and hit his face multiple times.

The sound of a gunshot made Parker freeze.

Chapter 39

AJ Hartford, 1995

AJ lay still and listened. She heard a dog barking. Then she heard a man growl *Shut up!* Then she heard the dog yipe. The car door shut, and another door opened.

"Hey!" the man yelled in sudden pain. AJ heard a scuffle and then a small scream. She assumed AJ2 had tried to get away, but the man overpowered her again. Her heart sank with the knowledge that this man was not going to be easy to defeat.

She waited until she was absolutely sure they were inside. Then AJ got on her knees and peeked over the truck bed. It was all clear. She quietly lifted one leg, then two, over the side and hopped down more gracefully and quietly than she normally would have. She was jealous of the balance the AJ of this world seemed to possess.

AJ crouched beside the truck, assessing the situation. The tiny shack house sat on a piece of land that stretched on for so many miles, she could not see any other houses. So much for help from neighbors. She was truly on her own here. A single lightbulb dangled from the porch ceiling.

Otherwise, she could see lights on and a sheet haphazardly thrown over a window.

Seeing no one else in the yard, save the lazy dog that now lay pouting with his chin resting on the porch, AJ ran on tiptoes to the window. She peeked in the corner where the sheet wasn't covering.

She could see AJ2 sitting in a chair in the middle of the room. A man was tying AJ2's wrists to the back of the chair. Her back was to the window so AJ could see they were held back by zip ties.

"What the—" the man stood up and angrily stalked out the back door.

It was now or never. AJ opened the front door, thankful to find it not locked. Wordlessly, she ran to the kitchen and found a knife. She came back into the room and met the eyes of a startled AJ2.

AJ froze for half a second. When their eyes connected, a shift occurred. It was almost unnoticeable, but AJ knew she knew her. In fact, she was so similar, AJ would have sworn they were sisters though she knew she'd never met this woman before.

"Who are you?" AJ2 whispered, fear in her eyes. They were damp from obvious tears she had been crying.

"I'm here to rescue you," AJ replied in an equally low voice. She ran around and squatted behind her chair. She used the knife and seesawed the zip ties.

AJ heard the sound of a gunshot and her hands stilled for a minute, then they started shaking. She took a deep breath and worked faster. She heard the back door open and close. She frantically increased the sawing.

The kidnapper had returned. AJ's heart raced. She

fought the urge to freeze or lay down and play dead. Who had he shot? She tried to make herself small to hide behind the chair, but she knew it was no use. She would be spotted the minute he entered the room. Her heart beat so fast and loud in her own ears she was sure the kidnapper would hear it too.

"Help!" AJ2 cried out loudly.

"Shh," AJ hissed. "I'm trying." The zip ties snapped then. With a flood of adrenaline, AJ jumped up. She held the knife in front of her and protectively pushed AJ2 behind her. She could feel a trickle of sweat roll off her forehead.

"Woah there!" Parker stepped through the door with a wide grin on his face. "Boy, am I glad to see you."

"Parker!" AJ dropped the knife and flung herself into Parker's arms. Sudden tears pricked her eyes. Parker hugged her tightly but addressed AJ2.

"Amy Jo, I presume?" Parker asked.

AJ stepped back. She didn't know AJ2 was named Amy Jo. She stood looking at this woman who could have been her double. An older version of herself.

"AJ," Amy Jo cleared her throat, tears in her eyes. "People call me AJ."

"Babe!" A deep male voice sounded behind them. Amy Jo ran into the arms of a light-brown-haired, blue-eyed man.

"Chance! You're here!" Amy Jo was crying now.

AJ turned to Parker, whose hand still held her around her waist. "We don't have any time. The man who kidnapped her will be back soon."

"Nah," Chance smiled impishly. "We took care of them."

"Them?" AJ asked.

"Yeah, there were two of them out back," Parker said.

"The gunshot?" AJ understood now what must have happened.

Parker nodded grimly. "They had us for a minute. I didn't know there were two of them. I had one under control. But just as the second perp came around the corner with a gun, Chance here had found the gun we dropped in the grass and he saved my life. They're both in handcuffs in the back of my car. I need to go clear the house. Then we need to get them back to the station. Be right back."

AJ nodded and stepped away, feeling suddenly cold.

"Thank you for rescuing me," Amy Jo said shyly. Her face was full of curiosity. "I'm AJ."

"I know." AJ didn't know if she wanted to shake her hand or hug her. She seemed to be waiting for AJ to speak.

"I'm Amanda Jane," AJ told her. The truth seemed very complicated right now.

The sound of a crash met their ears as something glass broke. Then the sound of a loud thump against the wall followed by a grunt occurred. At the sound of a struggle, AJ ran in that direction. Chance and Amy Jo ran right behind her. They arrived in a bedroom where Parker was securing a man. He was tall and lanky and his dirty, brown hair hung in his eyes. With defeat on his face, he turned to allow Parker to march him out of the room.

"Dad?" AJ said.

"Dad!" Amy Jo said at the exact same time.

Terrance Hartford looked surprised then laughed loudly.

"I'll be damned! I never thought I'd see my two girls in the same place at the same time!"

AJ's mouth swung open, and she turned to see shock in Amy Jo's eyes. Then the pieces fell into place. In AJ's world, Terrance had always had a job where he traveled and stayed overnights. Right up until the moment he'd died. Now, it was surreal to see her father alive again. He looked rougher than she'd ever seen him.

"What are you doing here?" he asked AJ as Parker navigated him out of the room.

"They kidnapped her because they found out you were a drug informant. I came to save her when I found out. They left a note for me, but they went after her instead."

"Well, that explains a lot. But it doesn't explain why they disposed of a dead sheriff—"

"Dead sheriff?" Parker asked, looking horrified.

"Yep, they threw Sheriff Rifkin out the vehicle after kidnapping us both. After they knocked you out," Terrance nodded toward Parker. "Put a bullet in Rifkin's head after he hit the ground."

"Oh no!" Parker groaned. "I need to call it in." He found a phone in the living room.

"You can," AJ said as she put her hand on his arm. "But they had already found him. The station had gotten a phone call when I left earlier."

"Okay," Parker said as he used his sleeve to pick up the phone. "I'll just let them know our situation here."

Within ten minutes, police officers and an ambulance had arrived. An EMT worker named Tammy assessed AJ for injuries.

"I'm fine," AJ said. "She's the one who was kidnapped." She pointed to Amy Jo whose face sported a big bruise.

After a quick check, EMT Tammy seemed satisfied that Amy Jo was fine. "You better follow up with your obstetrician just to make sure the baby is okay."

"Oh, I'm sure he's fine," Amy Jo smiled. "I've felt him moving around in there."

"Him?" Chance asked with a grin.

Amy Jo smirked at him. AJ could tell there was some inside joke there. AJ watched as Tammy, the EMT worker, approached Parker as if they were old friends. Tammy peered at Parker's temple. For the first time, AJ noticed the butterfly bandages on his face. She made a note to ask him what had happened later.

The man who had kidnapped Amy Jo was sitting securely in the back of Parker's police car. She knew he was handcuffed in there. She also knew from earlier experience the doors wouldn't open from the inside.

"Sisters, huh?" Chance grinned widely. He hadn't stopped hugging his fiancé and rubbing her pregnant belly since they'd found them. It was like he'd gotten a second chance. Only AJ knew just how true that really was.

As AJ looked at Amy Jo, she felt something she'd never felt before. Instant love for the person she'd just met.

"Apparently," AJ said in wonder.

"Did you know?" Amy Jo asked.

"No," AJ answered.

"But you came to rescue me anyway. How did you know where I would be?" Amy Jo asked.

AJ sighed. If only she had a logical answer. "There was a note. There was suspicion that my dad was here. He'd left my mom and me and moved away. The rest just fell into place."

Amy Jo looked skeptical. "Someday, when we know each other better, maybe you can tell me more."

"In the meantime, no more late night calls on payphones," Chance lectured Amy Jo.

"Are you kidding? I'm never leaving your side again!" Amy Jo wrapped her arms around his waist.

Chance comedically tried to walk. "Oh no, this will make things difficult!"

AJ laughed. Looking at Amanda's belly made her reach up to finger the place where her locket had hung around her neck. Sadness over the lost locket washed over her, but AJ knew it was only a short time before she would be going home.

Kiera was at home waiting.

Chapter 40

AJ Hartford, 1995

Well after midnight, AJ left Parker completing the interviews to file his reports. AJ could have left hours ago but had felt reluctant to leave Parker's side. AJ knew everything would change the instant she traveled back home, like it had for Cinderella at the stroke of midnight. She wanted to sit in this moment to remember it as long as she could. Her mom's car was within walking distance to the police station. AJ left the station and walked to the car.

AJ finally found herself alone behind the steering wheel. She had the urge to cry with relief and decompress what she had just been through. She started the car, debating where to go next. She hit the gas, deciding it would come to her as she drove. In truth, it didn't matter where she went because she was going home.

"You did it!" Amanda's voice was triumphant.

"Geez! Hi to you, too," AJ said. "Hold on, why are you still here?"

Amanda was quiet for a minute. "I need to help you get back home."

"Great! Just tell me where to go," AJ felt happy to have help. Truth be told, she had no idea what to do next. But she didn't miss the look of concern in Amanda's eyes.

"The nearest train station is three point five miles from here. It doesn't matter if—"

Sudden police lights lit up AJ's review mirror. Frowning, AJ pulled over by the tree near the payphone. She looked at the tree where she'd been sleeping when AJ2's screams had woken her up. So much had happened in such a short period of time. Yet she'd managed to circle right back to the place where it had all begun.

She hadn't had the best experience the last time a Chritten deputy had pulled her over. She debated not stopping this time. Instead, she rolled down her window a bit and leaned over to look for an insurance card. Amanda had disappeared.

"Ma'am, I'm going to need to ask you to step out of the car."

AJ's hand stilled. She knew his voice. She reluctantly met his eyes. She had hoped to leave without a word so the real AJ of this world could resume her life without Parker knowing she had even left.

AJ opened the door and got out of the car.

"Leaving without saying good-bye?" Parker asked. There was something in his eyes. Something that hadn't been there before.

"It's late and we still have a long way to drive before we get back." Her excuse sounded flimsy in her own ears.

"When I couldn't find you earlier," Parker's voice cracked a little. He cleared it and started again. "When I couldn't find you, I panicked. Not because I viewed you as a part of my job. It was more than that. This connection we have. You must feel it too. Please tell me you feel it too?" The vulnerability in Parker's eyes pulled AJ in.

Still, AJ hesitated. She wanted to push him away. She needed to leave. He was making it harder than she wanted it to be.

"I feel it too," she admitted.

"How did you know? How did you really know Amy Jo was going to be taken? It happened right here. You named the exact spot, at the exact time, and the exact person. But you'd never met her, and you didn't know your dad was here. I saw the surprise on your face. There was too much you didn't know. I might have bought that you knew she was your sister and a target. But I could see the shock on your face. Both of your faces. Neither of you knew."

"Parker," AJ began, searching for the right words. "I'm not from here."

"Right," he smiled. "You're like an alien?"

"I'm just somebody who was trying to change the past," AJ skirted the truth.

"You can't change the past," Parker said. He moved closer to AJ, his eyes staring intensely into hers.

"No, but maybe you can reroute the future a little," AJ whispered.

"Have you ever thought about those moments in life where you make a decision that's so important you know it's going to change your life forever?" Parker was now inches from her, his face stooped down to close the distance between them.

"All the time," she said.

Parker closed the gap and AJ fell into his embrace as

his lips found hers. She was pinned against the car as his body leaned into hers. She deepened the kiss, her arms around him, her hands found his hair and wrapped up in it. Parker groaned and kissed her until they both reluctantly broke apart, gasping for air.

Parker stared hard into her eyes.

"You're not part of the plan," AJ said sadly. It was then that she looked over and saw the gold glittering in the moonlight. AJ held up a finger and walked to the tree. It was Kiera's necklace. She picked it up and examined it. The clasp was fine. She put it back on. It was her sign. She had to choose Kiera, no matter what.

"You're leaving." Parker said when she walked back over. AJ thought she could see his heart breaking through the pain in his eyes.

"Yes."

"Can I go with you?" he asked.

AJ smiled sadly and shook her head no. The Parker of this world didn't belong in hers. "You can take me to the train station." It was as far as she could go with him.

"I'll escort you there."

Chapter 41
AJ Hartford, 1995

AJ could see the train. She could also see Parker Sheridan. She knew Amanda was here with them though she could not see her. She clasped the necklace that now hung around her neck in her hand.

I choose Kiera. The future of the world depended on it. Kiera's future depended on it. The survival of millions of people in economically developing countries depended on Kiera.

Still, tears streamed steadily down her face as Parker held her tight. It wasn't within AJ's right to change the future. This sliding-glass moment didn't belong to her. It belonged to the AJ who lived here in this dimension to choose her future. That thought hadn't occurred to AJ when she was running around trying to save Amy Jo.

At the thought of the sister she'd just met, AJ only cried harder. She was leaving two people whom she had connected with and wanted to stay and get to know. But Kiera was more important than all of that. She was AJ's priority.

AJ wondered if the AJ of this world, the one she was leaving behind, would remember any of this. She hoped she would. Having a sister and a boyfriend who cared for you sounded like a great start to a new life.

"I wish you would stay. I'd really like to see where this goes," Parker whispered into the top of AJ's head.

AJ took a deep breath and broke the embrace. She wiped her tears. "Maybe in a different timeline."

Parker looked confused. AJ leaned forward and kissed his cheek. Parker turned his face and connected with her lips. He kissed her in a way that almost made her forget she had a daughter waiting for her back home.

"Goodbye, Parker," AJ said as she broke the embrace. She bought a ticket, got on the train, and looked out the window to see him staring back at her. The look on his face was one of bewilderment, like he was watching the love of his life disappear before his very eyes. Little did he know...

The train lurched, as did AJ's stomach. She'd forgotten her intense motion sickness when it came to trains. Still, she positioned herself right by the window and stared out into the black night. She took deep breaths as the train picked up speed. Her eyes searched for Amanda.

Then she saw that boney hand that had once terrified her on the train from Chicago so long ago. AJ was startled to realize it actually hadn't been long at all. So much had happened in such a short period of time.

She saw Amanda's face then, and her other hand pressed against the window. AJ placed her hands against Amanda's hands. Their hands meshed through the glass that was suddenly not the window anymore. Body heat radiated from the touch of skin as Amanda firmly clasped

AJ's forearms. She pulled AJ out of the train. AJ screamed at the sudden jolt.

Then everything slowed down. They were floating between worlds in a place where no one would find them. AJ remembered this. The weightless feeling of floating off forever in the darkness with no real destination. Her only comfort was the fact that she had done this before, and she had arrived at her destination. Her confidence in Amanda's abilities was increasing as well.

AJ embraced the silence, thinking about the quick chain of events that had enabled them to save Amy Jo. She should feel triumphant. Instead, she felt a little lost.

"You did the right thing," Amanda said as if reading AJ's mind. She guessed it wasn't so far-fetched to think Amanda could read her mind. She was, after all, a version of AJ. AJ tried to remember how long ago they had floated around before Amanda had propelled her into 1995. Was that only days ago?

AJ sighed, feeling herself relax into the weightlessness. It was like she was floating down a river, only she knew she would not fall under the water and drown. She hadn't realized she had been holding her breath. Until she wasn't anymore.

"I hope you're right. That was hard. But then I thought of Kiera. That made the decision easier. What's she like as an adult? Your Kiera?"

"Taller," Amanda answered.

AJ laughed. It felt good to laugh. She felt so light and free. She was going home, back to the world where she belonged.

"Okay, prepare yourself," Amanda warned.

"Already?" AJ whined. Nothing could prepare AJ for the feeling of free falling and plummeting through time and space.

"Put your other hand on my arm and hold on tight," Amanda said with excitement in her tone. "Remember you're going to fall for a while. You'll be okay. You lived through it the last time. You'll make it through this time as well."

AJ clutched Amanda's arm. She tightened her gut as adrenaline kicked in. She began to free fall.

Fear shot through her body. AJ could see flashes of light and a swirling wind up ahead. Then her body was hurling toward the light. Her body sucked into the blackness, spinning out of control and flailing around. Then she was plunging toward a light, falling fast.

She landed hard with a loud smack. She was in the bathroom, and she had fallen against the cold, tiled wall. She felt momentarily dizzy and closed her eyes to steady herself. Then the dizziness passed.

AJ ran a hand over her body, her head, her hair, her arms, and looked in the mirror. She was her old self again. Relief flooded through her, and she'd never been so happy to see her thirty-plus face again. She suddenly loved the curvy figure and extra padding that had become so hard to keep off into her thirties. AJ felt herself again.

She left the train station as soon as she could get a taxi. She gave the driver her mother's address. She was finally going home. She was so close. Her heart was bursting with excitement to see her daughter again.

Chapter 42
AJ Hartford, 2015

Whoever said *you can't go home again* was lying. You can always go home. There's just no guarantee home will be exactly as you left it.

AJ paid the taxi driver and practically ran to the door of her mom's house where she'd last seen Kiera. She knocked with eager anticipation. The porch light turned on. Then the door opened. Her mother stood at the door.

"AJ, is that you? What are you doing knocking? Get in here, you crazy girl." Her mother smiled lightly at her.

Weird, AJ thought.

"Where's Kiera?" AJ asked, unable to wait. She really wanted to grab her daughter and head home. She couldn't wait to sleep in her own bed and convince herself it had all been a strange dream.

Before her mother could answer, AJ heard a male voice. "AJ? Is that you?"

The deep voice was slightly familiar, but AJ couldn't quite place it. "Yes?"

Parker Sheridan strode into her mother's living room. It

was the same living room, in the same house, at the same address but an older, more distinguished version of Parker Sheridan was standing in her mother's living room. Like he belonged there.

Before she could say another word, he scooped her up and spun her around. He set her on her feet and kissed her until she was breathless. She kissed him back. He had been cute as a young rookie cop, but now... AJ couldn't figure out why she wasn't running for the nearest bedroom to be with him.

"Sweetheart, how was your trip? How did you do on the train?" he asked.

"Umm..."

Parker took her hand and led her into the kitchen. Only then did she notice he was wearing an apron.

"You're cooking?" AJ asked. She could see spaghetti sauce boiling and remnants of scratch onions, mushrooms, and tomatoes on a cutting board. The smell of oregano, parsley, and cloves filled the air and made AJ's stomach rumble.

Parker gave her a patient look with a twinkle in his eyes. "Of course I cooked."

"It smells wonderful," she breathed.

"You still haven't answered my question about your trip," Parker reminded her.

"You know me and traveling," AJ replied with a casual shrug. Did he know her? She saw the ring on his finger and looked down at hers. She was wearing one too. It was a simple but elegant ring with a large square-cut diamond.

Parker stirred the sauce and looked at her with sympathy. "I do. That bad, huh?"

AJ nodded but her eyes wandered around the room.

"Where's Kiera?" AJ asked.

"Who?" both Parker and her mother asked simultaneously. They were staring at her quizzically.

"Kiera," AJ felt panic rise as her heart beat faster. "Where's Kiera?"

"I'm sorry, sweetheart, were you meeting someone here? Someone you traveled with?" Parker asked.

"My daughter," AJ's voice was raised near the point of hysteria. She could see the way her mom's eyes widened in shock.

Parker took a cautious step forward. He leaned in and lowered his voice. "AJ, you didn't want kids, don't you remember? We agreed on that—"

"No, no, no..." AJ groaned loudly as she took three steps backwards out of the room.

"AJ?" Her mother called after her.

"I'll be right back," AJ responded. "Not feeling well." Then she ran. She ran from room to room in the house looking for Kiera. Sweat trickled down the side of her face. Panic and anxiety had taken over. After she'd looked in the last possible place in the house, AJ had her answer. It was an answer she couldn't accept. She opened the front door and ran outside.

Chapter 43
AJ Hartford, 2015

AJ had no more than run off the porch when a large lightning bolt hurled from the sky and hit the Earth angrily. AJ yelped and jumped back to the porch. Amanda showed up beside her.

"There's a big problem," AJ panted. "A big, gigantic problem!"

"I know," Amanda said. "There's a problem in my universe too. I think it's why I'm still here."

"Kiera, she's—"

"I know. Mine too."

"What do you think happened?" AJ asked. Even as the question left her mouth, her brain formed a hypothesis. She stopped talking suddenly with a realization. It was too horrible to consider.

"Parker." AJ gasped. She put her hands on her knees and tried to catch her breath.

"Parker?" Amanda asked.

AJ nodded as she walked around in circles, her anxiety

making it difficult to breathe. "It's the only thing that changed in the other world. My preference was for Parker, not Johnny."

"And?" Amanda's voice was laced with panic. Thunder boomed loudly overhead. "I told you not to change anything."

"I think I might already have changed the single most important thing before you even said something," AJ admitted. She paused to think for a minute. "When you appeared to me in the bathroom, I had just seen Johnny in the hallway. I blew him off. He was asking when we were going on our next date, and I blew him off."

"And Parker is not Kiera's father," Amanda said, realization dawning on her as well.

"When I met Parker in the other dimension, everything changed. Even though nothing actually happened, the absence of something happening caused everything to change. I blew off Johnny and my heart chose Parker. Only, Parker and I aren't the ones who had Kiera."

AJ yelped again as lightning struck and she smelled burnt, singed earth that took her back to the very beginning of this quest. AJ knew neither she nor Amanda were supposed to be there.

"Can you fix it?" Amanda asked.

AJ thought for a minute. She remembered how Johnny had leaned over her in the high school hallway hitting on her. That was the moment where she'd chosen wrong.

"I think so."

AJ knew what she needed to do. Even as the thought came to her, her stomach felt queasy. Knowing what she had to do with Johnny and doing it were two different things. Johnny had ruined her and Kiera's life, which made it difficult to accept that she would have to purposely choose to go through it all again. She'd been pregnant with Kiera by the end of her senior year. She had to make that happen again.

"We have to go back. Can you get me back?" AJ asked.

"I think so," Amanda answered.

"You think so?" AJ heard her own voice rise. "I don't think I could handle another dimension. It has to be the exact same one."

"I got you there once. I can get you there again."

A plan was beginning to form in AJ's mind. All she had to do was stay away from Parker. If she never ran into him, he'd never know she'd returned. Once AJ did the deed, she didn't have to stick around to experience what happened next. But she knew better. Kiera was the bond that had tied her and Johnny together in her dimension and she hated the thought of putting that on the AJ in the other dimension. But it was the only solution for the future.

She walked back into her mother's home with newfound clarity and AJ worked to calm her brain. She quietly opened the door and latched it shut. She casually walked into the dining room where Parker was dishing his homemade spaghetti onto plates.

"There you are. You're just in time," he greeted brightly. Then he lowered his voice. "You okay?"

"Yeah, sorry, I was looking for something."

"Just wait until you try this spaghetti, AJ," her mother said. "It's to die for."

"I actually have to run back to the train station. I left something. I'm so sorry," AJ smiled apologetically.

"What did you leave?" Parker looked up. His disappointed eyes met hers.

"My... credit card. I left my credit card in a bathroom stall. I was still carrying it after I paid my ticket."

"Okay, why don't I come with you?" Parker asked.

"No, it's fine, really. I just need to grab it before someone else does and starts charging it up. I'll be back soon."

"Wait," Parker followed her out of the room. He grabbed her arm gently and spun her around.

AJ found herself in Parker's arms and cuddled into his warm embrace. He kissed her gently at first, then with more urgency. His warm, hot breath smelled like herbs and spices. His tongue found the inside of her mouth. For minutes, AJ lost herself in his kiss. She had to be crazy to leave this.

Finally, Parker broke away. He took a step backwards.

"What was that for?" AJ asked.

"I really missed you," he said with a flirtatious smile and smacked her butt as she turned to leave. "Hurry back."

AJ stared at him half a second longer than necessary. She was memorizing his ruggedly handsome face. He had aged well. Strands of gray lined Parker's hair and he had a short beard. He looked like he was in good shape too. Did AJ have time to find out what was under those clothes? She shook her head. She was only prolonging the inevitable. When she returned, this Parker would be but a distant memory.

"I'll miss you too," AJ said, choking back the emotion that followed *goodbye for a lifetime.*

Parker handed her the car keys. "You might need these."

"Right," AJ laughed and went out the door.

Chapter 44
AJ Hartford, 1995

Sneaking back into a universe was a lot harder than leaving had been. And it wasn't a peaceful transition into the sleeping version of herself this time either. She was at cheerleading practice of all places. As if AJ wasn't clumsy enough, her body jolted forward when she entered the AJ from this dimension.

Unfortunately, AJ from this dimension had been holding another girl's foot in an L-stand. When she jolted forward, the flyer had lost her balance and fell backwards, causing her to land on the spotter—who was not paying attention.

AJ was relieved to find she was in the same body she had been when she rescued Amy Jo in Chritten. These were the same mean girls who she'd practiced cheer with before. Though she couldn't remember each of their names.

"Ow, Lisa!" the spotter whined as she hit the floor.

"You would've caught me if you hadn't been daydreaming, Becka!" Lisa snapped. She jumped up and offered her hand to Becka. "Are you hurt?"

Becka shrugged and rubbed her bottom. "My butt hit pretty hard."

This caused a round of snickers and giggles.

"What happened?" a pretty, blond girl who did not look amused looked around at all of them accusingly.

AJ found her voice. "I lost my balance."

The pretty girl whirled on AJ with venom in her eyes. "Lost your balance?"

AJ shrugged. "Sorry."

"You gonna lose your balance on game day?" she asked impatiently.

"I hope not!" AJ thought, feeling suddenly horrified. Would she have to perform on a game day? She felt sick. Or maybe that was the effect of the rose-colored universe on her vision again. No, it was definitely nerves over the prospect of cheering at a game.

"It was just an accident, Amber. AJ wouldn't drop me on purpose... Would you, AJ?" Lisa looked nervous and bit her fingernail.

"Of course not." AJ was shocked that this girl, or any of them here, would think such a thing.

"Let's call it, girls," Amber announced loudly.

Only then did AJ notice there were a handful of other girls milling around watching the whole thing.

Relieved, AJ turned to walk away, slowly. She was processing that somehow she didn't feel dizzy or nauseated and wondered what that meant. Was she acclimating to this world?

"Hey, AJ," Amber was suddenly at her elbow and AJ noticed they were walking alone separated from the other girls. AJ felt dread in her stomach. "You didn't drop her on purpose, did you?"

AJ stopped walking and stared at the girl with wide eyes. "No! I would never! Why on earth would you think that?"

Amber shrugged but AJ could see sympathy in her eyes. She put her arm in AJ's and started walking slowly. "I think she went out with Johnny. Did you know?"

Now AJ halted abruptly. "What?"

"Oh no! You didn't know? It's just... I thought... We all thought..."

"What, spit it out!" AJ didn't have time for such games. She needed to get her life back on track. Fast. This little girl could not stand in her way.

"We thought you were with the cop now."

"I see," AJ said, irritation evident in her tone. "No one thought to ask me?"

"Well, Lisa said Johnny told her you blew him off and you weren't together. You need to pick, AJ. You can't have them both."

AJ saw the truth in this and felt her anger deflate. She *had* blown Johnny off. She didn't want him then, nor did she want him now. She just had a job to do. One that made her stomach hurt.

"Yeah, I know," AJ mumbled. "It's just not that easy."

Amber patted her arm and lowered her voice. "If I were you, I'd go for the cute cop. He's older, has a job, and is way hotter than Johnny. Plus, Johnny is just kinda bad news, ya know?"

"Oh yes," AJ agreed. "I know."

She broke away then and said *goodbye*. AJ was off to

seduce said bad news guy. She was not prepared for the scene that met her when she left the school. Johnny had Lisa pinned against the school building. His body melded against hers. As he mauled her face, his fingers made their way up into Lisa's short, softie shorts. Lisa giggled but slapped at his hand.

Lisa's eyes were closed but Johnny's were wide open and looking right at AJ. What a creep. He was checking her out while making out with her friend. Why should she feel surprised by that?

Still, AJ remembered how to play the game with him. She rolled her eyes and walked on by. Johnny had always wanted what he couldn't have and when he got it, he lost all interest. This was going to play to AJ's favor.

"Hey, AJ, is your car still in the shop?" Amber pulled up beside AJ in her car and had rolled down the window.

AJ looked around the parking lot. By process of elimination and deducing that the IROC-Z Camaro left in the parking lot had to be Johnny's, AJ nodded.

"Get in, slut. I'll drive you home," Amber called playfully.

Johnny walked by at that moment, Lisa walking ahead of him. He slowed his pace.

"Yeah, slut," he whispered in AJ's ear as he walked by. "Maybe you could ride me—I mean—with me."

"No way in hell, Johnny," AJ hissed back. "Your car is full." She pointed to Lisa, turned, and quickly got in Amber's car. Johnny would be back. She hadn't lost him. AJ just needed to figure out the right time to make this all work perfectly. She didn't plan to take multiple tries at this.

She needed to let Johnny knock her up and then move away forever. Talk about the past repeating itself in the worst possible way! Who knew AJ's biggest mistake in life would end up her greatest accomplishment?

All that mattered right now was Kiera. As long as Kiera was born, the timeline would get back on track. Then AJ could live a long, happy life. Parker was right. You can't change the past. She had been wrong. She shouldn't have tried to reroute it. Even a little bit.

Chapter 45
AJ Hartford, 1995

"AJ is that you?" her mother called as AJ stepped through the door.

"Yeah, I'm home, mom," AJ answered. She suddenly felt like she needed a hot bath to get past her interaction with Johnny earlier.

"What time do you need to be back up at the school?" her mom asked, coming into the room.

"Back up to the school?" AJ asked blankly.

"AJ, it's the Spring Formal dance tonight!" her mother clucked at her. "Go get ready. You probably only have an hour."

"Spring Formal," AJ repeated, her brain processing. "Do I have to go?"

This time her mom laughed. "Well, if you don't, I'll take back that dress I got you. It was not cheap."

"It's just a dance, right?" AJ asked.

"Of course, what's gotten into you?" Maria gave AJ a weird look.

AJ felt relieved. For a minute, she was afraid there was a game where she would have to cheer.

"Okay, but why do I have to be there so early?" AJ wondered.

"Aren't you part of the decorating committee?" Her mother frowned at her. "Are you feeling alright?"

AJ almost told her she didn't, but her mom promptly felt her forehead.

"You're not even hot. Go get ready. Oh, and one more thing. I really like Parker Sheridan. I think you do, too. You officially have my permission to date him."

"What?" AJ almost tripped on her own feet. "What changed?"

"I see the way he looks at you. I like that he went after you and saved you from your father. He made sure you got back here safe and sound. Such a nice boy."

Oh brother, AJ thought. She had no clue what story he'd given her when he'd returned but Parker must have really charmed her mom. The timing was terrible, and AJ felt herself falling into a dark hole of depression. She already hated herself for what she was about to do to the AJ in this dimension. AJ had already paid her dues in her dimension. It just broke her heart to know this AJ had to endure the same fate.

Once in her room, AJ thought about going out the window and running away. But that wouldn't help her any. Instead, she found the dress her mom had bought her for the dance tonight.

"Oh boy," AJ said. She couldn't believe her mom had allowed this tiny dress. It was bright red with a short, fluffy skirt. The top was so low cut, AJ imagined it would show a fair amount of cleavage. This night could not get any less exciting.

She focused on her hair and makeup first. When she had curled her hair with just the right amount of beach wave, AJ felt doubt. In this era, they wore their hair very curly or very straight. She shrugged. She liked her hair, so she was going to keep the wave. It looked classy. Not that what she was trying to accomplish was very classy.

She'd chosen darker colors for her makeup and found a tube of bright red lipstick. If she had to wear such a revealing dress, she might as well wear lipstick that brought the eyes up.

No such luck. When she wiggled into the dress, it was just as revealing as she'd assumed. The top was a single strap that circled around her neck. The scalloped edge plunged just low enough to show her cleavage and tight enough to give it a boost. She tried tugging it up, but it was no use. The dress only fit one way. The skirt had a bit of a flounce to it, with several petticoats under it, causing the skirt to poof out and cut off drastically at her upper thighs.

AJ looked around and found a pair of dress shoes with a small heel on them. They laced up like ballet shoes. They looked new and must have been intended to go with this outfit.

Finally, AJ emerged.

"Oh, AJ! You look incredible! I love your hair like that," her mother stared hard at her. It was a dead giveaway that no one was wearing their hair like this yet.

"I know no one wears their hair this way yet," AJ quipped, thinking of the line from *Back to the Future* when

Marty McFly overplayed "Johnny B. Goode" at the "Enchantment Under the Sea" high school dance. "But your kids are gonna love it," AJ finished the iconic line with a mumble as she walked away.

"What?" her mom asked quizzically.

"I said I just wanted to be different," AJ said a bit louder. Everything about this night was starting to feel like her own version of that movie. Whatever she had to tell herself to get through it, she supposed.

"You're quiet tonight," Maria commented a few minutes into the drive toward school.

"Yeah, I've just been thinking about the future. When you were my age, was there anything you wish you would have done differently? I don't want to get older and have regrets," AJ told her.

"Wow, that's a heavy subject," Maria laughed lightly.

"I know," AJ said. "It's just my senior year and I'm looking at what comes next."

"When I was your age, all I was thinking about was who I was going to marry. I had this list. He would be tall, dark, and handsome. He would be rich. He would treat me like a queen. He would want a family... Oh, Lord, I was so idealistic back then."

"What changed?" AJ asked. She wanted to ask *Why dad?*

"Every man is flawed, AJ. No one is perfect. There's no black and white, just degrees of gray. Your dad was the only man I dated who wanted kids. That became more important to me than anything else on my list. And I don't regret that. Your dad is a great dad. At the time, nothing else mattered to me. I made the best decision I could at that moment."

AJ let the words roll around in her head. The car rolled to a stop. "Thanks, mom." AJ leaned over and kissed her mom goodbye.

Her mother drove off and AJ walked into the auditorium where she worked with the other kids to transform their high school gym into a magical party kingdom. She had to admit she was a little in awe when it was done.

"Hey, AJ, give me a hand with this punch?" someone called out.

Gladly, AJ followed the sound of the voice to the cafeteria kitchen. She rounded the corner in time to see a tall, skinny boy grinning wickedly while he poured a fifth of vodka into a large punchbowl of floating sherbet.

The punch bowl sat atop a rolling cart so there was no need for AJ's help but when he offered her a cup, she gladly took it. She would need liquid courage to survive this night.

When she was properly buzzed, she and the skinny kid pushed the cart out and lifted the punchbowl clumsily onto the table. The punch sloshed dangerously but only a few drops hit the tablecloth.

"Oopsie!" AJ giggled as she wiped it up with her fingers and licked them.

"Ew, gross!" The skinny kid made a face as he stuck his finger in the punch.

AJ collapsed in a chair in a fit of giggles.

"Someone's already having a good time," the principal said as she walked by.

AJ felt her eyes go round as she looked into the

startled eyes of her partner in crime. When the principal kept walking, they quietly giggled again.

Within a half hour, the DJ showed up and music began playing. Shortly after, kids arrived one at a time, then two, then in groups until the gym was full. AJ stood against the wall. She remembered high school dances. They were fun at the time but nothing about this seemed fun.

She saw Johnny walk in with Lisa. Johnny had charisma. No matter that he was bad news, it only lent to his charm. AJ watched many girls turn their heads as he walked in. This was getting complicated. AJ had to make sure he left with her. AJ watched as Lisa broke away from Johnny. AJ headed for the bathroom.

Before she made it, she felt a hand on her arm. She whipped around and found herself face to face with Johnny.

"You look pretty, AJ," Johnny said, his face inches from her. AJ's stomach revolted. She took a deep breath. Even in her foggy state, she had a hard time conjuring a smile for him. So, she didn't.

"You're here with another girl, you creep!" she mouthed.

"Only because you weren't available," he said sweetly, his eyes roaming up and down her chest.

"I wasn't available?" AJ repeated blankly.

"Don't think I don't see you whoring around with that cop when you could've had me. He's a nobody. Graduated from here last year. Didn't even leave this town," Johnny whispered, tightly gripping her arm now. He was clearly jealous. This meant AJ still had his attention.

"You're hurting me," AJ said through gritted teeth. "And that's none of your business."

"I know your type," Johnny's smile had turned mean. AJ remembered this smile. She had memorized it from the years in the prison she'd served as his wife in her dimension. "All tease but no payout. You're not worth my time."

"Good, because I wouldn't want any of it," AJ smarted as she yanked her hand away just in time to see Lisa exit the bathroom.

"AJ?" Lisa asked as she passed her.

AJ kept walking. But she heard Lisa's voice behind her as she addressed Johnny.

"What was that about?" Lisa loudly asked Johnny so she could be heard over the music.

"Don't worry about it," Johnny replied. AJ could feel his eyes boring into her back as she went back for more punch. This buzz was wearing off a little too quickly for her. It was going to be a long night.

AJ sat back and watched as Johnny and Lisa got progressively madder at each other as the night went on. She watched as Lisa pouted and Johnny rolled his eyes. She wasn't surprised. Johnny had no respect for females. It was always a matter of time before girls left him. To her knowledge, AJ was the only one who kept trying to make a toxic relationship work. She'd done it for Kiera. Only, she'd stayed too long at the party.

Which was precisely what she was thinking when Lisa stormed off and Johnny immediately stalked over to her.

"We need to talk," he announced.

"I can't imagine what we have to talk about," AJ said, still playing hard to get knowing it would only fuel Johnny's flame.

Johnny grabbed her arm again. "Come on, let's go outside. We can sit in my car."

"Stop grabbing my arm," AJ said. She tried to get up the courage to leave with him. She knew what she needed to do. But she was fighting herself.

"Leave her alone, Johnny." The skinny boy who'd spiked the punch earlier was standing there trying to look mean.

Johnny started laughing. "Beat it, Lockwood. Come back when you learn to be a man."

"She said stop grabbing her arm," Lockwood squeaked.

Johnny dropped AJ's arm and AJ could see him ball up a fist.

"Okay, okay, enough," AJ said quickly. She didn't want to see Johnny lay this kid out. "I'll go talk to you."

"AJ, you sure?" Lockwood asked.

"I'll be fine. Thanks, Lockwood," AJ repeated the name Johnny had called him.

The kid opened his mouth to protest but seemed to change his mind. AJ waved *goodbye* to Lockwood, not feeling fine at all.

Johnny grabbed her hand and AJ allowed herself to be pulled out of the school. Johnny opened the door of a Camaro IROC-Z and pulled the front seat forward, pointing to the back seat.

"We can have more privacy there," he said.

AJ reluctantly obeyed. *Just get this over with*, she told herself.

Then she was alone in the back seat of Johnny's Camaro. She wondered vaguely how many girls he'd had back here. She'd never been with anyone before Johnny in her dimension. The backseat was a tight fit once Johnny jumped in. He immediately put his hand on her knee. He leaned over and pinned her against the seat, kissing her roughly.

"Hey!" she protested.

"Don't tell me you're a tease," Johnny jeered at her, his face inches from hers. His hand rode up her leg and planted firmly on her inner thigh. He applied enough pressure so AJ knew she couldn't move if she wanted to. "No one likes a tease."

He kissed her again, his lips so hard against hers. They felt instantly bruised. Warning bells went off in AJ's head.

This isn't right, her head screamed. But it was familiar. Her mind transported her to a time in her own dimension. It had been the first time she'd been with him and most likely the night she'd gotten pregnant. It had started exactly like this. It was like the memory she had locked away was now trying to warn her about what was going to happen. It was like déjà vu.

AJ felt Johnny's hand creep even higher, and she gasped. He kissed her harder, his body angled against hers. AJ couldn't move and she couldn't breathe. She froze up. In this world, in the 90s, the term post-traumatic stress disorder wasn't talked about or known. This was the closest AJ had ever come to feeling that. She was panicking and having a hard time breathing over something that had already happened in her past. In fact, she might even be subconsciously holding her breath. This wasn't right. It had never been right.

"That's right, baby. Don't fight it. Just let it happen," Johnny's sleazy words registered in her brain.

That's when it all came back to her. The first time she'd

been with Johnny hadn't been consensual. In fact, she'd said *no*. But it hadn't stopped him. When she'd found out she was pregnant, she'd been so terrified, she'd stayed with him. Who else would want anyone at such a young age with a baby? She never considered her choices, and she was sure now that she had blocked all of this out.

"No!" AJ surprised herself with the force of the word. She needed to let this happen, but her brain had shut down and she was just reacting defensively now.

Johnny laughed and she heard fabric rip as he tugged at her underclothes. "Come on, baby. You know you want it. You can't leave a guy in a position like this. Don't you know what blue balls does to a guy?"

"It's never killed anyone." AJ found strength in her sudden anger and pushed him hard. Gone was the plan to conceive Kiera. The only thoughts in AJ's brain were to get out of there fast. "I said *no*!"

Johnny pulled back, anger in his eyes. In a flash, the back of his hand connected with her face.

AJ felt momentarily dizzy. Then she felt stunned. Johnny had abandoned his efforts of violating her for a moment to unbutton his pants. AJ loudly screamed.

"Shut up, bitch!" Johnny hit her again and pinned her down. He worked his pants down his hips with one hand. He impatiently ripped the fabric she wore under her dress.

AJ felt hot tears and she screamed again as loud as she could before Johnny pulled out a pocketknife. He held it against her throat. AJ went still.

"That's a good girl," he cooed. "This will go easier if you stop fighting and let it happen. You might even like it. You know what they say about uptight girls. They just need a good f—" Johnny's words died in his throat as his car door yanked open, then his body was yanked through the door.

AJ squinted through her tears. She could see a man cuff Johnny and roughly push him against the car. Johnny's pants were still unbuckled, the belt buckle dangled and hit the side of his car. She saw an officer lead Johnny away in handcuffs.

AJ sat up and smoothed down her dress. In minutes, the officer peeked his face into the car.

"AJ, are you okay?" It was Parker. Parker held out his hand to help her out of the car, but AJ recoiled from it. "It's okay, AJ, I'm here to help you, not hurt you."

AJ's body was trembling from head to toe. Conflicting emotions coursed through her like the adrenaline that made her veins feel hot and cold at the same time.

"He raped me," she whispered.

"Almost," Parker said, compassion in his eyes. He approached her like she was a feral animal. He squatted outside the car and waited patiently for her to come out. AJ knew her mind was not in the present but stuck in the distant past. She remembered all of this too clearly now. Only, there had been no one to save her then.

Now thoughts of Kiera paraded around her mind. How had someone so amazing come out of something so horrific? She jolted to the present with panic and horror again at the thought of Kiera. She had just ruined her one shot of having Kiera.

AJ felt the tears fall like a torrent and loud sobs racked her body. She wasn't crying for her younger, abused self though she could have. She was crying for Kiera. The child she would never have.

She managed to get herself out of Johnny's car. She could smell his lingering cologne on her and felt repulsed. His cologne and aftershave permeated his leather seats. The smell had brought it all back. She got out of the car and threw up from the memory and all the vodka she had drank earlier. Parker stood back.

"AJ, what can I do?" Parker asked. He put out a hand to rub her back, but AJ held out a hand to keep him back.

She stood up after the vomiting stopped and looked at Parker through blurry, self-induced, hate-filled eyes. "This is all my fault."

"What?" he gasped. "No! Rape is never the victim's fault. *No* means *no*, AJ. We could hear you screaming."

"No, really, it's my fault. I needed to... I thought if I... Wait, *we*?"

"Yes, your friend, Larry Lockwood found me. I was on duty tonight. I knew there was a dance. I was in the car parked just over there. He found me when he heard you scream the first time. He told me this Johnny guy bullied you into *talking* in his car," Parker threw an agitated thumb over his shoulder to where he'd put Johnny in the squad car, "and was up to no good."

"Larry?" AJ asked. It was then that she peeked around Parker to see the kid Johnny had called Lockwood standing awkwardly nearby. He looked nervous.

"Thank you, Larry," AJ said.

Larry looked instantly relieved.

"Larry, do you know where the nearest phone is for AJ to call her mom?" Parker asked.

Larry nodded.

"Where are you going?" AJ asked, not wanting Parker to leave.

"Nowhere until your mom gets here. Then I need to take that guy to the station to book him for the night. You can press charges or at the very least get a restraining order."

"Can I think about it?" AJ's teeth chattered as she spoke. She still felt this was her fault. She had lured Johnny out here with the intention of conceiving Kiera. Hadn't she? Because right now, it sure seemed like the other way around.

"Let's call your mom," Parker said softly. His caring eyes stared into hers. "You have blood on your neck," he said suddenly.

AJ reached up and felt the damage the knife had done that Johnny had pulled on her. She shivered as she felt the small scratch. She couldn't help but feel lucky. She knew Johnny was a loose cannon. She was just surprised to find it had all started so early and she had missed the signs in her universe.

Less than twenty minutes later, AJ's mom showed up, took one look at her, and wordlessly put her in the car. Then, Maria stood outside and had a hushed conversation with Parker. AJ could see her mom's anger. She would be angry too if it had been *her* daughter. But they didn't know the full story. Nor would they ever.

This wouldn't happen to AJ's daughter because AJ had ruined all chances of having Kiera. When her mom got in the car, she folded AJ in her arms as AJ sobbed. But not for the reason her mom thought.

AJ was crying because she had failed her daughter.

Now she would never know Kiera. As a result, Kiera would not be inventing a water purification system for economically developing countries. Which meant AJ had also failed the world. Not just her world, she'd failed Amanda's world too. There were at least three worlds, maybe more, who were all affected by this one night. AJ had never felt so low. How had refusing to do the thing that had felt the most wrong become the worst mistake of her life?

Chapter 46
AJ Hartford, 1995

The weeks after the dance passed in a blur. AJ had lost all hope. Her whole purpose had been to save Kiera. To bring Kiera to life. AJ had failed. She had no purpose left. AJ stared off into the distance through the back window of her house.

She remembered when she first saw Amanda through the glass. Then she thought about Amanda explaining the decisions people make becoming sliding-glass moments that could change their lives. AJ had changed their lives but not for the better. No amount of staring through the glass now would change that.

AJ stirred her oatmeal absently.

"AJ, are you going to eat that?" Maria broke into her despondence. "Your oatmeal is getting cold."

"No," AJ pushed the bowl away as if seeing for the first time she had food in front of her.

"AJ, I'm worried about you," her mother started quietly. "What happened to you was not your fault. It was violent and senseless. I'm sorry you had to go through that. Do you think talking to a counselor would help?"

AJ looked at her mother. There were tears in Maria's eyes. It was then that AJ realized what her mother must think. She must think AJ was still upset about the almost-rape. But that situation was the least of AJ's concerns.

In fact, she had decided not to press charges against Johnny. She still felt like she'd led him on and put herself in that situation. AJ felt she was to blame. She'd listened to Parker as he encouraged her to fill out the paperwork.

It might save someone else, Parker had informed her.

How? AJ had challenged him.

With a felony on his record, it will make people aware of who he is. And a restraining order will protect you—

It won't. On both cases. People like Johnny think they're above the law. Do you think he'll volunteer that information? There's no way for girls he dates to search that information. Not at this time, she almost added. *I just want to go on my way. Move forward...*

Only, AJ wasn't moving forward. She wasn't moving in any direction at all. But something worse had happened. Amanda had disappeared. Not in the way she normally did where AJ knew she was still there lurking somewhere and would come out to give her advice. It was something more permanent. AJ felt it. She felt the finality of her destiny. This new destiny. Amanda was gone. AJ was stuck in this dimension. Not that she had anything to go home for. Sure, Parker had been there. But Parker was here too.

"We need to go, AJ." Her mother got up from the table and carried dishes to the sink.

"Go where?" AJ asked. "It's a Saturday."

"Get dressed. We need to run an errand."

"Do I have to?" AJ had become used to her routine of listless napping any time she wasn't in school. She hated to give up a whole Saturday of that.

"Yes, you do," Maria's tone was final.

AJ sighed loudly and reluctantly left the table. She didn't make a lot of effort with her appearance. She couldn't imagine why she would. She threw on a pair of bell-bottom jeans, clunky boots, a snug t-shirt, and grabbed a jacket on the way out.

AJ didn't ask where they were going. She recognized this as an attempt to get her out of the house. She appreciated her mother for it. What she could not explain was the feeling that she'd had a child once and now she didn't. Nor would she ever have this child. It was like mourning a death. At least, AJ assumed this is what it would feel like.

AJ leaned forward in surprise as her mother drove the car up to the police station. "Mom, I don't—"

Her mother patiently turned off the car. She turned to AJ. "I was wrong to keep you from your father. I knew where he went all this time, and I hid that from you. I was trying to protect you. I was wrong in my approach. I realize now, you have a right to determine what kind of relationship you have with him."

"Mom, why are we here though?" AJ felt confused.

"Your father is here, and he's requested to speak to you. It's up to you but from what I understand, he's going away for quite some time. This might be your only chance to ask him questions or make your peace with him."

"He's not dying, right?" AJ felt afraid, remembering that

her dad had died so abruptly in her world. She hadn't had the best relationship with him there. But his death was so sudden, she hadn't had time to say *goodbye.*

"No. He's going into the witness relocation program. He'll be unreachable. Who knows for how long."

"Oh," AJ said.

"It's up to you if you want to talk to him. I just didn't want you to miss this short window."

"Okay," AJ thought about it a moment longer. Then she opened the car door. "Are you coming in with me?"

"No," her mother gently shook her head. "I'll wait right here for you. After this, we can go pick up your car from the mechanic."

"Great," AJ said and shut the car door. She found herself in the police station then. When she walked through the door, she didn't notice the receptionist who greeted her. She saw the memory of when she'd first come to this world. It was the day she'd met Parker. His second day on the job. She smiled fleetingly as she thought about how nervous she'd made him by fainting every five seconds like that. Her equilibrium had balanced out since then. She was accustomed to this rose-colored world now.

"I'm here to see Terrance Hartford," AJ told the receptionist.

"Right this way," the receptionist guided AJ into a small interrogation room.

When she saw him, Terrance Hartford looked more peaceful than she'd remembered. He had clearly bathed, and his wild hair now lay down nicely on his head. It was still long, and he had a beard, but it had been trimmed up.

"AJ," he said as she sat down.

AJ looked at him. Her heart didn't flood with love, but she didn't feel anger or animosity either. Instead, she felt a sort of compassion.

"Hi, dad."

"I'm goin' away," he said.

"I know," AJ responded.

"I've done some bad things but I'm trying to make it right."

"That's good."

"These people—there are more than one—I need to help stop them. So, they're puttin' me in protection until they're all caught."

"Will they come after me or Amy Jo again?" AJ wondered.

"No. We took down the local cell. But this thing is bigger than we'd thought. I knew for a while. That's why I tried to hide on my own. It didn't work."

"Yeah," AJ wasn't sure what to say to that.

"They're taking me out of here in a couple hours. We don't have much time. I just wanted to apologize and say goodbye."

"But I have so many questions." AJ felt time was running out and she needed answers.

"Now's the time to ask."

"What about Amy Jo? Did you have two families?" AJ wondered.

"Yes. But you and your mom were the second family. I got married to her mom because I'd knocked her up. We named her Amy Jo and called her AJ. Then I met your mom on a trip. I married her too. We had you. I named you Amanda Jane and called you AJ because I have a bad memory and I didn't want to accidentally call either of you the wrong name someday. I thought, *There's no way my two wives would ever meet since they live an hour apart.* And they didn't. But one day, your mom came looking for me—after I'd left. She'd found me in Chritten, and she wanted answers. She didn't tell you this, did she?"

AJ shook her head.

"I'd screwed things up pretty bad. She told me not to come home. So, I stayed in Chritten. It was all working out until you showed up. I guess they left you a threat note. But they meant it for Amy Jo?"

AJ shrugged. "They might have known about both of us."

Terrance shook his head. "Man, when I saw you two together... I did a double take. You look so much alike. But it's more than that. It's the way you stand. Your mannerisms, facial expressions, and your eyes. You had the same reactions. My genetics must be strong because you just look and act so much alike."

There was a knock at the door. They looked up as Parker stuck his head in. "We need to wrap this up, Terrance. Sorry, we need to get you on the road."

"You said I had a few hours!" Terrance protested in a whiny voice.

"We say a lot of things when people go into protection and do the opposite." Parker looked at AJ. His heart was in his eyes as they swung to hers. "Hi."

"Hi," AJ said with a small smile. She hadn't talked to him much since the incident. She'd assumed he was giving her space. She'd been fine with that.

"Finish up, Terrance." Parker shut the door behind him. She was alone with her dad again.

"See," Terrance said. "It's weird. How did two people who were so perfect come from someone who was such a mess?"

AJ stared at him as she processed his words. She had thought something similar when she realized Kiera had come from Johnny, a horrible, abusive human being, but would still turn out to be a person who created a solution for clean water in economically developing countries.

My genetics must be strong because you look and act so much alike.

What if her genetics were strong too? What if Johnny didn't have to be the father of Kiera for Kiera to still exist? AJ's heart beat strong in her chest. Maybe it wasn't too late to save Kiera after all.

AJ got up, went around the table, and hugged her dad, catching him off guard.

"What the—"

"I forgive you, dad. For all of it. I love you. Be safe." AJ left him there in the room. It was the last time she ever saw her dad.

It wasn't hard to find Parker. In fact, AJ was sure he was loitering nearby to make sure he didn't miss her. AJ walked up to Parker and stopped inches from him.

"I—" she started to speak.

Parker opened the door to an office and pulled her in. He locked the door behind him and closed the gap between them.

"I know," Parker said. "I missed you, too." He dropped his face to close the distance between her face and his.

His lips were warm and welcoming. The connection she had with him felt like home. With Amanda gone, AJ knew she had set this life on a new path, and she had no choice now but to live it.

When Parker released her, AJ blurted out the first thing that came to her mind. "I'll be eighteen in three months."

Parker smiled. "Your mom gave me permission to date you before that."

AJ smiled but felt sadness in her heart. She already cared so deeply for Parker. Maybe she could still save this after all. But reliving the life she'd already lived was something her brain was going to have to adjust to.

Chapter 47

AJ Hartford, 1997

(Two Years Later)

It was a warm, beautiful September day. The smell of charcoal and sizzling meat permeated the air, making AJ's stomach growl. That wasn't surprising since she was hungry all the time these days. She rubbed her stomach. Her reward was a small kick. She was due in three months.

AJ smiled as she watched Amy Jo, her husband Chance, and Parker talk as Parker flipped burgers. Behind them was a sparkly Rainbow Bright tablecloth over a table with a bright pink and purple birthday cake.

"You seen one yet?" She heard Chance ask Parker.

"One what?" Parker asked.

"One of the new computers. Geez, Parker, where's your brain these days? I've been telling you about it for the past hour." Chance reached over Parker's shoulder and flipped a burger that was getting a little too done.

"Oh right," Parker grinned sheepishly. "My brain's been a little preoccupied."

All heads swiveled in AJ's direction. She sat on a swing,

one barefoot tucked underneath her and her other barefoot pushing off the grassy ground, moving the swing forward and back. AJ smiled back knowing full well they were talking about the baby.

"Auntie AJ!" Two-year-old Grace Miller came running up to AJ as fast as her short little legs would carry her and she flopped her belly onto the swing next to AJ, pumping her legs to get up.

AJ laughed and helped Grace up onto the swing. Grace cuddled her little body into AJ's big pregnant cushion. AJ hugged her back.

"Happy birthday, you big two-year-old! Where did your friends go?"

"Hidin'."

"Like hide-and-seek?" AJ asked.

Grace shrugged. "They said *you're it* and ran away."

"Oh, you're supposed to go find them," AJ tried to coax her.

Grace made a face. "No!" She poked at AJ's belly. "The baby's fat!"

"Grace Elizabeth!" Amy Jo was suddenly there with her hands on her hips.

Grace sat up, wide-eyed, startled by her mother's presence. "Sorry, Auntie AJ."

AJ just laughed.

Amy Jo scooped up Grace and settled her back on her lap, cuddling her close. "I swear to God, AJ. When I think about what would've happened if you hadn't been there—"

"Well, I was and we're all here now," AJ smiled happily. Not one day went by that her sister didn't thank her for saving her life and Grace's life. But today was a special day.

It was Grace's two-year-old birthday. AJ had learned to take the compliment when it came. But the truth was, she had accepted her fate here and moved forward.

AJ glanced at the ring on her finger that sparkled in the sunlight. Lucky for her, swelling had not been bad enough to make it necessary to stop wearing her ring. It was a simple ring. She and Parker were just starting out after all. While Parker had gotten the respect he'd needed to launch his career after helping save her and Amy Jo, he'd only gotten a small raise. But to AJ, the ring was perfect. It was a square-shaped diamond with a simple band of small diamonds that danced in the rose-colored sunlight.

"Have you decided on a name yet?" Amy Jo asked with a smile. "I know how bad Parker's suggestions have been."

"Kiera," AJ said decisively.

"Oh, I like that!" Amy Jo said. "Very pretty. And if it's a boy?"

"She's not," AJ smiled confidently.

Amy Jo rolled her eyes. "Yeah, we were pretty sure we were having a boy." She tickled Grace's ribs. Grace giggled. "We were wrong."

"We'll see," AJ shrugged with a smug smile.

"Burgers are done," Chance called.

The women stood up and joined the men. Three kids a little older than Grace materialized, having decided their bellies were more important than being found.

As they sat down, someone found a stereo and turned it on. It was the top 90s count-down and "Whoomp! (There It Is)" by Tag Team was playing. The kids abandoned their plates and started dancing.

Amy Jo took out a camera and Chance got his video

recorder, which was a big contraption he had to put on his shoulder to balance as he looked through it. AJ didn't miss much about her world. But the updated electronics sure made things more convenient. Then she thought of Kiera. Her teenage daughter she'd left back home. It was easy to get submerged in the world where she'd made new happy memories, but she would never forget Kiera. She rubbed her belly, mindlessly wondering if Kiera would exist in that world after the baby was born here. Had she saved her after all?

It took quite an effort to calm the kids down and get them to eat. They hadn't even had cake yet. AJ shook her head with a smile thinking what a fiasco that would be. She didn't have to wait long to find out.

"Who wants cake?" Amy Jo called out.

The kids went berserk.

"Oh no! I forgot to bring out the candles!" Amy Jo exclaimed.

"I'll get them," AJ responded.

"You're a lifesaver! On the kitchen counter by the coffeemaker."

"Okay!"

AJ slid the glass door open but didn't have time to close it. She froze in utter shock. If she had anything in her hands, she would have dropped it. Her heart fluttered. Her eyes misted. She blinked three times to make sure what she was seeing was real.

For half a second, AJ thought she'd glitched back to her original universe. It would be the only explanation for who AJ saw standing in front of her. But no, as AJ ran a hand over her large, pregnant belly, it confirmed she was still very much in 1997.

"Hi, mom!"

AJ was speechless.

Chapter 48
AJ Hartford, 1997

"Kiera!" AJ gasped in a shocked whisper. "I was so worried I would never see you again."

The girl standing before AJ was Kiera but different. She was taller than AJ. AJ remembered two years had gone by which would make Kiera eighteen now. At the thought that AJ had missed Kiera's two-year transition into adulthood, tears spilled down AJ's face. Kiera had that same face AJ remembered but her hair was dishwater blond and straight. She had a smattering of freckles that brushed over her nose and cheeks. They reminded AJ of Parker's freckles.

AJ rushed forward and hugged Kiera. So many questions flooded her mind.

"Is that me in there?" Kiera asked rhetorically with a smile. "Trippy."

Before AJ could ask a question, Kiera broke the embrace and took half a step back.

"We don't have much time, mom. I partnered with a scientist who created a device to move us through dimensions. After you disappeared, I never stopped researching multiverses. I have a journal full of theories. I can explain more, but right now, you have to come with me. There's no time left."

"Time for what?" AJ asked. "I can't just leave here."

Kiera took AJ's hand in response and squeezed it hard. Harder than AJ would have expected. It actually hurt and AJ realized a hard object had pierced her skin.

"Ow!" AJ yelped.

"Sorry, mom," Kiera said in a quiet voice.

The dimension went black.

Chapter 49
AJ Hartford, 2017

AJ and Kiera were floating into the nothing. That dark void where they were weightless and relaxed. The space that AJ had come to enjoy regardless of the free fall that she knew would come next. It was as if time ceased to exist as did all her worries. The only thing that felt real was Kiera's hand in hers.

"Kiera, I miss you. I did everything I could to get back to you. Then I sort of got trapped. How did you get here?" AJ asked in her dream-like state.

"Time passed differently after you left," Kiera began. "I immediately started researching parallel universes. I started with my science teacher. He connected me to some college professors. Those professors referred me to other scientists who had been researching multiple dimensions, which they call the multiverse. I explained your story. They got excited. I wrote everything they taught me in my red journal."

"I remember that journal," AJ said with a smile.

"Well, I forgot about the journal for a long while," Kiera said in a serious voice. "I forgot about a lot of things. The best I can understand, time reset itself. I still loved science, but I didn't remember it holding such an important place in my life. I didn't remember the journal or that you'd traveled. I always felt more mature than kids in my grade, smarter and older, like I didn't really belong. None of it made sense."

AJ thought about this. When she got pregnant with Kiera in the universe that was 1997, it was two years after Kiera was set to be born originally.

"Kiera, how old are you?" AJ asked.

"Sixteen," Kiera giggled. "Gosh, mom. Is that dimension travel or old age kicking in?" she teased.

"Watch it, young lady, I'm still your mom," AJ practiced her best *mom voice*, which came out in a matching light tone. In truth, she felt so relieved, she thought she would cry. She hadn't missed two years of Kiera's life after all. Her theory must be correct. She must have pushed back the timeline by marrying Parker and not getting pregnant with Kiera for two years. That would mean AJ had been gone for two years but Kiera might have only experienced her being gone for days.

"Sorry, mom," Kiera said with a smile in her voice that said she wasn't sorry at all.

"You were saying, about school...?" AJ prompted.

"Well, one day I was sitting in my room thinking about how I didn't fit in and how despondent I felt—you know, typical teenage stuff—when this lady showed up. She just walked through my bedroom wall! Literally, she walked through the wall. It was you, only it wasn't you. You had just left on a work trip. This lady was older. Like you ten years in the future—"

"Amanda." Relief flooded through AJ. Amanda had still been watching out for AJ and Kiera this whole time.

"Yes! Anyway, she gave me the red journal and told me this crazy story. At first, I was too terrified to blink. This ghost just walked through my wall! But when I reached out to grab the journal, I remembered everything. It was like this crazy montage of you leaving to go save AJ2 because it would save all of us. I saw myself researching and I saw scientists I had talked to. It all made sense but none of it had happened in my lifetime."

"I think I understand why," AJ said. "You were supposed to be born two years prior but it reset the entire timeline when I got pregnant with you."

"Woah, that's crazy!" Kiera said, awe in her voice.

"So, Amanda gave you the journal. Then what?"

"I opened it up and it was in my handwriting. I flipped further back, and I saw all these journal entries from when you left. The dates were from two years ago.

My mom isn't missing, she's just on a work trip. She'll be home tomorrow, I'd told Amanda.

"She told me you wouldn't make it back. Not until I finished what I'd started. She flipped to the back of the journal. I had notes about traveling to dimensions. I had the names of the scientists.

"Why didn't you travel back the way I did?" AJ wondered.

"We tried that, and it didn't work. Not the way it had when she was connected to you. She thought it was because she and I didn't share exact DNA. She couldn't move me through time the way she did with you. She couldn't explain why, but Amanda had somehow disconnected from you as well."

"So you were talking to the scientists?" AJ asked.

"Yeah, I went back to a scientist I had written about in my journal. I explained the whole story. He believed me. He had just created this device.

"*It's a travel prototype,* he'd said. But he didn't want to use me because it was still in beta testing. I begged him. After a few hours, I'd worn him down.

"He set the timeline and pushed the device into my skin. All I had to do when I got to you was pierce your skin with the second travel prototype. Our devices would link up. He couldn't even guarantee it was safe. No one had ever successfully traveled with one. Amanda thought the timing would be right because I had been conceived in the other dimension and therefore could exist in 1997. As long as I could get back there."

AJ was stunned. "Kiera! That was horribly dangerous. It wasn't worth it!"

"Of course it was, mom! I can't live the rest of my life without a mother. Anyway, Amanda explained it was a little like your soul leaves the body in that dimension and you go back into the body in the dimension where you belong."

"So, that's what we are right now? Souls?" AJ asked feeling a little creeped out. "Can you see me?"

"I can't see anything. It's all dark. But your hand is in my hand and our DNA and the device connects us together. Pretty incredible, huh?"

"Yeah... and what happened to Amanda?" AJ asked.

"Well, if this all works right, we'll never see her again.

She'll be alive in her dimension," Kiera announced cheerfully.

"Oh." It made perfect sense and AJ wanted that for her, but she felt a sadness over the finality of this disconnect from her older self. She had missed her for these past two years and kept waiting for her to pop up and scare her like she used to.

"No one knows a thing. According to dad and grandma, you've just been away at a conference, and I went to go pick you up."

"And your dad is...?"

"Mom!" Kiera giggled. "Parker Sheridan. You remember him, right?"

AJ felt relieved thinking how wonderful it was that he was the dad Kiera had known her whole life. "Of course I do."

"Thank God!"

"Kiera?"

"Yeah, mom?"

"I know I haven't exactly been gone long from your world, but I missed you every single day I was in the other world. My whole mission was to get back to you."

"I know, mom. You were only gone for two days to that conference. I missed you every single day, too. I can't imagine two years without you."

AJ didn't have time to brush the tears away because she was free falling. Only this time, she embraced the rush. She was falling back to the world where she was born to live.

Chapter 50
AJ Hartford, 1997

(The Original AJ of 1997)

It was the year 1997. It was a beautiful, sunny day. At least that's what she saw when she opened her eyes. For some reason, AJ Hartford was laying on the floor. She had no memory of how she'd gotten there. She didn't even recognize the floor where she was laying. She opened her eyes to find three people all looking down at her. She didn't recognize them. Anxiety triggered her pulse to speed up.

"AJ! Babe, you okay?" a cute man asked her as he peered down at her with concern. He was tall with dishwater blond hair and a smattering of freckles across his nose. He had nice green eyes. She felt his love for her.

The woman looking at her was pretty with blond hair and blue eyes. She looked a lot like AJ, actually. "AJ? Are you okay, sister?"

Why was she calling her *sister*? AJ didn't have a sister.

"Should we call an ambulance?" the cute man asked.

"I'm not sure," the sister replied. "AJ, can you sit up?"

AJ tried but found it very difficult to do so. She felt so

bulky and awkward. She looked down at her stomach which was large and swollen. She gasped with sudden understanding.

"What's wrong, are you okay?" the cute man reached down to help her sit up.

"I'm pregnant?" The shock AJ felt came through in an outraged howl.

"I'm calling an ambulance," another man, who AJ was also sure she she'd never seen before, left the group for a phone.

"AJ, do you know who I am?" the cute man asked.

AJ wracked her brain for some answer but came up empty. She shook her head. She could see the hurt in the man's eyes. He gently took her hand and showed her the sparkling ring on her finger.

"You're my wife," he whispered gently.

"I'm married!" AJ gasped in shock again. He looked nice enough, but AJ didn't know who he was.

They called an ambulance. That's when the testing began. Hours of testing confirmed that AJ Hartford was fine. There was nothing abnormal showing up in the testing. They had no explanation for why she'd passed out. The baby was fine. The fact that she was pregnant still shocked AJ.

During the time AJ spent in a room in between waiting on the doctor and more testing, the three people told AJ stories to jog her memory. Stories about who these people were and how they'd all met.

But to hear she'd met Parker after fainting in a police station on his second day on the job only to insist that she was there to save the other AJ Hartford sounded insane.

How had anyone believed her? She didn't believe it herself and she'd supposedly done it. And yet, that AJ Hartford, who now stood before her and went by Amy Jo, swore they'd all shown up at AJ's insistence to save Amy Jo's life. This also saved the life of her unborn child, Grace. AJ felt like an alien had snatched her body and driven her around for quite a while.

Finally, the people switched tactics. "AJ, what's the last thing you remember?"

AJ thought for a moment. "Senior year in high school. My car was in the shop. The Spring Formal dance was coming up."

The four of them laughed like this was a scene from *Wizard of Oz* when Dorothy insists that her adventure wasn't a dream. Only, AJ was having the opposite effect. Whatever they'd experienced together must have been a dream they'd all had because AJ had no recollection of it.

Still, as AJ looked hard at each of their faces, she decided they were familiar to her after all. They were familiar in the way a long-lost relative who had returned to visit every few years would be familiar. She'd swear she'd never known them, yet they felt like they were a part of her.

As she looked at the ring on her finger, she knew she must love this man to have married him. He'd been here in the emergency room holding her hand the whole time. She didn't know if she felt love at this moment, but she was at least comforted by his presence.

"Amanda Jane! Are you okay?" Her mother burst through the door. "I would've been here sooner, but someone forgot to call me." She gave Parker an annoyed glance.

"I'm sorry, it all happened pretty fast," Parker said sheepishly. He waited until Maria had leaned down to kiss AJ's cheek, then he gave Maria a hug. "All tests came back fine. She and the baby are fine."

"Remember when you and AJ first met, and she kept fainting on you?" Maria asked quizzically.

Parker grinned. "Yeah, we were just talking about that."

"Well, she ended up in the ER that day, too. She was dehydrated, if I remember correctly."

"Oh yeah!" Parker said. "I'm gonna find a nurse..." Parker left the room.

"Actually," AJ smiled kindly at the couple left in the room. "Can I have a moment alone with my mom?"

"Absolutely!" Amy Jo grabbed Chance's hand and they left.

"Mom!" AJ pushed herself up and looked into her mother's eyes with alarm. "I don't remember them!"

"Remember who?" Maria asked with confusion.

"Any of them—Amy Jo, Chance, Parker—I have no memory of any of them, but they all seem familiar at the same time."

"Oh no! What do you mean you don't remember them?" she asked with concern in her eyes.

"My last memory is of senior year before graduation."

"You don't remember your wedding?" she asked.

AJ shook her head.

"Did you remember you were pregnant?"

AJ shook her head again.

Tears filled her mother's eyes. "That's too bad. I had never seen you more ecstatic in your life than the day you announced that news. It's like your life's purpose was realized. You were dead set on naming her Kiera, too. No one could talk you out of it. No clue where you got that name. It's very original."

"I want to remember," AJ said slowly. It sounded like it was a wonderful memory. "How long ago was high school?"

"Oh, AJ! It was two years ago," her mother said quietly.

Now it was AJ's turn to feel the tears puddle. How did she not have any recollection of the last two years of her life?

"How was the wedding?" AJ asked with a sad smile on her face.

"Everything you'd dreamed of since you were a little girl. Don't you worry, AJ. You must have bumped your head when you passed out. It will all come back to you. You'll remember everything. You were happier than I'd ever seen you."

AJ nodded and closed her eyes. She wasn't sleepy. It was just so much to process. If she slept, maybe she'd be able to regain the wonderful memories her mom and her family were trying to remind her about. It sounded like she was loved and living her best life. Maybe, in time, surrounded by these caring and patient people, she would remember them. As she feigned sleep, a foreign thought came to her.

Kiera is a beautiful name. It's the perfect name for a daughter...

Chapter 51
AJ Hartford, 2017

AJ was home. She was in the kitchen at her mom's house, which was the last place she'd been before she'd left home. It was odd that the one place she'd never called home had changed the most in the two years since she'd been gone. AJ now felt comfortable and safe in her mom's house. It felt as if she belonged here. She was snuggled up against Parker's side.

Parker was Kiera's father. Kiera had no memory of that ever being different. Not even after getting the journal back. Kiera was close to her grandmother and always had been. AJ's family went over to her mother's house for dinner every Sunday night. It was the same house her mother had built after her father had died but that appeared to be the only similarity.

Here in AJ's home dimension, things had changed slightly. For one thing, AJ was very close to her mom. She sensed it and felt it before her mom had whisked her off to her room to warn her that Kiera had met someone while AJ was away on her trip and was waiting until the right time to tell AJ. But Kiera had reasoned, since AJ was just returning home from her work trip, Kiera would give her some time to get back into a routine.

AJ knew the real truth. Kiera wanted to make sure AJ acclimated back to her home dimension before she popped any more surprises on her.

The four of them sat down to dinner. As the hot, homemade food began to pass in front of her, AJ's heart felt full. She looked around the table, watching her mother talk to Kiera about a book she was reading. Parker was staring down at AJ with warmth and love in his eyes. He grabbed her hand. He brought it to his mouth and kissed it.

"Ew!" Kiera broke in, grinning childishly. "Get a room."

"Right now?" Parker asked, comically half rising from the table. "I didn't know that was an option. Come on, AJ!"

AJ just laughed. "Kiera, what's new in the world of science these days?"

For a moment, Kiera's eyes widened. Kiera recovered when she realized AJ wasn't trying to bust her on parallel universe jumping. Then Kiera's green eyes sparkled—eyes that were once blue before AJ rerouted life with Parker. AJ couldn't get over it. It was like Kiera was highlighting her hair blond and wearing green-colored contacts. The freckles across her nose were so like her father's. Thankfully, Kiera's personality was the same. AJ supposed that spoke to the way she'd raised Kiera to just be herself. Not to mention, her strong genetics.

"Are you ready for this?" Kiera asked, leaning forward.

Parker groaned. "You had to ask..."

"Water!" Kiera announced. "Did you know around two million people die a year due to unsafe water sources and eight percent of them are from economically developing countries? Eighty percent of illnesses are due to water and sanitation problems. In America, we have resources and funding to fix it. But who is looking out for Lebanon? I'm in a group with five other sophomores and that's the topic we —well, I—came up with for our group science lab. What resources do we have to help economically developing countries and what are some practical steps to take to put in clean water sources?"

AJ grinned with relief. She had put life back on track in this world and she hoped the other worlds as well. She remembered the conversation she'd had with Amanda about sliding-glass moments. We can choose our fate. But we are predisposed to choose what we might have already chosen in another universe.

AJ leaned over and kissed Kiera's forehead. "I'm beyond proud of you, daughter! Keep following your passion."

"Even if my passion is clean water?" Kiera asked looking doubtfully at her dad.

"Especially if your passion is clean water! You're going to change the world someday."

"To Kiera!" Parker raised his glass, responding to AJ's excitement.

"To Kiera!" They all answered in unison.

Epilogue

AJ Hartford, 2017

AJ Hartford was lounging on her couch, reading a book, taking advantage of the last days of summer before school started and she went back to teaching. Not a day went by that she didn't feel grateful for the way her life had been rerouted.

A knock at the door surprised her. Kiera was at soccer camp and Parker was at work. She put the book face down on the coffee table and approached the door cautiously. She still feared some glitch in the universe might come back to haunt her.

She peeked out the window and saw a UPS truck. Guard down, she flung open the door and grabbed for the large box the man was holding out to her. Once the box was in her grasp, she looked up.

"Thank you," AJ said kindly. Her eyes connected with the UPS driver and felt instant shock and alarm. It was Johnny. His intense blue eyes stared back at her for half a second.

"Well?" he asked abruptly. The irritation in his voice

took AJ back to memories of a soon-to-be forgotten lifetime. "Anything else? I need to get back before my boss bitches me out for taking too long."

"No, thank you." AJ turned to go back into the house.

"Wait a minute," Johnny's voice sounded puzzled. "I think I know you."

AJ reluctantly turned back around, feeling curious.

"Did we go to the same school?" he asked.

"No," AJ lied and shook her head. "Just one of those familiar faces, I guess."

Johnny shook his head and shrugged. "Huh." He turned and bounded off the porch and as he got into his truck, AJ could see an ankle monitor peeking above his sock.

AJ went back into her house, shut the door, and leaned against it, package still in hand.

"Dodged a bullet with that one," she said.

The End

If you liked *The Other AJ Hartford*, check out book 1
of A Mynart Mystery Thriller series—
WHAT COMES BEFORE DAWN

PROLOGUE

KRYSTA MYNART

Icy cold winter wind pushed its way through the window that was not supposed to be open. It wrapped its frozen fingers around her wrist, her face, and her neck. The chill settled in her heart. Krysta Mynart gasped loudly, coming awake from a deep, dark slumber.

She snuggled into her husband for warmth. His body always radiated heat but right now, nothing seemed to help. She was so very cold. Her brain was waking but her eyes refused to open as she processed one eerie fact. Her husband, Jason, woke religiously before the sun rose every single day.

"Jason?" Her voice came out in a hoarse but hopeful whisper. His arm was hanging over her body, limp and heavy, a dead weight across her stomach. She struggled to breathe as she felt hysteria rising inside of her. Something was wrong. She was afraid to open her eyes. She began to shiver and then shake from head to toe. Jason was always a light sleeper.

She could feel her head stuck in place to the pillow. She was so twisted in her sheets she could not move. Frozen air was blowing through the room. Senses suddenly heightened, Krysta noticed the sheets had wrapped her into a mummy-like cocoon as if she had tossed and turned violently. As if there had been a struggle. She gasped at the thought and tried to lift her head. She refused to open her eyes. Strands of hair pulled painfully. That wasn't the only thing that hurt. Her head throbbed, right at the temple. She was literally stuck. Stuck how? Her heart sank in her chest because the answer came to her with absolute clarity.

Krysta could smell a light, faint metallic odor. Not a foreign smell exactly, and she was able to place it instantly. She lay very still and finally opened her green eyes. She could no longer deny what her mind was telling her. There was no arguing the trails of brown-red she saw on her white sheets.

Jason was dead.

She sat up now, throwing the blankets and sheets up with her, ripping her blond hair off the pillow. Red blood matted her normally silky strands. Unearthing the tangle of sheets, she saw the horrific truth.

Jason was not just dead. He had been massacred. In his sleep. There was blood everywhere. Blood seeped from under the sheets, soaking through to the oversized comforter. Fresh pools of blood so vast it seemed no number of blankets would sop it all up.

Then she saw the knife. There was a knife laying at the foot of the bed. Her knife. Jason had given it to her as a wedding gift. She remembered it now as if it had happened yesterday, not seven years ago.

What in the world would I do with a knife? She had protested.

It's pretty. A souvenir... Consider it a wedding present?

Jason had said. His eyes were full of mischief and he was amused. He had leaned forward and kissed the tip of her nose with his full, red lips. His beard tickled her.

You're lying! She had pushed his broad chest. She had gently touched the knife.

Okay, he had shrugged sheepishly. *You may need to defend yourself someday. Don't worry. I'll show you how to do it...*

Her mind worked quickly backwards through the night, but she had no explanation. Too shocked to cry, she stared into space. Why couldn't she remember anything?

She willed herself to remember but she knew it would not work. It was a thing she did. Chunks of time were missing from her life. One minute, she was in the moment, living life, the next, she was just... somewhere else. Always with the sensation that she had been teleported into a new scene in a movie. She just blacked out. And she knew, with absolute certainty, that she had done it again at the exact wrong moment. It had cost her husband his life. It was her fault that Jason was dead. No one would convince her otherwise.

"Jason?" she whimpered. "No!" She willed herself to cry. To take time to grieve for the loss of her beloved husband. But she couldn't. There was no time. She had to clean this mess up.

Forty-five minutes later, Krysta realized that the only blood she could clean up and make disappear was her own. All showered with a clean set of clothes on, she looked in the mirror. She had such a thin, long pixie face. Her blond hair fell just past her shoulders. Her big green eyes looked around as she said good-bye in her heart to her home. She packed a small bag. In the bag was a wad of cash, a few changes of clothes, and a passport with the name "Krysta Deffer."

Jason had told her this day would come. The day when she would have to run. She was prepared. She could grieve later. But for now, she needed to give herself as much time and distance as possible to get away. Once they found her husband's body, she would be the prime suspect. She had no alibi. None that she could remember anyway. For all she knew, she *had* killed him. Some witness she would be on the stand! She would only incriminate herself. The only thing she knew was she had been there when it happened. She was alive and he wasn't.

She could hear her mother's words floating in her head. The voice she had heard all the years of her childhood but tried to forget.

You're a wicked child, Krysta Suzanna, and one day the whole world will see you for who you are...

Now Krysta knew the truth. Her mother was right. All mothers are. She had no choice now but to believe her. Krysta was wicked. Soon, everyone would know as well.

Krysta opened the door to her home and paused. The sun was just creeping into the sky and a beautiful sunrise had dawned. She was struck by the evil that lurks in the night. *It's what comes before dawn,* she thought.

The ride to the airport took several hours from her rural home. Finding a plane ticket took even longer. Finally, at approximately 10:35 p.m., Krysta Mynart stepped off the plane in Canada and embraced a new identity, Krysta Deffer. No one ever questioned her.

The one thing Krysta hadn't counted on and had no

plan for was her barely conceived embryo. Her daughter Paige would be born within the year and she would have to work hard to make sure Paige didn't turn out just like her. But that's all Krysta knew. The rest of the story would belong to Paige.

Also by Addison Michael

A Mynart Mystery Thriller series is ghostly suspense with psychological elements. If you like complex heroines, paranormal twists and turns, and gripping suspense, then you'll love Addison Michael's dark glimpse into the psyche. Tap the links to buy these books today!

Book 1 - *What Comes Before Dawn* - A tragic death too close to home. A young woman seeking answers. But will the truth prove fatal?

Book 2 - *Dawn That Brings Death* - Two men are dead at the Mynart Murder House. Paige, a newly single mom, is hiding in Canada. Will she be able to keep her daughter safe when a new enemy emerges?

Book 3 - *Truth That Dawns* - When Paige's secrets are exposed, she must face the consequences including a serial killer looking for revenge. He'll stop at nothing. Will Paige live to see her daughter again?

Book 4 - *Dawn That Breaks* - Anna is gone. It starts with a deadly car accident that creates too many questions. Will Paige learn the truth about her daughter, Anna, *before* a deadly ghost from her past ends Paige's life?

Join the Addison Michael Newsletter to receive the FREE story *How it Began*!

Review Request

If you enjoyed this book, I would be extremely grateful if you would leave a brief review on the store site where you purchased your book or on Goodreads. Your review helps fellow readers know what to expect when they read this book.

~ Addison Michael

About the Author

 Addison Michael is an author who lives in the Midwest. She believes in writing what she knows so her stories are often set in the Midwest region. Addison Michael writes mystery thrillers with psychological and ghostly elements. From cabins surrounded by acres of desolate woods to rural police departments and eclectic personalities, Addison Michael captures the essence of small-town living.

You'll find the following tropes in Addison Michael thriller books:

- Cabin in the woods
- You can't go home again
- Unreliable narrator
- Kidnapping/missing person
- Addiction/recovery
- Femme fatale
- Serial killer